BEYOND THE LIES

ABBI COOK

BEYOND THE LIES

I'm not who I appear to be. Who I am is a lie.

I have a job to do, but in one night that all changes when a beautiful girl turns my world upside down.

She has no idea how much danger she's in, but it's too late now.

Because once we start on this path, there's no turning back. Everything I am is a lie.

Except when it comes to her.

CHAPTER ONE

ing

THE LAST JOB OF THE NIGHT ALWAYS TURNS OUT TO be a pain in the ass, and when a guy like Tap comes along, it usually becomes a shitshow. He's fucked in the head, and no matter what the boss says, things get screwed up when he's added to the mix.

From behind me, I hear him already start to cock off. "What do you say we bust some motherfucking heads tonight?"

Kroger chuckles next to me and gives me a knowing glance. He and I work together fine. Not that we don't bust heads when it's necessary, but we do the job we have to and get out. Tap's constant need to prove he's the biggest asskicker around only proves over and over he's the biggest asshole going.

I can deal with someone being an asshole if they

1

don't get in my way. The problem is Tap's need to show he's a bad ass always gets in the fucking way and whoever's stuck with him ends up having to clean up the mess.

"We have a job to do, man. This guy's never an issue, so you're going to have to find your head busting somewhere else," I say as casually as I can, hoping to dismiss his nonsense as quickly as possible.

Out of the corner of my eye, I see relief settle into Kroger's expression. A lot like me, he doesn't need to deal with shit tonight either. Unlike me, he's got something to go home to. The last thing he wants is to get caught in some goddamned crossfire and never see that pretty little girl he shacks up with again.

"One of us should tell Duke we don't need this guy's help anymore," he whispers barely loud enough for me to hear him.

I do, though, and I can't agree enough. When we get back tonight, I need to do just that. Duke has to have something else for this crazy motherfucker to do other than tagging along with the two of us and fucking shit up.

"Kro, what'd you say?" Tap asks with more than a hint of accusation in his tone.

Fuck. I'd hoped he didn't hear us talking up here. We don't need him starting shit now.

Turning back to face Tap, I nod to give him the sense he's among friends here even as I fight to keep the scowl at how ugly he is from my face. Too many fights with too many sharp objects have left him looking like some kind of thrift store jigsaw puzzle that's missing a piece or two. Between the scars on his cheeks and forehead and his overall ugliness because of bulging eyes and a nose that faces somewhere around seven o'clock, he's nothing but hideous.

"Kroger says he's hoping we get this done quick so we can get out of here. Lucky him, he's got something waiting for him at home."

For a second, Tap looks confused, like he doesn't know whether to believe me or not. Then, after a few steps, he stops on the sidewalk and nods. "I hear that. The faster we get done, the faster I get back to the house and my knives. Got to keep them sharp since you never know what's going to come down the pike."

I give him another nod like I think his knife obsession is cool and then turn back to focus on the house we're at. Fucking knives. It's not the seventeenth fucking century, for God's sake. Who the fuck gets that goddamned jacked up about knives anymore?

This guy pisses me off. He makes me want to pound the hell out of something, and it's all because he's such an asshole. But Duke made me pledge not to get into it with him again, so I'm forced to keep my mouth shut and pretend like he doesn't irritate the fuck out of me.

"So this guy isn't usually a problem? I wonder why the boss sent me with you two then," Tap asks behind Kroger and me in a way that makes it sound like he suspects we need his help.

I have no real idea why he was sent to tag along with us, but I suspect it has more to do with Duke not wanting to have to deal with him tonight and pushing him off on us since he can than the two of us needing any help from the likes of Tap. His oversized ego makes him think he's necessary.

He's not.

The house in front of us looks like any ordinary mid-century house in an American suburb. One floor, enormous window in the living room, and a small, concrete front porch. Nothing special. Inside, the man who owes Duke money is nothing special either. Like every other guy who's gotten in too deep with gambling, drugs, or whatever else it is that forces him to look for someone like the boss to finance his habits, he's pretending to live one life when he's actually living another, very different one.

Not that I can't sympathize on that issue.

But I don't care what life John Carney thinks he's living. All I need is for him to hand over the money he owes Duke so we can be on our merry way and Tap won't feel like he has to cause any hassle. It's simple, really. Borrow money? Then pay it back.

Not that Carney has ever been a problem, but I've found in the past there comes a time when every man thinks he can outsmart reality. Maybe they fall in love or find Jesus. Or maybe they give up all hope and slip into a depression. Whatever happens, when that time comes and a man can't accept the truth of how much trouble he's gotten himself into, it's men like me who have to yank them back to reality.

Hopefully, tonight isn't that night for this guy.

We make it halfway down the sidewalk before

something inside me says Tap should stay outside. I learned a long time ago to always follow my gut, no matter how out of left field it seems at the moment.

Spinning around, I see him walking toward Kroger and me with his gun out already. Christ, this guy is a walking, talking trainwreck.

"Hey, Tap, you stay out here and watch for any issues. We got this. It's simple shit, but we don't need any problems sneaking up on us, you know?"

He looks up and focuses his bulgy eyes on my face when he stops walking. "Problems? Like what kind?" he asks, gripping his gun in anticipation.

Whatever I tell him is a complete lie. Kroger knows it as well as I do. Carney isn't some badass who's going to throw down instead of forking over the money. He's a goddamned accountant with a penchant for betting on sports and little luck, at least lately. That's why we don't need Tap blowing up the situation.

With a shrug, I point toward the front door of Carney's house. "It's all good in there, but you never know what's going to happen out here. That's why having you here is a good idea."

It doesn't take long for him to accept my bullshit reason. With a big smile that showcases his crooked teeth, he nods like he had the same idea.

"Got it. I'll take care of anything that comes up out here."

Kroger and I glance at one another, and all I can think is how quiet it is in Carney's neighborhood. It's suburbia at its finest. The most that might come up out here while we're dealing with him is a dog getting out or a raccoon digging through a garbage can.

But better to have Tap think he's doing something useful than have him fuck things up inside. Accountants don't require the hard sell.

"Let's go, Kroger. Time to shake down the suit for what he owes us."

I get a rare smile from my partner before we turn to knock on the front door. Carney answers less than a minute later and lets us in with no hassle, just as I knew he would. With one last look at Tap standing on the sidewalk stroking his gun, we head in to do our business.

"You know why we're here, John," I say in a low voice, making it sound intentionally ominous, just in case he's got any ideas of not doing the right thing.

"Yeah, I know. Just give me a couple seconds, okay?" he says as he flails his hands nervously.

"I'll give you a few minutes," I answer as I look around his house and notice his TV in the living room looks new.

"Okay. Thanks. I just have to go to the bedroom since I left my wallet in my pants. My wife is already in bed, so I have to keep it quiet, you know?"

Smiling, I nod like I know anything about that, but I don't. I've never been married, and the closest I've come to being committed to a woman was when I dated that girl in high school for a few months. The thought of having to tiptoe around my own damn house because I don't want someone I supposedly love and respect to know what I'm up to is utterly foreign to me.

Kroger looks around the living room and then smiles like he approves of this kind of place. "I could live in a house like this. Lots of space and pretty nice."

"Planning on settling down, man?" I ask with a chuckle.

He shrugs and gives me a sheepish look. "You never know. Life can change at the drop of a hat. Maybe someday."

Younger than me by a few years at least, Kroger looks like he's thought a lot about leaving the life. I can imagine him living in some house with that girlfriend of his and a few kids. Maybe with a yard he can mow and a kiddie pool like the one we all used to hold the ice to keep our beer cold last Fourth of July. He would probably be happy living like that.

I give him a supportive slap on the shoulder. "If any of us can be that guy, it's you, Kroger. Grab that brass ring, man."

Rolling his eyes, he laughs. "I'm not saying I'm planning on doing it any time soon. I'm just saying I wouldn't be against it is all."

Carney shuffles toward us, still looking shakier than usual. Holding out his hand full of money, he says, "Here. It's all there."

I can't tell if that's the truth or not since he seems to have raided some piggy bank and grabbed any bill he could grab. Hundreds mix in with twenties and even a few ones, and I can't believe I'm going to have to count it all out like some kind of middle manager after a shift at some fucking family restaurant.

"Jesus. What the hell is all this, Carney?" I ask in disgust as a couple bills fall out onto the floor.

"Sorry. Things are tight this month, but I swear it's all there, King."

As Kroger bends down to pick up Carney's wayward bills, out of the corner of my eye I see out the big picture window something happening out on the lawn. I turn my head and see Tap take off into a full sprint across the grass. Fuck! I have no idea what he's up to, but it can't be good to have a madman with a gun running around a suburban neighborhood.

"Get the money and follow me!" I order Kroger as I rush toward the front door.

I stuff the bills into my front pocket and run out to catch up with Tap as Kroger follows a few seconds behind. Quickly, I scan the yards nearby and see no sight of the fucker. Damnit! I knew it would be a mistake to have him come with us.

Pointing toward the house on the left, I bark out, "Look for him over there, and I'll head the opposite direction. Let me know if you find him. Go!"

I take off toward the yard on the right side of Carney's house, my rage practically exploding out of my body that I have to deal with this shit from Tap. What the fuck would make him run off like that?

Christ, I hope it wasn't some animal. Shooting some kid's pet dog in the middle of a quiet neighborhood isn't the way to stay low. He should fucking know that.

He isn't anywhere in the next-door-neighbor's yard, so I head back out toward the street. Just as I step foot onto the asphalt, I hear a noise that makes the hair on the back of my neck stand at attention in pure terror. The muffled sound of a woman crying for help, like she's screaming behind someone's hand over her mouth.

Did Tap grab some woman? Holy hell! Why the fuck would he do that?

I race down the street toward the sound I think is coming from where I sent Kroger. He comes running out to the street, clearly panicked since he's heard the same thing I have.

"That sounds like a woman, King. Did he go after someone here in this neighborhood?" Kroger asks in utter disbelief.

Opening my mouth to answer his question, I've got nothing but stunned disgust. As we stand there, the sound hits our ears even clearer this time.

"Let me go! Help! Help!" a woman's voice calls out in pure terror.

A second later, Kroger and I take off down the street toward the corner. I get there first and under the streetlight, I see Tap struggling to subdue a brunette wearing a pair of blue shorts and a pale pink T-shirt.

"What the fuck do you think you're doing? This is a fucking residential neighborhood. Someone's going to call the cops, you asshole!" I snap in a hoarse whisper.

"I got her for Duke!" he says far too loudly as the

girl continues to cry out for help. "I'm going to be the golden boy after this."

As I take a step toward him and the girl, I look around at the houses nearby and hope nobody can hear him ranting. "Put her the fuck down and let's go. What the hell would he want with her? We don't have time for this nonsense, so let's get the hell out of here."

Tap shakes his head like a rabid dog and refuses to release her. "No way! Duke's going to freak out when he gets this prize from me."

I look over at Kroger in confusion to see if he understands what the hell Tap is talking about, but he seems just as baffled. Any moment, one of the neighbors is going to look out and see us holding this girl, so we need to get Tap to let her go so we can get the fuck out of here.

Unfortunately, Tap is as single-minded as he is ugly, and he's got other plans. He drags her toward the car parked two houses away while all the while bragging that the boss is going to be thrilled.

Convinced he's lost his mind, Kroger and I catch up to him just as he's about to stuff her into the back seat. She's crying, Tap's acting like he's going to be made king of the world because of her, and the two of us are staring at all of this like we can't believe our shitty luck.

"He's not going to want some random girl, Tap," Kroger says in a calm voice I'm not sure I could muster at this moment.

But I jump on that idea and add, "Yeah, man. She's

just some girl out for a night run. Drop her and let's go."

Turning her toward us, he roughly tilts her head up so we can see her face. Fuck. This is not what I need right now. This will only makes things messier.

Beaming his happiness at the prize in his arms, he says, "Do you know who this is? Sophie Varens, motherfuckers! I remember her from that picture Duke was looking at a couple weeks ago when her uncle took out Ozzy. When Duke sees her, I'm going to be the favorite from now on. Let's go, or I'll drive away and leave the two of you here."

Fucking-A. Sophie Varens, oldest niece of Victor Varens, Duke's biggest rival. Tap may have just found a surefire way to become the boss's favorite.

"Fine. Put her in the car and let's get the fuck out of here before the cops show up," I bark as I jump into the driver's seat, my mind whirling with the possibilities of what will happen when we get back to Duke's.

CHAPTER TWO

ing

TAP RACES OUT OF THE CAR WITH THE GIRL BEFORE I even put it in park, so goddamned eager to show off what he found on what was supposed to be a regular job to get money. Kroger and I follow them into Duke's office, my pocket full of Carney's payment that should be the main reason for any celebration.

"Boss, look what I have for you," Tap brags, practically cooing his words.

Duke stands at his bar in the back corner of his office pouring himself a drink as he usually does at this time of night. Nearly as tall as me at six foot four, he tends to be heavier, especially when he goes through periods of drinking too much. I've been working for him for nearly eight months, and in that time, he's given up booze twice—once last winter right after I started here and once in late February as what he gave up for Lent. Both times he lost twenty pounds and looked like a new man.

Now, two months since his last dry period ended, he looks like he's swallowed a small keg. For some reason this time, the booze has made all his weight settle in his gut. He likes to slap my flat stomach and joke that if only he stopped drinking, he'd look more like me and less like Humpty Dumpty's twin brother.

Tap's announcement makes the two men sitting in front of Duke's desk turn around to look at us, and their eyes get wide like he's not holding a female in his arms but a chest filled with gold.

"Boss, you're going to want to see this," Marsh says in his usual whisper, unable to talk any louder after someone crushed his larynx in a fight a few years ago.

Duke slowly turns around, and the first thing I see is not his enormous gut hanging over his dress pants but his dark eyes opening wide like he can't believe what he's seeing. Tap may have been right with his prediction that grabbing Sophie Varens would make him the new favorite of the boss's.

For her part, Sophie refuses to pretend to be a willing participant in any of this and flails against Tap's hold. Against his hand, she cries out the same words she's screamed the whole drive there.

"Let me go!"

"Holy shit! Is that who I think it is?" Duke asks, putting down his glass of whisky without taking a drink.

"Sophie Varens, the niece of Victor Varens himself. I saw her when we went to get Carney's payment and grabbed her," Tap brags, all too proud of his capture. "I knew you'd want her, boss."

His eyes still wide as saucers, Duke slowly walks over toward where Tap holds her tightly, even as she continues to fight him. "I've heard she's Victor's favorite niece. When he finds out I have her, he's going to lose his fucking mind."

I had a feeling Duke would enjoy the idea of having this kind of leverage over the boss of the Varens family. Tap becoming the favorite of all his guys isn't going to be good for any of us, especially me. We barely tolerate one another, and that's when all things are equal between us. Tap having power over me isn't going to work.

"You've done well, Tap. Very well," Duke says slowly as his eyes scan Sophie.

"That's all well and good, boss, but she's mine. Tap owes me, and I'm calling in his debt," I say flatly, needing to turn the tables on this shitshow now.

Everyone in the office turns to look at me, including Tap. The girl's eyes fill with horror, as if being with me would be worse than being with that ugly motherfucker.

"Tap owes me for that fuck up last month. I took the heat for it, but now I want my due."

I know how Duke thinks. He likely doesn't want to strip Tap of his take, but he can't let my claim go unanswered. He looks over at me and then back at him before saying, "King's got a point. You know how things work here, Tap. I told you last week he'd come calling when something good came in."

"No way! She's mine. I saw her and grabbed her for you, boss. He did nothing!" Tap shrieks, clutching the girl closer to him.

From over near the desk, Stills laughs and says, "I think we should share her. Seems only right so nobody gets their nose out of joint."

Tall and thin, he's cornered the market on being the clown here, so I don't take him too seriously until I see Duke nodding, like he thinks that's a good idea. I must not have made myself clear.

I take a step toward Tap and stop, pointing at the girl. "She's payment and I want it. It's that simple. Tap owes me, boss. It's only right that he pays me, and she's how he needs to do it."

For a long moment, no one says anything. I watch as Tap waits to hear Duke's decision, glancing over at Sophie to see her eyes darting back and forth between my boss and me. If she thinks I'm the worst choice, she's clearly not seeing this situation clearly.

Finally, Duke nods. "King's right. You owe him, Tap. There's nothing else to be said. Hand her over."

I don't expect to take her without him causing some trouble, so when he pushes her away into Duke and pulls a knife on me, it's not surprising. While Duke grabs hold of the girl, Tap and I stare each other down, both of us waiting for the moment when we'll start this fight.

He's smaller than me by about three inches and forty pounds, so I can take him no problem. The knife is a whole different story. He spends every spare fucking moment with his goddamned knives and knows how to use them. If I'm not careful, he'll cut me bad enough to take me out.

"You can't have her, King. She's my prize, not yours," Tap says, practically whining as he moves that damn knife of his back and forth in front of him.

"You owe me, man. You know how that works. I told you I'd handle things, but you knew I'd be calling in the debt. Pay up."

I'm not sure which of those words enrages him more than before, but he lunges at me, ending our little dance around the room, and I easily take him down. His back slams off the floor, momentarily knocking the wind out of him. That's my chance to overcome him before he can recover, so I send my fist into his face, pounding his cheekbone.

But it's not enough, and a second later, he's back to swinging that fucking knife at me, even from his position on his back. I move left and right, avoiding the sharp edge of the weapon he'll use to carve me up like a Thanksgiving turkey if he gets the chance, but he catches me in the leg.

The pain from the blade slicing into my skin becomes secondary to my rage at having to deal with this asshole all night only to get fucking cut. Something snaps inside me, and a moment later, I'm ramming my fist into his ugly face like a jackhammer, his blood and teeth flying back at me as I beat the hell out of him.

By the time Marsh and Stills pull me off him, Tap

is unconscious and his face looks like something a dog puked up. I struggle against their hold, still wanting nothing more than to beat this guy into the ground, and fight them as they stand me up to lead me away.

"King, man! You got him! Now we have to do something about that leg," Duke says like a referee as they drag me toward the bathroom right off his office.

"I'm not done with that motherfucker! Let me go!"

The last I see of Tap is the bloody mess I made of his face before Stills slams the bathroom door closed. I stop fighting them and sit down on the side of the bathtub. Looking down at my torn pants, I shake my head in disgust.

"I hate those fucking knives of his. He better watch or one night I'm going to bury one in his chest. Motherfucker needs to find an outlet for his aggression. Maybe he needs to jerk off more or something."

Marsh lets out a low chuckle and hands me a pair of scissors. "Open up your pants so we can stitch you up."

Cutting into the black fabric, I peel it apart to reveal the damage Tap did to me. A thin streak in my skin on the outside of my thigh is currently gushing enough bright red blood to cover my leg.

"Glad you can see the humor in this," I say, looking up at his meaty face before handing him back the scissors.

Stills and Marsh have together sewn me back up no less than a dozen times in the months I've worked for Duke. Closer to the boss's age than my thirty years, they've probably stitched up dozens, if not hundreds, of guys.

The two men stand staring down at me, each one smiling. "You pick. Stills or me," Marsh says in that whispery way of his.

"Stills. The last thing I need is that husky voice of yours giving me a hard on at this very moment," I joke.

Scowling, Marsh mumbles something that sounds like fuck you and steps back to let Stills work on me. He hates having his balls busted about how he sounds, but the more I make it seem like my leg doesn't hurt like a motherfucker, the better things will be for me.

Stills crouches down near my leg and laughs as he douses it in peroxide and then begins to sew the skin back together. "I would have personally chosen him, sexy voice or not. He's better at this."

The pain makes me feel like I'm about to explode through the roof, but I laugh at his comment, even as I worry I'm going to black out. I can't let them see this hurts so bad I'd kill for something to deaden my emotions at the moment. The world we all live in will eat a man alive if he shows weakness. Anyone who can't handle a few stitches after a knife fight with a pussy won't last long here, so whatever I have to do to show strength, I'll do it.

My life depends on it.

Ten minutes later, Stills looks up and smiles at me. He's done his usual good job, so I say, "I guess I'll live to fight another day. Thanks, man."

All this playacting that I'm not in pure agony and

watching someone sew up my leg didn't make me want to throw up is exhausting, but I have to keep it up, at least until I get away from Duke and the other guys. Just a few more minutes and I'll be in the clear.

I follow Stills and Marsh out into the office to find Duke's the one holding Sophie now. She's stopped squirming, which seems curious. Does she have a thing for old, fat bastards?

Putting on my best face, I smile at my boss and walk up to where he and Sophie stand. "All better now, so I'll be taking her with me."

The way I say that is meant to quash any questions he or anyone else may have about her being mine. Duke may be the boss of this organization, but even he follows rules, particularly ones he's set. My tone is intended to remind him of that.

She looks up at me like the mere idea of going anywhere with me terrifies her, again baffling me. How could I be the most upsetting choice among Tap, Duke, and me?

"Those are the rules, so she's all yours, King. Let me warn you, though. She's got fight in her, so don't turn your back for a second."

"I won't. No need to worry about that."

"And don't damage her. She could be useful at a future date, and having her look like she's been through a meat grinder wouldn't do us any good. Understand?" Duke says as he roughly pushes her toward me.

"I have no intention of damaging her, boss. In fact,

that's the last thing on my mind," I say with a wink I'm sure he'll understand as I pull her to me.

Duke throws his head back and lets out a hearty laugh before patting me on the back when he passes me to return to his glass of whisky. "That's exactly why I gave her to you, son. You see, there is a method to my madness."

As I wonder why Sophie isn't fighting my hold on her or saying a word, I keep up the pretense of everything being fine, even as the pain in my leg makes focusing on anything nearly impossible. "I never doubted it, boss."

Tipping his glass up, he takes a big swallow of whisky and waves his hand to dismiss me. "Have a good time with her, but don't forget I expect to see you back here bright and early tomorrow morning. I suspect you'll be tired, though."

Duke, Stills, and Marsh all laugh at his poorly concealed sex joke, but fucking Sophie is the last thing on my mind. I can't imagine my cock even getting hard at this point I'm in so much pain.

"See you tomorrow!" I say as I guide her toward the office door.

From behind me, Duke yells, "By the way, Tap's pretty hurt. I don't know if he's going to be okay after what you did to him."

I look over my shoulder and shrug. "You take a swipe at the king, you better kill the king. Maybe Tap learned that lesson now."

"If he can't come back, I'm going to make you responsible for breaking in his replacement. That's my job as the king of this organization," Duke says in a serious tone.

His message comes through loud and clear. Take on Tap, who's an asshole and causes us all trouble, and he doesn't care. But make his life and how he runs his business more difficult, and that's a whole different story.

"Got it."

Closing the door behind me, I walk a few feet with Sophie and stop as the pain overwhelms me. For the first time, she stirs in my hold, likely sensing her opportunity to escape.

Nothing could be a worse idea.

I pull her tightly to my body and squeeze my arms around her as the guard dogs bark in the distance. Leaning my head down, I whisper in her ear, "You hear that? Their sole job is to capture people. Try to escape, and they'll tear you limb from limb, sweetheart. And if they don't get you, the dozen or so guards with guns will. You're miles away from any house or anyone who can help you, so behave yourself. Your previous owner may have cut me with that fucking knife of his, but you lucked out when I took you. Trust me on that."

Sophie turns her head and frowns at me. "That's not much comfort since the first guy was a psychopath."

"Who knows? I might be a psychopath too. I did just beat one of my co-workers unconscious."

Her frown deepens. "Again, not comforting."

Wincing from the pain shooting up my leg into my

hip, I take a deep breath and let it out slowly. "Behave yourself and you won't be hurt. Don't behave and you'll wish Tap had won his claim on you. Understand?"

I wait for her to answer, but she simply nods. All the better. I don't feel like talking much at the moment anyway.

As we walk toward the outside, I look over and see her staring down toward my leg. "Don't get any ideas. If Tap couldn't take me, you have no chance."

We stop at the door and she quietly asks, "What are you going to do with me?"

She's not stupid. The show she got to see back in Duke's office tells her the kind of men holding her. I'm not different from any of them. Well, not that she can see.

I look into her dark eyes and force a smile as I push the door open. "You're in luck tonight, Sophie. I couldn't get hard if I wanted to."

Her breath hitches as we hit the balmy late June night air, and I can't decide if it's because the thought of being with me terrifies her.

Or excites her.

CHAPTER THREE

ophie

MY CAPTOR'S APARTMENT IS LOCATED ON THE FAR end of Duke Cantorini's estate, far enough away that I can imagine there must be a place nearby to escape through that the guards and dogs King mentioned might not check often. Then again, I might be delusional since I'm still in disbelief that I've been taken and brought to this place.

My father warned me since I was a little girl to never be alone. When I was young, I thought he said that because of the stories about the rest of my family that sounded too fantastical to believe. As I grew up, I came to understand the life they lived was exactly what everyone claimed it was and meant I would forever be in danger, despite never being a part of that world.

For years, I made sure I never went anywhere without someone with me, and nothing happened. Then a few months ago when I turned twenty-one, I decided my father had always been just an overprotective parent and all his warnings had been to simply scare me. I stopped forcing friends to accompany me to the mall or to the coffee shop simply to have someone with me. I started running alone at night, something I'd been cautioned never to do, even if I had someone with me.

But I didn't listen. I knew better. People didn't get snatched off a side street in a residential neighborhood, for God's sake. I carried mace sometimes, just in case, but I stopped doing that last month too since night after night proved to me I didn't need it.

Now I'm being held by one of Cantorini's men after he nearly killed the one who took me from that residential neighborhood.

I sit in the chair King shoved me into when we walked into his apartment and then immediately disappeared into the bathroom. My mind constructs a dozen plans to escape, but each one ends in dogs ripping my body apart and him standing there watching as they devour me.

Looking around, I wait a few seconds for him to appear, and when he doesn't, I stand up and tiptoe over to the door. This apartment is on the top floor and above another apartment that appeared empty when we walked up the stairs past it. I might be able to get away and make a run for the edge of the estate, which I imagine is nearby. King's injury made walking up all those stairs difficult for him, so I could outrun him if I sprint.

My heart slamming into my chest, I turn the doorknob and find it unlocked. I knew he was in too much agony to pay attention to details! All I have to do is get outside and then run as fast as I can before the alarm is sounded and those dogs are set after me.

"Bad move, sweetheart."

I freeze at the sound of his voice. Much angrier than before when we spoke right outside Duke's office, it practically stops my breathing.

Slowly, I turn around and see him behind me. He's huge and intimidating bearing down on me. I want to speak but don't know what to say that wouldn't anger him more.

Taking a step toward me, he stops and inhales a deep breath of air into his lungs. "I can smell your fear, little girl. But there's something else under that delicious scent coming off you."

"Oh, yeah? Like my perfume? I've been told it's pretty great, so you have good taste," I say to him, mustering all the bravado I can while everything inside me quakes in complete terror.

He shakes his head and smiles. "No, little girl. Not your perfume. Now sit back down and behave yourself or I'm not going to be responsible for what I do."

I want to answer that he'd be the only one responsible since he's the one in control of this get-together we have going on, but I don't. I may have a smart mouth, but I have the intelligence to go with it and I know better than to back talk a man like this one.

However, I can't stop myself from correcting him on the pet name he seems to have chosen for me.

"My name is Sophie, and I'm not a little girl."

His eyebrows slowly rise into his forehead, and he stares at me in surprise for a few seconds before he says, "This isn't a meet and greet. Sit down."

"Could I at least know what I should call you?" I ask, hoping I'm not pushing my luck.

Those eyebrows that just made him look shocked now dive in toward his nose to make him look very angry. Narrowing his eyes, he answers, "You don't listen very well, honey."

"I'm just asking your name."

Suddenly, he winces and shakes his head, clearly in pain as he grabs his thigh. With a groan, he finally gives me what I want. "King. Now if you don't sit down right the fuck now, I swear to God I'm going to do something you're going to regret."

Quickly, I return to that tan recliner he sat me in before and look up at him to assess my captor for the first time. I guess I always assumed if someone did grab me like my father warned me about, they'd look like my uncle Victor. I haven't seen him in a long time, but I remember him being a portly man more like King's boss.

King is nothing like that. My eyes scan his frame and I guess he's got to be at least six foot three, maybe taller. I felt how solid he was when he held me against his body. All muscle, he's much stronger looking than either my uncle or his boss.

And he's younger than I imagined the guy who might grab me would be. Again, I figured it would be some henchman of one of my uncle's rivals, a man in his forties or fifties with slicked back hair. Maybe he'd stink of cigar smoke and liquor. Maybe he'd have a gravelly voice after years of smoking and shitty living.

Then again, he could look like my cousins who work for the family. They're young like King. But he doesn't remind me of them either. Then again, Jaxon and Cason have never been anything other than my protectors when boys bullied me in grade school.

While all of this runs through my mind, I see him stop next to the couch on the far wall and grab on to the back of it like he can't walk another step. My natural instinct kicks in, and I want to help him. I hear his shallow breathing as he steadies himself. He's in agony from that knife wound. Memories from stories my mother told me from her time as an ER nurse rush back into my mind.

I open my mouth to ask him if he needs help but quickly clamp my lips together when he turns back and glares at me. Whatever then. Suffer, you son of a bitch.

Instead, I preoccupy myself with how my uncle will get me out of there. I have no doubt he can. These guys aren't any smarter than he is, so why not? And he's just as bad as they are, so I know he will.

But the more I try to convince myself that I won't be trapped in King's apartment for much longer, I feel hope begin to slip away. I've been gone for hours. Does anyone know I'm missing? My mother calls every night to check on me, something I normally roll my eyes at when I see her number show up on my cell phone at ten o'clock. Certainly she'll do that tonight.

A feeling of dread settles into me when I remember I left my phone at home tonight because I only planned to run around the neighborhood and didn't think I'd be gone long. Now when everyone realizes I'm gone, they won't have the clue that I was taken off that street near my house.

God, I've seen this in every real crime show I've ever watched. When my mother doesn't get an answer to her call, she or my father will go to my house eventually and see my phone there. Crucial hours when they could be asking people in the homes near where that asshole grabbed me will be lost because they'll assume I was taken from my home.

The more I think about it, the more I feel my hope begin to wane. What if they don't realize I'm gone until tomorrow? What if they don't make the connection between my uncle's life and mine?

I quickly assure myself that won't happen. My father is just as paranoid as he's always been about someone grabbing me one night. Unlike my mother, who married into the Varens family, my father knows all too well what Victor's done in his life. He may never have been part of his brother's business, but he's never completely turned a blind eye to it.

He'll make the connection when he doesn't find me

at home and sees my cell phone sitting on the kitchen counter. I have to believe that.

Over and over, I repeat that like a mantra to myself, but doubt creeps in with each time I silently say it. My emotions swell inside me, and finally, I can't stop myself from feeling despondent.

Turning away so King can't see me, I tear up with each second the worst settles into my mind. Sniffling, I wipe under my eyes, refusing to give up just yet.

"Crying? I would have thought a member of the Varens family would be tougher than that," he says with a taunting laugh.

I spin around to see him sitting on the couch leering at me like my pain amuses him. Hating him and how smug he seems even as he sits there in pain, I snap, "Fuck you. You don't know me. You don't know a thing about me or my family."

He sneers at my defense of myself like it doesn't impress him. "I know enough about your kind, sweetheart."

I wait for him to continue his insults, but he turns away, ignoring me. Infuriated by his dismissal, I don't stop myself and say, "Be a man and kill me, if that's your plan."

The words are barely out of my mouth when I fear I've poked the bear one time too often. He flashes me a wicked smile and stands from the couch to slowly walk over to where I sit. Even hurt, he emanates power with every step, and I'm intimidated more than I want to admit, even to myself.

Looking up at him, I struggle not to look away I'm

so scared, but if I'm going to die right here and now, I won't leave this life as a coward. I may not be as able to hurt him as a man may, but I'm a Varens.

King stares down at me, locking his gaze on mine, and I can't help but notice how unique the color of his eyes is. It's like a deep chocolate brown mixed with a forest green, and as I look up at him, I'm amazed at how unique they are.

Like two beautiful, exotic jewels in a vicious face.

His breath is labored again, and I sense he's in more pain than he wants to let on, but his power and strength continues to radiate from every inch of him as I wait for his response to my challenge. Each time he inhales, his broad chest expands, and when he exhales, his warm breath drifts over me. Seconds pass into a minute without him saying a word, though, keeping me on the edge of my seat waiting for what will come next.

Arching a single dark eyebrow, he lowers himself so his face is mere inches from mine. Those stunning eyes of his stare deeply into mine, making me feel like he knows every thought racing through my head.

When I don't think I can face him for another second more, he finally responds to my taunt and the room instantly feels like someone has sucked out every last ounce of air.

"I don't plan to kill you, little girl. I've got other plans for you."

His words send a chill down my spine. I don't know what he means, but that wicked smile of his makes me think he's even more vicious than I first thought.

As he steps away from me, I wonder if he's going to torture me. My father often warned me that if any of the Varens' enemies took me, they'd do unspeakable things to hurt me in order to get to my uncle. But they wouldn't kill me because I'd be useful to them as something to trade. They'd just cause me enough pain to make him want to give them what they want.

My mind whirls with possibilities, each one more terrible than the last, and tears fill my eyes once more. I won't let him have the satisfaction of seeing me afraid of him, though, so I quickly steel myself, forcing my tears away.

King may have all the power here, but I have control over myself and I won't give that up without a fight. If he thinks I'm some little girl, as he keeps calling me, he's confused. I might be only twenty-one and only a woman, but I'm a Varens.

He can try to do his worst. I won't break easily. His psychotic friend grabbed the wrong woman from that quiet side street. Soon King will see that for himself.

ing

My eyes fly open as a spike of pain tears through my thigh, taking my breath away. Fuck! When I feel better, I'm going to kill that son of a bitch Tap. I push myself up against the headboard and take a deep breath as another jolt of pain races toward my groin.

Jesus Christ! I've been cut before. Why does this hurt so much? Fuck, I've been shot before and didn't feel this bad.

Lifting the blankets, I look down and see my leg's bright red around where Stills stitched me up. A third wave of pain rolls over me, taking my breath away. It's infected. Son of a bitch. Fucking Stills must have used a dirty needle.

I grit my teeth and tighten my fists in the sheets as

I wait for the pain to subside. The last thing I want to do is have Sophie help me, but I don't have a choice, it seems. It's either her or Duke, and he'll set me off on the sidelines for God knows how long. In the meantime, Tap will recover from the beat down I gave him and be front and center again finding ways to get in the boss's good graces.

Including taking Sophie back.

"Fuck. No way I'm letting him one up me," I groan before calling out for her. "Sophie! Get in here now!"

A few seconds later, she appears in my doorway looking terrified. Her wide eyes stare at me filled with fear because she has no idea how little I could do to her at the moment.

Hovering near the door, she doesn't say a word. All she does is stare, which only makes me feel worse.

"Get in here. I need your help," I say between gritted teeth.

She slowly walks toward where I sit in bed, far more timid than when she dared me to kill her a few hours ago. Too frightened, she stops a few feet away and shakes her head.

Before she can say whatever the fuck she plans to, I lose my patience and bark, "Get the fuck over here and help me, goddamnit! Stop acting like some frightened mouse!"

Thankfully, she obeys and turns on the lamp sitting on the nightstand. "I don't know what to do," she says in a tiny voice.

In the light, I see how bad my leg truly is. Not only

is it red, but it's swollen around where that fucker Tap sliced me. Definitely infected.

"Get me a warm washcloth and some peroxide out of the bathroom."

It feels like she takes forever to get back. Maybe if she didn't walk at a goddamned snail's pace. I watch her take each step back toward the bed excruciatingly slowly, and every second that passes my leg throbs in tandem with my heartbeat.

She returns as a wave of pain washes over me. Throwing my head back, I grit my teeth and hold my breath as I pray it ends before I black out.

Suddenly, I feel warmth on my leg and open my eyes to see her pressing the washcloth to my outer thigh. It feels so good that for a few sweet moments I forget about the agony I'm in and relax a little. Unballing my fists from the covers, I take a deep breath and let it out slowly, happy for the relief she's giving me.

"I think you need a doctor."

Her suggestion tears me out of the first good moments I've had in hours. Dismissing her, I shake my head. "I'm fine. Just clean up the blood near it."

"Do you have any pain killers? I can get them for you. Just tell me where they are."

Again, I shake my head. "No. I'll be fine."

"If you took something, then you'd be able to at least get some rest. I can get you them since you can't walk. Just tell me where to go."

Her insistence on arguing with me makes all the good I feel from her pressing that washcloth to my leg disappear, and the pain comes roaring back again. Furious, I push her away, disgusted at having to listen to her tell me what I should do.

She falls back, landing on the floor with a thud. Closing my eyes, I try to push away the rage brewing inside me, but it mixes with the pain to make me want to kill someone.

I grab the washcloth, which feels like ice against my skin now, and throw it at her. "This is cold! Warm it up again and don't take forever to get back here!"

A minute later, she returns, clearly afraid of me. I'm tired of this shit. I can't deal with her problems and my leg, so I pull her down next to me and snap, "Unless you want to see what happens when I'm really angry, take care of my leg. Now!"

Her hands trembling, she gently presses the warm washcloth to my leg. I close my eyes to revel in how good it feels and hear her exhale softly as she relaxes next to me.

"How does that feel?" she asks after a minute of the two of us saying nothing.

A wave of pain hits me, so I answer through clenched teeth once more, "Fine."

Slowly, I relax again, and my breathing calms as the pain subsides and I sigh at the warmth of the washcloth against my skin calming me.

I feel her lift it off my leg and instantly open my eyes to see why. She looks at me like she's terrified and forces a smile before placing it back against my leg with such care I wonder if she's done this before.

"Are you a nurse?"

Sophie looks up and shakes her head. "I'm a hostage."

"I meant…" In disgust, I don't bother to finish my sentence.

But she continues. "My mother's a nurse. I'm going to school for art." She stops and looks away. "At least I was."

I groan as she tenderly cleans the wound, and a second later, she pulls away, recoiling in horror.

"Don't worry. I'm not a complete, fucking monster. I don't plan on hurting you while you're helping me."

My words fail to reassure her, though. "I saw what you did with that man you beat unconscious. Why would I expect anything better from you?" she asks.

Her mention of that asshole Tap makes my anger surge again. "He's a fucking dick. He got what he had coming to him."

When she doesn't say anything in response, I snap, "You should be thanking me. If Tap had gotten his hands on you, I can promise you wouldn't be able to talk. You'd be fucking lucky to be conscious after he got done with you."

And yet still she doesn't seem to see she's gotten a good deal by coming with me.

"I guess I should be thankful then," she says with a healthy hint of defiance.

"That smart mouth is going to get you into trouble," I warn.

My threat makes her afraid once more. I see the fear fill her dark eyes. Good. I might be stuck in this bed and in fucking agony, but I'm not a man she or anyone else should mess with.

Her hand slips off the washcloth and brushes the inside of my thigh before she quickly moves it away. A rush of arousal awakes need inside me, and my cock begins to harden. I'm naked under the sheet covering everything but my injured leg, and it doesn't take long before the outline of my hard-on is obvious.

I see her cheeks turn red when she notices it. She also seems nervous, all of a sudden, too.

"What's wrong, little one? Never seen a man's cock get hard? You're not a virgin, are you?" I ask, liking the idea that she might be untouched.

She frowns but won't look at me as she answers my question. "No, I'm not a virgin. I just…"

Laughing at how uncomfortable she is with seeing me get hard, I say, "You've obviously spent your time with the wrong boys. A man should get excited when you touch his thigh like that."

Confused, she shakes her head and looks back at me. "I just would have thought you'd be in too much pain to have that happen."

I lift my hips off the mattress, loving how getting hard has taken my mind off the pain in my leg, and palm my cock through the sheet. "You have a way of making a man forget how much pain he's in, little girl."

Once again, she blushes at the reality of my arousal hidden right below the covers. I like how sweet she looks at that moment, and quickly my mind moves to imagining what her pretty mouth would look like wrapped around my cock.

As I fantasize, she looks up at me with that same fear in her eyes as before. "What are you going to do with me? Are you going to kill me?"

I shake my head and run my palm over my hard cock again. "Not if I don't have to. I'd rather have you be useful in an entirely different way."

She blushes at the vague reference of being with me and stands, taking the washcloth away from my leg. Instantly, the pain comes rushing back and I grab her by the wrist.

Her eyes grow wide as I tighten my hold on her arm. "Make it warm and come right back."

"I cleaned it up. There's no more to do," she says tearfully.

"Just do as I say, damnit."

Releasing my hold on her arm, I watch her hurry to the bathroom to do as I ordered. I hear the water running and pray to God she doesn't do something stupid instead of returning. The last thing I want right now is to have to get out of this bed to pull her back through the window in there.

But I know she hasn't given up on the idea of escaping. Even the searing pain in my leg and the delicious thoughts of fucking her running through my head haven't made me blind to that.

As I sit there truly hoping she doesn't make the wrong choice at this moment, I hear the water stop and then see the light go dark. A few seconds later, she hurries back to my bedside and places the warm cloth on my thigh, making me breathe a sigh of relief.

"Better?" she asks, wide-eyed, not knowing how sure I'd been that she'd try to escape that time.

Suddenly exhausted, I nod and let my head fall back against the pillow. "Better."

"Why did you look so unhappy when I was walking back here?"

With a sigh, I open my eyes and smile. "I was in pain."

"That's it? You looked like something else was wrong," she says, searching my face for her answer.

"What else could be wrong? I'm lying here with a gash in my leg and more pain than I've ever felt in my life. I'm basically living the dream."

My smart ass answer confuses her, and she frowns. "Is your boss going to come here any time soon?"

"I fucking hope not. Pretending I'm not in agony takes more fucking energy than I have at this moment."

As soon as the words leave my mouth, I regret being so honest with her. Pushing myself up, I look her dead in the eye. "Don't tell anyone I said that. Got it?"

Sophie nods. "That's why I was asking. I don't know the whole story between you and that Tap guy, but I understood that you want to be the favorite in your boss's eyes."

Her ability to understand that amazes me. "What makes you think that?"

With a shrug, she lets out a tiny laugh and then says, "I don't know. I'm just a person who pays attention to interpersonal dynamics. You and Tap clearly don't like one another, but even more, you're fighting to be the top guy with Duke. At least that's how it looked back at his office."

"Then you definitely don't want to let him in on how much pain I'm in or he'll hand you back to that asshole Tap. I'm not exaggerating when I say you'll be lucky to be alive once he's done with you."

A sly smile slowly raises the sides of her mouth, and she gets a look in her eyes that surprises me. "Then I guess I'll keep my mouth shut if your boss shows up since I don't want to be sent to Tap."

"For an art student, you're pretty smart, little girl."

Her smile fades, like she's disappointed. "Could you not call me that?"

"How old are you?" I ask, curious why the nickname I'm using bothers her so much.

"I'm twenty-one, so I'm not a little girl anymore."

My gaze drifts down from her face to her T-shirt and shorts as my mind fills with curiosity about what her body looks like underneath them. "Twenty-one, huh? Sounds young to me."

"How old are you?" she asks, tearing me out of a sweet fantasy about her tits.

I consider lying to her but decide against it. Everything else about the two of us here isn't the truth, but I'll give her that small concession.

"Thirty."

"And still you want to call me little girl? You're not that much older than me."

"Nine years is a long time, Sophie. You probably

won't even recognize your twenty-one-year-old self when you're my age."

My use of her name brings the smile back, lighting up her face. "See? You said it right that time."

I feel sleep taking me over, so I don't want to continue discussing this anymore. Closing my eyes, I say, "Then I guess that's what I'll have to call you from now on. Little girl's out and Sophie's in. How's that?"

Her answer fades into the recesses of my mind, and then a moment later, I drift off to a place where pain doesn't exist.

CHAPTER FIVE

ophie

IN THE MIDDLE OF OUR CONVERSATION, HE FALLS silent, and then he's asleep moments later. I keep the washcloth gently pressed to his leg for a few minutes more, just in case he's not deep in sleep, careful not to make the pain come back again because he's much nastier when he's hurting.

After ten minutes pass, I gently pull the washcloth away and hold my breath. King doesn't move, so I sit down on the bed as carefully as possible so as not to wake him and let out a heavy sigh. My emotions swirl inside me, but more than anything else, I'm exhausted after all that's happened tonight.

Hanging my head, I try to sort out my thoughts about this night. I stupidly let myself get grabbed by a rival of my uncle's, something I'll regret for the rest of my life, assuming I live through this. That's not something I'm banking on yet. My strength will only take me so far, and the rest relies on the man lying next to me.

Or worse, if King is too hurt, on that Tap asshole.

I cringe as I remember his knife slicing through King's pants, cutting the skin beneath and drawing blood instantly as I watched in horror and their boss laughed like he enjoyed their barbaric show. Then when King beat him until he lay lifeless on the floor like some battered ragdoll, I had to turn away it was so awful. I've seen men fight before, but I've never seen someone so hell bent on causing another person to suffer like King wanted to do to Tap.

He's just as vicious as the rest of them, no matter what he thinks.

Looking up at his face, his expression belies that, though. His dark lashes rest on his cheeks, the kind of eyelashes women pay good money to possess and men seem to always have naturally. I don't know why I didn't notice them before this when I studied how beautiful his eyes were earlier. Maybe because their color is so unique I didn't pay attention to anything else.

My gaze drifts down to his mouth — the mouth that has been so nasty to me tonight. It looks hard, but a closer look tells me his lips appear soft. I have to fight the urge to reach out and touch them with my fingertip to see if I'm right.

His skin is tan above the dark beard just coming in along his jaw and around his mouth. For the first time,

I notice a tattoo on the back of his neck. It joins with those across his shoulders and seems different than the ones that cover his arms. I can't make out the detail, but if it's like those I can see, it's some kind of all-black rope design dotted with shapes like triangles and circles. I've seen guys with tattoos all through high school, but none of them looked like this.

Even more, none of those boys looked like King. He'd tower over them, dwarfing their bodies like a man would boys. Underneath those tattoos exists the body of a fighter, or at least that's what I imagine he looks like fully naked. Maybe that's because the only thing I've seen him do other than lie in this bed is attack someone. Perhaps he's just someone who spends hours at the gym to get a body so cut with muscles.

I don't know. All I do know is he felt hard against me when he led me back here hours ago, and now as I watch his broad chest rise and fall with every breath he takes, I can't help but wonder what his body feels like with nothing covering him.

As much as I wish I could stop myself, I continue to study him, dropping my gaze below his chest. Hard peaks and valleys ripple across his abs, firm muscles I can't look away from. I imagine what they'd feel under my touch, his skin quivering when I glide over sensitive areas near his hipbones.

I feel my cheeks heat as sensual thoughts fill my mind, but I don't stop looking at him. He moves, tearing me from my fantasy, and I see something strange under the sheet where it hits near his hips.

After watching for nearly a minute to see if he'll wake, I gingerly lift the sheet to see what that odd shape outlined underneath could be.

My breath catches in my chest at what I see. No longer hard, his cock is long and thick even now, but even more amazing is it's pierced with two silver studs, one on each side of the head. I stare in shock as I've never seen anything like this in my life.

I can't help but wonder what it feels like when he's inside a woman. What do those smooth studs feel like when he's thrusting his cock inside you? Do they hurt? Do they touch parts of you that can't be reached any other way?

My mind fills with downright erotic thoughts of what it must be like to be fucked by him. I imagine he's a hard lover, much like the rest of him. He doesn't make love or just have sex.

No, he fucks and fucks hard. He takes a woman for his own. Those large hands of his hold her to him as he rams his cock inside her, possessing every inch of her inside and out. That mouth that spews such cruel things speaks words that make a woman know she's his, her pussy his and his alone to do what he chooses.

A tiny moan escapes my lips, and a second later, King's hand runs over his abs and down his leg. I quickly drop the sheet and look for the washcloth. Hurrying to the bathroom, I run it under the hot water and hope I can get back before he realizes it isn't on his leg anymore.

I see his eyes are still closed when I walk out into the bedroom, so I breathe a sigh of relief and sit down on the bed next to him. Pressing the cloth to the outside of his thigh, I'm happy when he doesn't move.

A second later, he lets out a chuckle. "Like what you saw?"

Horror rushes through me at the sound of his words. He knew I was looking at his body! My face feels like it's on fire, and I turn away just as he opens his eyes and stares up at me like he knows every wicked thought I had about him as he slept.

"I thought…I just saw something odd…I didn't mean to wake you up," I say, my words staggering out of my mouth.

Turning back to focus on the washcloth and his leg, I see out of the corner of my eye he's wearing a smile that's utterly sexual. It makes his mouth look like nothing as awful as he's said before could come out of it again.

"I know what you saw. I asked if you like it."

Touching my cheek with my free hand, I feel heat worse than any fever I've ever experienced. I can only hope I haven't turned beet red to match the temperature of my skin.

As casually as I can, I say with a shrug, "If you've seen one penis, you've seen them all, to be honest."

But he sees right through my attempt to be nonchalant. "So you've seen others that were pierced before? Who'd have thought innocent little Sophie lived such a dangerous life."

"Why do you want to make me out to be some untouched little girl who knows nothing about sex? Does that get you off or something?"

His smile grows even as he shakes his head. "There's that smart mouth again. One of these times that's going to get you in trouble," he says in a low voice tinged with the threat of punishment.

And yet, all I can think of is how he must feel inside a woman with those piercings on that big cock.

I OPEN MY EYES AND LOOK AROUND, UNSURE WHERE I am for a few seconds. Scrubbing the sleep from my head, I feel someone next to me and look to see King still sleeping.

The sound of the floor creaking startles me, and I sit bolt upright on the bed. We aren't alone. King's boss stands a few feet away with a glint in his eyes that instantly frightens me. I don't know how long he's been there, and something tells me he's not here just to check on how King is feeling.

Quickly, I shake his shoulder. "King, your boss is here. Wake up."

He slowly opens his eyes and looks first at me for a moment. In them, I see a kindness in him I hadn't seen before. It disappears a few seconds later, replaced by the hardness I've come to expect from him when he realizes his boss is standing there.

Pulling the blankets over his leg, he pushes himself up against the headboard as Duke comes over to the side of the bed. Towering over me, he says, "By the look of what I saw when I walked in, you're feeling better. Ready to get back to work?"

"I'm ready. I'll be right there."

"Take your time. I want my best man at one hundred percent," Duke says as he turns to leave.

King smiles, but I sense it's forced when he laughs and says, "I'm fine. No worries, boss."

Duke doesn't seem to pick up on how much pain his best guy is in and leaves without another word. As soon as the door closes, King's body sags back onto the bed as he lets out a low groan.

"Get the washcloth warm," he orders, clearly in pain.

I do as I'm told and return less than a minute later to find him in a pair of boxer briefs sitting on the side of the bed, his head hung. Crouching down in front of him, I gently press the washcloth to his leg.

"You're not ready to get out of bed. I wouldn't be surprised if you can't even walk."

Shaking his head, he mumbles, "I'm fine. I'm just fine."

When he tries to stand up, he falls back onto the bed, just as I assumed he would. I lean over to help him, but he barks, "Get off me!"

He angrily pushes me away, and I fall back onto the floor, hurting my arm. "Ow! I was just trying to help," I cry out while pain radiates through my wrist.

"I don't need your fucking help, little girl," he snaps with all the anger he has inside him.

The second time he tries to stand up, he succeeds and limps away, leaving me sitting on the floor as he slams the door behind him. A spark of hope ignites inside me, and I rush over to see if he left it unlocked.

But I try the doorknob and it doesn't move. The door's locked from the outside.

Disappointed and raw from emotions too close to the surface, I collapse on the floor and let the tears come that I've been holding back ever since that fucker Tap grabbed a hold of me. I'm never getting out of this place. Whatever kindness I thought I saw in King's eyes a few moments ago doesn't exist.

He's as vicious as any of the men my father warned me about for so long.

CHAPTER SIX

ing

DUKE'S OFFICE IS EMPTY WHEN I GET THERE, AND I silently thank the universe for not forcing me to perform my bullshit I'm fine act for a room full of people. I'm not fucking fine in any possible definition of that word. Not at all.

Pain radiates up toward my hip, taking my breath away for a moment, and then ebbs away. I grab hold of the doorframe to steady myself and hope I'm not shaking so anyone can see.

"How's my best man doing today?" Duke asks in his most chipper voice as he walks out of the bathroom where fucking Stills probably infected me with some kind of skeevy disease when he sewed me back up the other night.

It's an effort to tilt my head up to look at him, but I

have to keep this façade up for now. I can't risk Duke thinking I'm not able to do my job, just in case I didn't fuck Tap up enough and he's back on his feet.

"Ready to go, boss. What's going on today?" I ask as a wave of pain rolls over me and I tighten my hold on the doorframe. Did my voice falter on the word today? I hope not.

He stops just before he reaches his desk and studies me for a long moment. Remaining perfectly still, I watch for any sign he knows how fucked up I truly feel, but he simply smiles and shakes his head.

"You're one cool customer, King. Meanwhile, Tap is still laid up in bed. You really messed him up. I hear he just woke up, but there's no way he can work anytime soon, I'm guessing."

As Duke takes his seat, I force a laugh that makes my body feel like it's splitting apart down the middle. "Pussy. He's lucky I didn't fuck him up even worse."

Throwing his head back, Duke lets out a chuckle. "That's why you're the king, right?"

I nod, hating every fucking syllable of this small talk he seems interested in having with me today. Dane comes up behind me and brushes against my side on his way into the office. It takes every ounce of restraint in me to not spin him around and cold-cock him, but I stop myself. I can't go around beating the hell out of people because I feel like shit or they'll all figure out how bad I'm doing.

Holding out a sheet of paper, Duke says, "You and Dane go out and gather up these guys. Bring them back here. I'll be waiting."

Thankfully, Dane grabs the paper so I don't have to walk across the office to get it, but I ask, "Anything we should look out for?"

"Nah. Just the usual types who need to be reminded of how the world works. They got a visit from Marsh and Stills the other day, but I feel like they need a face-to-face meeting to get my point across."

"Got it." Turning toward Dane, I push down the urge to scream from the pain in my thigh and nod toward the door. "Ready to go?"

With a shrug, he starts walking toward the hallway. "Sure. Let's go. You driving or me?"

"You drive," I answer as I take a step and the pain crushes me.

And then everything goes black.

MY EYES OPEN AND I'M LOOKING UP AT THE DOCTOR standing next to my bed with Duke right behind him. Both men stare down at me like they're surprised to see me awake.

Unsure what the hell is going on, I follow the doctor's gaze to the IV coming out of my right arm. Clearly, I didn't know how fucking sick I was.

"King, you've got an infection. That's what the IV is for."

I nod but ignore him and say to Duke, "Tell Stills I'm going to get him for this."

"Once we get this into you, we can take you off the

IV and move you to antibiotics that won't keep you in bed," the doctor continues, disregarding my joke.

"Leave it to you to not want to take a day off," Duke says, shaking his head. "I want you to stay in bed with your pretty nurse until you're better. No arguing this time either."

He has no idea how bad I feel at this moment. I couldn't argue if my life depended on it. Lifting the arm with the IV attached, I look up at the doctor. "Is this going to do anything for the pain because my leg feels like it's being fucking ripped apart."

Nodding, he smiles. "Yep. It should already be taking the edge off. Give it a few minutes and you'll feel it. I'll leave some painkillers too, just in case the pain gets too much."

"Thanks, doc."

After he leaves, Duke gives me a pat on the shoulder. "I'll leave you to get well."

I can't let him go without making sure he knows I'll be back to work as soon as I can. "Thanks, but it won't take long. Now that the doctor is pumping me full of drugs, I'll be up and around in no time. Just give me a day or two."

"Just get better. I know you're not anyone who'd ever slack off, so take your time and get back to one hundred percent. And I'll be sure to tell Stills you're going to want to talk to him."

He leaves smiling, which means I'm still in a good place with him. I can't afford to let this thing with my leg ruin everything I've worked so hard for. I won't.

Not because that asshole wanted to fuck me up with one of his bullshit knives.

Out of the corner of my eye, I see Sophie cowering in the corner of the room. For a few minutes, I'd forgotten she was still here when I was busy with the doctor and Duke.

"Come here, little one. I need your help."

She walks over to the side of my bed but says nothing, avoiding making eye contact with me. Did something happen with Duke while I was out of it?

It takes all the energy I can muster to sit up, and once I do, I feel like someone's used my body as their own personal punching bag. "Help me get my clothes off. And don't think you can run away. I'll happily rip this thing out of my arm, and when I catch up with you, you'll find out what happens when you make me angry."

Still, she doesn't look at me, but I see in her expression what I said bothered her. I obviously don't look as fucked up as I feel.

Tentatively, she reaches for the bottom of my T-shirt and begins to ease it over my head. "I've seen what happens when you're angry."

When she finally tugs it off, I look up at her and force myself to smile. "Good. Then don't do anything stupid."

Sophie begins to pull back the sheet but quickly covers me again. Sheepishly, she mumbles, "Sorry. I forgot you don't have pants on after the doctor took them off."

Dressed only in my underwear, I lean back against

the headboard and let out a heavy sigh. Just taking off my clothes with Sophie's help sapped every ounce of energy I had. If she decided to take off now, I couldn't do a damn thing about it.

Then again, I probably wouldn't have to since the dogs would find her in less than a few minutes and there wouldn't be much left after they got through with her. The image of her being torn apart flashes through my mind, and for a brief second, I think about warning her again about leaving.

But I don't. If she's going to be stupid, I'm in no shape to stop her. Let her take her chances with hungry dogs or Tap. She'll find out too late she got the best deal she could when I claimed her.

When I look up after daydreaming, I notice she's looking at my crotch. Filled with curiosity, her wide-eyed gaze doesn't veer away even when I clear my throat.

"Not today, little one. I'm in too much pain. Another time I'll get hard for you."

That pretty pink I've grown to like colors her cheeks, but she doesn't look away. Little one liked what she saw. Good.

"Then again, if you keep blushing in that innocent way, I might not be able to control myself."

For the first time, she lifts her head and her gaze meets mine. Frowning, she says, "I'm not as innocent as you seem to think I am. I'm not sure how many twenty-one year old women you've known in your life, but we aren't virginal schoolgirls, you know."

The image of Sophie dressed in a Catholic school

uniform with the skirt barely reaching the middle of her thighs runs through my mind, and I wonder if maybe I could get hard. Probably not. All the better. I need to recuperate, and I don't have the energy to fuck anyway.

"I swear to God you're trying to tempt me tonight, little one. Just the mention of you as a virginal schoolgirl is enough to make me think I can handle doing more than just lying in this bed."

A tiny smile lights up her face. "Do you believe in God?"

So, she wants to play? Okay, little one. We'll play.

Pushing myself up against the headboard, I look her up and down and smile as I fantasize about how good it will be when I finally feel better and can act on what's in my mind. "When I'm balls deep inside a woman and she's yelling my name, I have to admit I believe in God then. When my face is drenched with a woman's juices after I finish eating her pussy and her thighs are quivering against the sides of my head, I believe in God then. And when a woman's mouth is taking all of my cock down to the base and she flicks her tongue over my balls, I believe in God then. Other than that, I don't see much evidence that God is anywhere around these days."

By the time I finish, her brown eyes are as wide as saucers and her mouth is hanging open. I like this look on her. She looks cute when she's shocked into silence.

"Did I say something to offend you, little one?" I ask, enjoying how teasing her makes me feel better.

Or maybe the drugs the doctor claimed would take the pain away are finally kicking in.

"No. I'm not a child, so you talking dirty like that doesn't affect me one way or another," she answers, but I can see she's clearly flustered.

"Oh, that's not dirty talk, honey. If I was talking dirty, you'd be dripping wet and close to coming." Looking down her body, I let my gaze settle on her pussy. "Or maybe I was. You tell me."

"You don't have that kind of effect on me. You're not my type."

I sense she likes talking about this subject, even though she doesn't give me much to go on. That's okay. This is a hell of a lot better way to pass the time than lying in bed and watching bad TV.

Looking up at her, I ask, "And what's your type, little one? Let me guess. High school football team captain. Acts like a badass but in real life he's just as clumsy as the other boys. He thinks he's got the moves, but unless he's been blessed by God with a giant cock, he spends most of his time fumbling around your pretty little panties trying to find your clit."

Sophie rolls her eyes and grimaces at my mention of the senior class jock. "Nice pun. No, thanks. I prefer men, not boys. And the men I like create things like music and art."

I cringe at her description of her type of guy. Artsy fartsy douchebags with shitty beards? I think I'm disappointed with where this conversation has gone.

"I thought better of you, little one. Your type

makes my dick go limp. The very thought of you wasting your time on that kind of guy makes me think I misjudged you."

"I'm a little surprised to hear my type does anything to your dick, to be honest," she says with a sly smile.

"Clever, Sophie. I walked right into that one," I admit, appreciating how bright and confident she truly is. Too bad she wastes her time with those artistic assholes.

We stare at one another, neither of us saying anything after my compliment until she smiles and straightens the sheets over my legs. "I have a feeling those drugs are starting to work. You don't seem to be in as much pain as before. Do you need me to do anything or get you anything?"

Shaking my head, I close my eyes as I slide down onto the bed. "I'm fine, little one."

"Sophie."

I open my eyes and smile. "I'm fine, Sophie. Now don't do anything stupid like try to escape or kill me in my sleep, okay?"

She avoids answering what was more of a rhetorical question anyway and asks, "Would you like me to fix your pillow, or are you good?"

Her voice sounds like it's coming from somewhere far away, like she's fading into the distance with every word she speaks. I consider answering her question, but my eyelids flutter shut and then I'm lost to a drug-induced sleep.

CHAPTER SEVEN

ophie

AN AGONIZING CRY LIKE THAT OF A WOUNDED animal wakes me out of the soundest sleep I've had since coming here. My feet are on the floor and moving toward him before I'm even fully awake. Working on instinct alone, I stumble into his room and stop next to his bed. His eyes closed, he doesn't move, but I watch him sleep and wait to find out why he made that sound.

He's pushed down the covers to around his hips, so his entire torso is bared to me. As much as I don't want to admit it, seeing his body creates a need in me I've never felt before with any other man.

There must be something wrong with me. He's my captor, and at any moment, he's liable to threaten me instead of uttering a single kind word to make me feel better. Why would anything about him affect me in that way?

Yet there I stand in the darkness of his bedroom watching his chest rise and fall with each breath he takes, the tattoos on his shoulders illuminated by the moonlight coming in through the window behind the bed. I should want to smother him with a pillow, but instead all I can think of is how it would feel to run my hands over his body and if his skin near his hipbones is as soft as it seems.

I didn't lie when I told him about the kind of man I've always preferred. I don't know if there was ever a time I consciously decided I liked artistic guys, but everyone I've ever dated looked about the same and nothing like King.

Thin with patchy facial hair that never quite makes it to a full beard, with bald spots in some places and scraggly, too long clumps of hair in others. They love to talk about art and music and how it affects them deep in their souls. They crave long talks to explain their creativity, spending their nights drinking popular brands of beer in trendy bars with women like me who hang on every word that pops into their heads and out their mouths.

Not that I've ever found any of that sexy. I've sat through countless hours of intense conversations with artistic guys, but not a single moment of that time ever made me feel like I do when I look at King. I just assumed I was the problem, that I simply didn't appreciate men like a woman should.

My eyes roam over his body now as I wonder if I

just wasn't meeting the right men to excite me. But how can someone like King be that kind of man? He's vicious and heartless. Just because he isn't as horrible as that Tap psychopath doesn't mean he's a good man.

And still need coils tightly inside me with every moment I'm near him.

He shifts his position and quietly moans, tearing me out of my thoughts. I turn away, terrified he knows I've been watching him, but when I don't hear him say anything for a few seconds, I glance back and see that same angelic look he gets when he sleeps.

How is it possible such an evil soul can look so gentle?

It's like he touches me deep inside in a way that makes me feel weak. Even now as he lies there in bed, his body fighting off infection, strength and power practically ooze out of him, exciting me and terrifying me at the same time.

I let my gaze travel from his tattooed, broad shoulders down over his muscular chest and chiseled abs partially covered by the bedsheet. Never before have I seen such a perfect physical specimen of a man.

My mind drifts to what's hidden beneath that sheet. The vision of those piercings is fixed in my brain, and question after question bounces around my head. Why did he do that to himself? Did it hurt? Was it part of some initiation into his boss's group? Do all of the men around King also have cock piercings?

I don't think I've ever been so fixated on a man's cock before in my life. Jesus, most of the men I've slept with I haven't thought about their cock as much as I've thought about King's in the past few days.

Turning away, I shake my head, trying to push out the last of the images of those piercings still in my brain. This must be some reaction to being a hostage. What do they call that? Some kind of syndrome. It has something to do with Vikings, doesn't it? Denmark? Is that it? Denmark syndrome?

No, that doesn't sound right. Copenhagen syndrome? No. That's not it either.

Stockholm syndrome! That's it! Stockholm. But doesn't that usually take a little while before the hostage begins to care for the captor?

I quickly correct myself on that ridiculous idea. I do not care for King. Not in the least. He may be better than Tap or his disgusting boss, but I don't care for him.

Why I'm borderline obsessed with those piercings I have no idea.

My cheeks heat at that admission, even though it was silent and only I know the truth. I've never been the type of woman who spends her time ogling men's crotches. I went to a male revue show with my friends last year, and even there, where every inch of men seemed to be available for all to see, I didn't think once about a single man's cock.

God, now all I can think about is that word! Cock. Christ, maybe I'm going crazy.

"What are you doing standing there? Why are you in here?"

King's angry voice rips me out of my thoughts,

thankfully, and I look up to see him glaring at me. My happiness to not be thinking about that particular part of his body is quickly swept away and replaced by fear.

"You...you were in pain. You ma-made a noise, so I came in, but I saw you were asleep. I didn't meant to wake you," I stammer out as he continues to look up at me in pure disgust.

He doesn't respond to my rambling, terrified explanation. Stretching his leg, he grimaces and groans.

"Are you in pain? Do you want more of those pills the doctor left?"

As if he doesn't hear me, King ignores my questions but groans again. I wait for him to tell me how he wants me to help him, but instead he waves me away.

"I'm fine. I'm not in pain."

"Oh, okay."

I don't believe him, but what else can I do? Part of me wonders if there's any way to escape if only I can get more of those painkillers into him.

But another part I don't understand craves being near him. How can that be? What the fuck is wrong with me? How could I think something so utterly perverse?

Cringing, I turn to leave, as disgusted with myself as he is with me. Maybe if I spend some time alone out on the couch I'll be able to get my head on straight and stop thinking these ridiculous things.

"I need a drink of water," he croaks out.

With a look back at him, I nod and head toward the bathroom. As I fill a glass with the water he wants, I think about smashing it against the sink and running in to slit his throat. He's in enough pain that I could probably take him by surprise. He won't know what to do when I come at him, and in seconds, I could be free of him and this place.

The water overflows the top of the glass just as reality rushes back into my brain. Even if I killed him and got free, how would I get by the guards and those vicious dogs that protect the estate?

Dejected, I turn off the faucet and return to give him his glass of water. He eagerly takes it and gulps down a mouthful as I reach for the bottle of painkillers. I tip out two pills and place them on his nightstand.

"Just in case. No use suffering if you don't have to."

He looks up at me with a curious expression, so I force a smile. I might not have a plan to get away, but it can't hurt to have him knocked out. I can't let him know that, though, or God only knows what he'll do to me.

When he doesn't say anything for a few seconds, I move to leave, but he grabs my arm to hold me there. "Stay here."

Confused by his demand, but even more by how my body is reacting to his touch, I look down at him lying there staring up at me with a hint of need in his eyes. My gaze moves to where his hand is tightly wrapped around my wrist. As if to convince me to do as he wants, he loosens his hold.

"Stay."

The urge to run away as fast as I can fights against one that makes me want to be close to him, and for a moment, I stare down at him as the tug-of-war inside me makes it impossible to move. The touch of his fingers on my skin sends a thrill through me, but the truth of who he is remains uppermost in my thoughts, tempering that urge I don't understand.

"Okay."

The word comes out of my mouth like a whisper, like I don't want anyone to hear me agree to stay there with him. Not that I have much of a choice. We aren't equals here. I can't forget that.

Ever.

His hand falls to the bed, and he inches over so there's room for me to sit. I watch in shock, confused that he wants me so close to him. My thoughts about his body that just made me feel so sickened race through my mind again, and I blush, my cheeks flush with searing heat.

I don't want to get too close to him, but I sit in the spot he's made for me. Maybe he's being nice. I don't know. All I know is his mood changes too fast for me to risk angering him.

He doesn't speak as I perch myself on the edge of the bed, not knowing what to say. He's holding me hostage, even if he does seem like he can't do much physically at the moment to keep me there.

A low moan fills the space around us, and I look over to see him cringing in pain. My nature isn't to be cruel, although I wish it could be. The thought of how easily I might smother him with a pillow makes me reach to grab the one propped up behind me, but I think twice about it, remembering the truth that stops me all the time.

I might be able to escape from King, but what awaits me outside this apartment is likely far worse and possibly deadly.

"Is there anything I can do to help?" I quietly ask as he writhes in pain.

A few moments later, he seems better and turns his head to face me. "So now you want to help me?"

"I've always wanted to help you. Well, maybe not always, but at least since the doctor said you needed medicine to get better."

My answer amuses him, although I don't understand why, and he smiles, shaking his head. "Well, well. You must be the little girl with the heart of gold. Here I am keeping you hostage, and you still want to help me."

All I hear, other than the complete disdain he has for my genuine attempt at kindness, is his use of that nickname I hate. "Is there anything I can do to make you stop calling me that?"

My frustration makes his smile grow bigger. "Calling you what, little girl?"

"That! I thought we agreed to call me by my name. Why do you keep using that nickname I hate?"

Pleasure dances in his eyes as he admits the truth. "Because you hate it."

"Nice. I bet you would pull my pigtails if I had them too."

That smile of his turns absolutely sinful, and he laughs at me. "I can't decide if you're trying to tease me or you really don't know how suggestive some of things you say are. Now I'm going to be thinking all night about you in pigtails and me pulling on them while you're bent over in front of me."

My stomach flips at the mere mention of the two of us together like that, and once again, he's succeeded in making me blush. Looking away so he doesn't see how he affects me, I mumble, "Typical guy. Everything is about sex."

"I can't think of anything better for everything to be about. What I don't understand is why you're so uptight about sex. I'm betting it's because you've never had anyone do you right," he says with a chuckle.

Hopeful my face has returned to its normal shade, I snap my head around to look at him and roll my eyes. "Again, so typical. If only a woman can have some of your magic wand, she'll have a perfect life full of sunshine, rainbows, and unicorns."

For a second, he just stares up at me, and I wonder if I've said too much. Even in his injured state, he's dangerous. I forgot that for a moment.

But then he lets out a hearty laugh that tells me I'm okay, if only for the time being. "Did your parents read you too many fairy tales as a little girl? Magic wand? I've never had it called that before. And as for a woman having sunny days, rainbows, and unicorns after I fuck her, I can't say if any of those happen. I'm not usually around after we're done."

Although he's making fun of me, at least he's laughing. I can handle someone having a laugh at my expense if it means I get to stay safe for another night. That saying about laughter soothing the savage beast runs through my mind. No, it isn't laughter that does that. It's music. Or maybe not. I'm not sure. All I know is a smiling King is better than the other variety of the man.

"So no reports of post-sex unicorn sightings by the women you've been with? Maybe those piercings aren't that impressive, after all."

I know as soon as I finish speaking that I've shown him exactly how much I can't stop thinking about that cock of his. He arches a dark eyebrow and shakes his head.

"My, my, Sophie. And here I was thinking that you didn't care at all about me. I had no idea those two silver studs enchanted you so much. Or is it my cock, in general, that you can't stop thinking about?"

Now I know I'm blushing, but there's no point in turning away or trying to hide it. He's figured me out, at least the part of me that's fascinated by those piercings.

That doesn't mean I have to let him think that cock of his is the be-all and end-all. "You have a one-track mind. You're literally the physical personification of the idea of thinking with the wrong head."

"Don't worry, Sophie. I use my other head when it comes to you, too."

And just like that, I've said something to make his smile disappear.

I think if I can get us to be more than captor and captive, maybe I can stay alive. Even though I've asked him if he's going to kill me and he said no, I don't want to rely on his mercurial moods. Perhaps if he sees me as a person instead of a thing he's keeping for himself, it won't be easy for him to kill me.

Trying to repair any damage I've done with my comment, I smile and ask, "Are you feeling any better?"

King thinks about the question for a moment and nods. "I guess I am. For a while there, I forgot about how much my leg fucking hurts."

"Well, if you want to go back to poking fun at me, feel free if it makes your leg hurt less. I can handle it."

With a smile, he rolls his eyes and sighs, making me think we can get back on track. "It's like everything out of your mouth is a double entendre, little one. What I can't decide is if you're doing it on purpose to tease me or by accident because you're just that innocent."

I grimace at his use of that damn nickname again, so he quickly says, "Sophie."

"Thank you. And if I'm being truthful, I didn't mean for anything to sound sexual there. I think you just have that on your mind."

"Poking?" he asks with a chuckle.

"Sex, in general. I don't know how someone in so much pain could think of that. I know I couldn't."

Closing his eyes, he sighs. "It's a hell of a lot better

than thinking about how my leg feels like it's being torn apart from the inside."

"You should take some painkillers. They'd let you sleep, and you'd be out of pain, at least for a while," I suggest, hoping I don't sound too eager.

He turns his head and looks up at me, and for a split second, his eyes seem to be filled with hurt. "Can't wait to be finished playing nursemaid, Sophie?"

Quickly, I try to convince him that this isn't a bad way to spend my time. "No. That's not it at all."

Whatever I saw in him hardens before my eyes. "Oh, I get it. You figure if you can get enough of those drugs into me that you'll find a way to escape. Trust me. The safest place on this estate is right here with me."

"No, that's not it either. I just figured if you're in pain you should do something to fix that. As for escaping, I've given up on that. The thought of guard dogs ripping my flesh from my bones does that to a girl."

For a moment, he studies me, like something I said makes him even more suspicious. His eyes narrowing to slits, he doesn't say a word, which makes me more nervous than I've felt around him since the last time he barked at me yesterday. I know he can't read my mind and know that I haven't given up on finding a way off this goddamned estate and away from him and all these wretched men, but is it possible my facial expression is telling him something I don't want him to know?

"You're smarter than that, Sophie. I don't believe

for a second you've given up on figuring out how to escape from here. Not that I blame you one bit. I would never accept being held prisoner, and I don't think you should either."

"Yet you'd kill me as quickly as look at me if I tried."

"True, but I wouldn't disrespect you for trying."

"Respect doesn't do much for a person when their bones are broken. Or worse."

King stretches his arm to rest his hand on my thigh. As excitement races over my skin, he says, "I told you I wouldn't kill you, Sophie. I'm a man of my word. If you die here, it won't be at my hands."

"Those were comforting words until you mentioned if I die here."

"Then let me change what I said. I won't kill you, and if there's anything I can do about it, I won't let anyone else kill you either. Better?"

I can't decide if it's the pain in his leg making him want to deal with me like this or the latent effects of those painkillers he took hours ago, but his promise makes me breathe a little easier. "I want to believe you. I don't want to die, no matter whose hands are involved."

"We all die sometime, little one. It's just a fact of life," he says in a faraway voice that makes me think he's no longer talking about my death at this terrible place.

"Well, I always thought I'd live long enough to have some life to look back on. As it is, I'm twenty-one years old and dying now would mean I lived very little."

His eyes flutter closed, and right before he drifts off to sleep, he says, "Then I guess we better make sure you get some living in."

I don't know what he means by that. All I know is something inside me says I'm safer with him than I am with anyone else at this moment.

The problem is I don't know what's going to happen in the next moment.

ing

FROM SOMEWHERE FAR AWAY, I HEAR A NOISE THAT sounds like a chime. Am I dreaming, or is that a doorbell? Whatever it is, someone needs to shut it the fuck up.

Rolling over, I stuff my face into the pillow, but the sound continues. Half-asleep, I open my eyes and look around. I'm in my bed, and Sophie is nowhere to be found.

As I become fully conscious, I realize the chiming noise is my phone. Snatching it off the nightstand, I clear my throat and groan, "Hello?"

"King, I need you in my office. You're feeling better, right? Dane and Marsh said they saw you outside your apartment late last night, so I'm assuming you're good to go."

I push myself up and sit back against the headboard, silently cursing those two for having big mouths. Would one more day of not having me around have killed them?

"Yeah, I'm fine. Those antibiotics the doctor gave me did the trick, and I feel like a million bucks," I lie. In truth, I feel about seventy-five percent good, but that's a hell of a lot better than two days ago.

"Great. Get yourself down here, and bring the girl. See you in a few minutes!"

"Okay. See you then."

As I swing my legs off the bed, I wait for the rush of pain to explode through my thigh. A second goes by and then two…and then nothing. I breathe a sigh of relief and smile. Thank God for the magic of antibiotics.

Free of the fear of the pain that's ravaged me for the past few days, I can't help but think that Duke has finally decided to let Sophie go. All the better. Tap should have never taken her in the first place. Grabbing girls off the street isn't the way to fucking do business.

At least not a smart way.

I slowly walk out to the living room and see Sophie still asleep on the couch. For a moment, I watch her and can't believe how peaceful she looks lying there in a place she doesn't belong. She'll be gone soon, though. As that thought settles into my brain, I have to admit I'll miss her.

But she shouldn't be here. I've known that since

the minute I saw Tap standing there on that neighborhood street holding her to him.

And she doesn't belong with me. Not here or anywhere else.

"Sophie, you need to wake up," I say, shaking her shoulder gently.

Her eyes fly open, and she sits bolt upright a second later. "Why? What's going on?"

The terror in her voice confuses me. Does she always wake up like this?

"We need to go. I'm going to grab a shower, so get ready."

I don't give her a chance to ask any questions and head into the bathroom. The less we talk, the better. She'll go home, and I'll go back to living my life the way I always have. Everyone will be where they belong again.

The hot water rolling over my skin feels better than anything I can imagine. The steam rises around me, fogging up the glass enclosure, and I wish I could stay here forever. Why the hell do I have to go back to work today? Would one more day without me truly have made anyone's life worse?

Fucking Dane and Marsh. Tattletales like little girls.

"King, why do I have to come with you this morning?" I hear Sophie ask practically in tears.

Through the steam, I'm surprised to see her standing there in front of the sink staring in at me. "Duke told me to bring you down to his office."

"But why? What's going to happen?"

Wiping the glass, I see the fear in her eyes telegraphing what she's worried about loud and clear.

"I don't plan to kill you or let anyone else hurt you, and unless you're going home, you'll be staying right where you are. With me."

"Going home? Is there a chance of that?"

"Yeah, so get ready."

But even hearing that doesn't change that look in her eyes. I wait for her to ask me something else I probably can't give her an answer for, but after a few seconds, she simply turns and walks out of the bathroom without another word. I don't know why, but her unhappiness bothers me. Why wouldn't that news put a smile on her face?

Even more, why do I care? Hanging my head, I look down at my cock already hard and wonder why this woman has such an effect on me. It's only been a few days, so why should I give a damn one way or the other whether she's happy or not? I have a job to do here, and I'm doing it. Period.

Pushing down whatever the fuck I'm going through, I finish my shower and dress to get down to Duke's office. When we reach the bottom of the stairs and start walking across the estate, she stops and grabs my arm.

Confused, I look down at where her fingers are clamped down onto me and shake my head. "What are you doing?"

Looking up at me, her dark eyes wide in fear, she says, "Please don't let them kill me."

My fucking emotions swirl around inside me, like

everything she's feeling has wound its way into my soul. "I told you. If you're not going home, you're staying with me, and I'm not going to kill you."

"Promise?" she asks in a tiny voice that hits me squarely in the chest.

It hangs in the air between us, joining me to her in a way I hope doesn't end up betraying both of us.

"I give you my word."

I start walking again, tugging her along as I struggle to force down my emotions to someplace inside me where no one can see. The last thing I need is to walk into an office full of men looking like she and I share some kind of secret.

"Whatever your word means in this world, I'm trusting you."

To myself, I think how dangerous that might be for her. I won't kill her, and I don't plan to let anyone else hurt her, but that leaves a lot that could possibly happen.

By the time we reach Duke's office, I'm ready for this thing with Sophie to be over. She's gotten too close to me already. Letting her in any more would be too dangerous.

The first person I see as we walk through the door is Tap, and he looks like he's fully healed, except for the black and blue colors along his jaw and under his right eye. All it makes me think is I should have fucked him up more.

He twists his ugly face into a smirk that makes the hair on the back of my neck stand up. Something's wrong. Along the wall, Marsh and Dane give me quick smiles that fade even faster. And Stills' expression looks like he is barely keeping down his dinner from last night.

Something is very wrong.

Before I can say anything, Tap steps forward and says, "So you've been laid up. Is that right?"

"I could ask the same question of you. Guess I went easier on you than I thought."

But he doesn't take the bait and instead points at Sophie. "The point is if he's been laid up, he couldn't claim her yet. So she's up for grabs. That means I claim her right now."

Terror races through me. He can't be fucking serious. We're going to do this again? I silently promise to fucking kill him this time. With his own goddamned knife, the asshole.

I look over at Duke, and for a split second, I'm stunned. He agrees with Tap.

"He did take her, so by rights, he should be able to claim her, King."

Sophie steps behind me to hide as I fight to keep my expression as blank as possible. Maybe I can talk myself out of another go round with that asshole.

It's no use, though. Tap's got Duke on his side, so we're going to do this again. I only hope my thigh can take it.

"That fuck owes me, and even if he didn't, I beat him already. That gives me the right to her."

"Not if you haven't had her yet."

Duke's words slam into me, and I struggle to keep myself calm. Out of the corner of my eye, I see Tap move toward Sophie and feel her grasp at the back of my pants. The fear comes off her in waves that threaten to overwhelm me.

Shaking my head, I don't say a word to him, but this isn't going to happen.

There's no way I'm letting him have her. I know he'll beat the hell out of her. The guy is a fuck.

Even more, I gave her my word. I didn't sign up to be her hero, but she won't be going with Tap.

As every man in front of me waits to see what will happen next, my mind races to figure out a way to stop Tap. I can beat him again, but I know that's not what he or Duke mean this time.

There's only one answer.

Reaching around, I grab Sophie's hand and pull her around to stand in front of me. Utter fear fills her eyes, but then I see something like trust replace that fear, and she gives me a tiny, hopeful smile.

I stare at her and if she could read my mind, she'd hear, "Don't. This isn't going to be good."

For a moment, everything around us freezes in place, until I place my hands on her shoulders and push her down to the floor. "On your knees, little one."

I hear her inhale a sharp breath, and when I look down at her, I see that trust she had in me is gone. Now there's nothing but fear in her eyes as they well up with tears.

Turning my head to look at Duke, I get a momentary reprieve from her hurt and smile like none of this bothers me. "Time to solve our problem."

Of all the things I've had to do since I came to this

place, this one takes the most strength. I can beat the hell out of people. Fuck, I can kill with little effort. Always could. But this is different. This is cruel.

I don't have a choice, though.

Moving my hand to my zipper, I slowly lower it and pull out my cock. It's been semi-hard since seeing her standing outside my shower, so hopefully I won't take long to come since I'm not a fan of putting on a fucking sex show for these assholes.

Sophie stares up at me in horror while Duke laughs from my left side and Tap whines, "This isn't fair. I took her. She should be mine. If anyone's going to get their cock sucked, it should be me."

After I throw him a smug glance, I look down into Sophie's eyes. They're all glassy from tears, and for a few seconds, I don't know if I can make her do this. I have to, though. There's no other choice. She has to be seen as fully mine or Tap will continue to question my claim to her.

I steel myself and replay the words I said to her over and over to force this.

I won't kill you, little one.

Well, this is how I make sure no one hurts her. Unless she does this now, she's going to end up with Tap and then she'll be forced to do much worse.

I push all of that out of my mind and feed her my cock without saying a word. What is there to say? We both have our parts in this terrible play. Now we have to act them out convincingly so the rest of these men believe us.

Her mouth rests on the head of my cock for a few

seconds, and I look down in fear that she doesn't understand her role. If she doesn't do this now, she'll end up with Tap. I won't be able to protect her, and she'll likely end up dead.

As if she hears these thoughts racing through my mind, Sophie begins to move up and down my cock, her mouth taking me inside her before she closes her eyes. A tiny sob escapes her lips when she reaches the base, and she quickly pushes me out of her with a groan.

It doesn't take long for me to get rock hard. Pushing out the noise of Tap, who's complaining loudly about this being unfair, I focus on the top of Sophie's dark head and her perfectly straight part down the middle of her scalp that's pale white compared to her deep brown hair. Everything goes silent, and all I can hear is the sound of my heartbeat pounding in my ears.

Sophie's mouth feels like heaven on me, and just a minute in, I'm thrusting my hips and fucking her mouth. She whimpers from the fierceness of my movements, and I bury my hands in her hair, holding her head still while I ram my cock down her throat.

In the haze of need and wanting to come, I think about how good she feels like this and wish she'd open her eyes and look up at me, but she keeps them tightly shut. Beneath them, the skin glistens from tears that began to flow right after I ordered her onto her knees.

Little one. I almost said her name when I told her to kneel in front of me. I couldn't, though. That would make it too much like I wanted to hurt her intentionally with this. It would be too personal. Too intimate.

Better to use the nickname I chose for her that first night. That name means nothing. I use it mostly to taunt her. Nothing personal about it. Just a nickname I'd give anyone like her.

I feel my balls tighten, tearing me out of my thoughts, and a moment later, I come in her mouth as the noise of the office filters back into my consciousness. Looking down, I watch Sophie wipe her tears and struggle to deal with what I just shot into her.

Only a few seconds more of this performance, Sophie. You're almost there.

While I stuff my cock back into my pants, I turn my head to look at Duke and say as casually as I can, "So is that settled? She's mine."

It's not really a question I want an answer to. Sophie's mine. Period. Now go fuck off, Tap.

"I guess so. Do with her as you like."

Pulling her up to her feet, I don't listen to Tap's continued protests. It's fucking settled. "She's mine. End of story."

Duke nods, giving the matter a definitive end as I quietly breathe a sigh of relief. "Enough! Tap, she's King's. And that's all I want to hear about this. Fuck, you guys have become like a fucking soap opera. Let's get to work."

"Now that's done, I'm going to take her back to my apartment. I'll be right back."

No one says a word, so I quickly guide Sophie out

of the office. We walk in silence back to my place as I try to think of a way to tell her I did what I did to protect her.

The problem is she refuses to look at me. I'm not even sure I could get her to face me if I ordered her to now.

Finally, we climb the stairs and reach my apartment. Once inside and out of view of anyone who might see, she yanks her arm from my hold.

Spinning around to face me, she screams, "I hate you! I should have known you were all alike. I fucking trusted you! I trusted you!"

She barely gets the words out before she begins to cry. With each sob, I feel sick and want to make her understand why I forced her to do that back there.

"I did that to make sure Tap couldn't claim you," I explain, but my voice is drowned out by her sobs.

Somehow, she hears me and shakes her head. "As if you and that pig are any different. I'm sure you've convinced yourself you are, but you're wrong. You did that for you, not me."

Her words tear at me. I don't have time to listen to this, though.

"Believe what you want, but I told you I'd keep you with me, and I kept my word. Make yourself comfortable, little one. While you're here, this is where you'll stay."

I turn to leave, and just before I close the door behind me, I hear her say, "I fucking hate you. I hope that pig slits your throat and you bleed to death. I hope you suffer too."

Looking back, I see nothing but hate in her eyes now. As I lock the door from the outside and begin walking back to Duke's office, I can't push away the memory of how much hate she has inside her for me.

It shouldn't bother me, but it does.

By the time I get to Duke's, my stomach's twisted into a tight knot. I can't let my boss or any of these guys see anything that's happened affects me, though. Any hint of weakness and Tap will be challenging my claim to Sophie every fucking day.

So I have to be the man she hates.

Strolling into the office, I grin like the cat who just ate the canary, pretending to be the cocksure fuck I've always been. "So what's on tap for today?"

They all look at me, and I see admiration in Dane's eyes while something that looks like grudging respect fills Marsh and Still's expressions. Tap is still whining like a little bitch about life not being fair, and Duke seems amused by me, like he often is.

"Life is never dull since you came around, King," he says with a chuckle and then pats me on the back.

"Don't blame me for any excitement. That's all Tap over there. I was happy to just go on living my life, and now I get to add performer in a live sex show to my resume," I joke.

Everyone but Tap bursts out laughing, instantly making me believe they buy my act. Good. I've worked too fucking hard since I got here to have it all blown up by the likes of that asshole.

As for Sophie, I did what I had to in order to keep her safe. I'd do it again, too. One blowjob and the hate she has for me now is worth it if I don't have to constantly go up against Tap for her.

Hopefully, she'll see that. If not, then I better get used to sleeping with one eye open.

Better me than that asshole who would kill her just as soon as fuck her. At least I only want to do one of those.

CHAPTER NINE

ophie

THE SILENCE OF THIS HORRIBLE PLACE PRESSES down on me like King's filthy hand on the top of my head. Every breath in is filled with his fucking scent. My ears ring with the sound of him panting above me as he forced his cock into my mouth. My brain is filled with one all-consuming thought.

I hate him. I hate him so much it makes me shake.

Pacing through his apartment, I look at his things and assign that hate to them. His bed. I hate it because he sleeps there. I want to rip the sheets off that fucking bed and lie in wait for him until he returns. Then I want to wrap them around his neck and tighten them until his face turns blue. Maybe for good measure, I could hang him from the hook on the back of the closet door and sit on the edge of that goddamned bed as he slowly dies and I watch with nothing but the purest happiness in my heart.

I want him dead. I want to watch him when the life drains from his face. My mind fills with the fantasy of being able to see that. I want to be there when he has no control over his tormentor and see the fear and dread in his eyes.

Step by step, I pace through this fucking place and hate every inch of it. I'm filled with so much of that one emotion that I don't think I can keep it in. I sense tears welling in my eyes and fight like I've never fought before to stop them from coming.

I don't want to cry. I'm not weak. I won't cry because of him. I won't.

Midway through the living room, I stop next to the couch that's become my makeshift bed and the tears begin to come. No matter what I do, I can't stop them. They roll down over my cheeks into my mouth and down my neck. They keep coming even as I scream, "I'm not fucking weak! I'm not!"

They blur my vision so I can't see to walk anymore. I stand there sobbing like a baby until I collapse, exhausted from all that's happened this morning. Last night. Every minute since that fucking asshole Tap grabbed me and stuffed me into the backseat of that car.

I sit there crying in a crumpled heap on the floor next to the couch, like some filthy pile of clothes discarded after being used. Crying morphs into hyperventilating, and then I taste the first hint of bile in my mouth.

After barely making it to the bathroom, I throw up in the toilet. My stomach contracts violently with each push my body makes to get all of King out of my system. I flush it all away and pray that's the end of it, but another wave of nausea washes over me and soon I'm bent over once more, puking all that's left in my stomach into the bowl. After a while, I begin retching and nothing comes up. Dry heave after dry heave tears at me, and my insides feel like they're fighting to exit through my mouth but can't.

Pain tears at my sides and my ribs feel like someone's used them for sparring practice, but I can't stand over the toilet anymore. Staggering back, I lose my footing on the tile and tumble to the floor in front of the shower enclosure.

I have nothing more inside me. No more of King. No more tears. Nothing. I'm hollow, emptied out of all the good and the bad.

Then why the fuck do I still feel so terrible?

I ease myself up, first on my hands and knees and then slowly until I'm standing on the floor which just betrayed me. Fucking tile. No wonder. It's just like him.

Looking into the mirror, my reflection startles me at first. I look so weak. My mascara that's days old now has run under my eyes, which are all sunken in. I look pathetic.

My cheeks are hollowed out, like some hideous almost skull-looking thing. Just a few days of this world and I'm already sickened by my own appearance.

I'm someone's prisoner. A man's sex slave. A disgusting thing paraded in front of other disgusting things by the most disgusting one of all.

How could I have ever thought I felt anything for him?

I peel my clothes off and step into the shower, desperate to feel clean again. I turn the water to as hot as I can make it and flinch when the first scorching beads hit my skin. It stings like someone running sharp blades over my body. God, I wish that was the case. To be free of the layer of skin that endured what King forced me to do in front of those horrid creatures so I could start over fresh and clean again is all I can dream of.

But no amount of hot water or soap makes that happen. I scrub my arms and legs with that disgusting green soap he uses, yet I don't feel clean. The overly sweet scent of it threatens to make me retch, even though there's nothing left inside me to come out.

I stand so long in the shower with the water pouring over me that it begins to cool, but I don't care. I'm not clean yet. I don't know if I'll ever be clean again, but I can't leave this spot yet.

By the time the water runs ice cold, my empty insides are filled with the singular emotion that fuels me.

Hate.

It increases with every second my brain can't do anything else but replay those moments in his boss's office when he made me less than human. The moment he pushed me down onto my knees. The moment he smirked at one of his fellow despicable creatures, as if forcing me to suck his cock was amusing. The moment he put it into my mouth, degrading me like some fucking whore whose sole purpose in life is to please him.

I'd cry if I had any tears left, but I have nothing but my hate and rage. They fill me until I think they're about to seep out of every pore and hole in my body.

As I step out of the shower, I stand on the mat and stare down at my clothes I've worn for days. I don't want to wear them ever again. They remind me of what he did.

But what choice do I have? Nothing in this fucking place is mine. Jailed in his apartment, the only other choice is to wear something of his, but the very idea makes me want to hit something.

I wrap a towel around myself and grab my clothes from the floor, disgusted and angry. Storming through the apartment, I make my way to the kitchen and find a washing machine and dryer I hadn't noticed before.

Maybe if I wash them in the hottest water possible with bleach I can put them on without wanting to throw up.

I toss them into the washing machine and grab the bottle of bleach from the shelf above me. I don't care that my pink shirt and blue shorts will be ruined. Anything to get rid of the proof of what happened.

The smell of the bleach as I pour it onto my clothes nearly chokes me, but I drown them in the stuff before slamming the lid down and starting the machine. With the amount I used, I'll likely have all-white clothes. I don't care. As long as I don't look at them and think of him and what he made me do.

My hands shake at the thought of him. I want to scream. I want to run away. I want to hit my fists against something.

Against his face.

The mere thought of him repulses me now. The metallic taste of those silver metal studs on his cock sits on my tongue like some horrible memory I'm forced to relive over and over. It mixes with the salty taste of his cum I can't get rid of. Even after throwing up, I can still taste him.

Or maybe it's some phantom sensory memory that will never go away.

I walk back into the bathroom and search the vanity for toothpaste to rid myself of these disgusting reminders. He uses the same peppermint flavor that I have at home, and instantly when I grab the tube to squeeze out a glob onto my fingertip, my heart drops in despair.

Will I ever be free of this place and him and return to my life?

Then a horrible thought enters my brain, upending all my misery. What will I be if I ever do return to that life?

Pushing that out of my head, I rub the toothpaste over my teeth and tongue. But still the taste of him remains. So I squeeze out a second glob and press it to the center of my tongue. A memory of some article I read or heard about years ago on taste buds flashes through my mind, so I rub the minty stuff along the sides of my tongue too, hoping to get to every possible place where those taste memories of his cock, those metal studs, and his cum exist.

But none of it works. I can still taste him in my mouth.

Disgusted, I throw the tube of toothpaste back into the vanity and slam the cabinet door before walking back to the living room. Exhausted from too much emotion and all that's happened this morning, I lay down and close my eyes.

The last thought I have before falling asleep is my uncle and his men coming to this awful place and killing every single one of the men who stood in that office and watched King strip me of the last shred of my dignity. Then they turn to him and cut him up into pieces while he screams in agony and begs for mercy from me.

My eyes fly open at the sound of someone turning the doorknob, and I wake up to see him coming through the door. He glances at me but says nothing before walking into his bedroom and closing the door.

"Nothing to say to the woman you dehumanized this morning, King? Asshole. I hate you," I mumble under my breath as I work to shake off the last vestiges of my long nap.

My hate pushes against every inch of my insides as I sit there loathing his very existence. I hear his bedroom door open and brace myself for him to return to the living room. He likely has something to say. What could he possibly say after this morning?

I don't know, and I don't care.

After a few minutes, he doesn't come to where I'm sitting in a towel, my clothes finished in the washer hours ago while I slept. I hear him making some kind of clanging noise in the kitchen and hate that I have to walk in there to put my clothes in the dryer, but I can't stay in this towel.

Marching past him as he sits at the kitchen table surrounded by pots and pans and a package of some kind of meat, I clutch my towel to make sure I'm covered and head for the washer. He doesn't look up from reading some label on the food, thankfully, and I look into the machine to see my clothes are all white. The pink top, the blue running shorts, the tan bra and blue underwear. All stark white.

The smell of bleach sends me backwards a few steps, and I shake my head to get my bearings. One quick grab into the washer and I have all my clothes in my hand before I toss them into the dryer and start it.

As I walk past him again, he says in a low voice, "I don't know how much bleach you used, but that smell is enough to knock me over."

I don't answer him, but silently I tell him to fuck off and die. I'm not sure I'm brave enough at that moment to say those words out loud. I don't know what he'll do to me if I do.

Then again, does it really matter? After what he's done so far, how much worse could it get?

A few minutes later, the tempting aroma of something cooking drifts into the living room where I sit in the only spot in this goddamned place that doesn't feel like it's entirely his. Not that I have any ownership of the couch, but at least it doesn't reek of him.

With every second that passes, the smell of food makes me hungrier and hungrier. I don't want to even see him, much less ask for something to eat. Not from him. I won't beg for anything from him.

Lost in thought about how what I really want to do is jam a knife into his jugular and watch as the blood spurts out like a geyser, I don't see him enter the room. He stops in front of the coffee table between us and places a plate with a hamburger and fries down in front of me. Instantly, my mouth waters since I'm so hungry. I don't want to take anything from him, though.

He doesn't speak a word to me, and a second later, he walks away, leaving me with the dinner he's made, my hate that makes even thinking about eating something he's made revolting, and my empty stomach that doesn't give a damn about how I feel about him.

The first bite of the hamburger makes me drool like a starving dog it tastes so good. I don't usually like hamburgers, but beggars can't be choosers.

No. I won't beg. I'd rather starve, no matter what my fucking stomach wants to say about it.

After a few bites of the burger and a handful of

fries, I'm parched and need a drink. That means I have to walk into the kitchen where he is.

I march to the refrigerator, making sure not to look over at him, and open the door to see nothing but beer. No containers of juice. No jug of milk. No food at all either.

Add that to the plethora of reasons I hate him.

Staring into the empty depths of the refrigerator, I say flatly, "I need a drink."

"All I have is beer," he answers before smacking his lips after taking a sip of that very drink.

I can't stop myself from spinning around to snap, "Beer will make me throw up. Since I spent the morning doing that, I'd like to avoid a repeat performance now."

He winces at my mention of getting sick and then looks down at his plate. "There's water from the faucet."

Disgusted by his answer, I grab a glass out of the cabinet and get a drink of water. The taste of it when it hits my tongue reminds me of the taste of those metal studs on his cock. Forcing the water down, I swallow quickly and leave to go back to my perch on the couch.

As I eat the rest of my food, I can't help but think about how he winced when I said I spent the morning throwing up. Were his feeling hurt by that? Too fucking bad. After what he did, I don't give a single fuck about his feelings.

From there, I can't stop myself from wondering what happened when he went back to his boss's office afterward. Did they all congratulate him for being a big man who could force a terrified woman to give him a blow job? I imagine them all slapping him on the back for his grand achievement as he stood there grinning with pride.

Big man on campus.

My hate surges inside me, making my stomach feel like it's going to purge my hamburger and fries. No, don't do that. I don't want to be hungry again, and I don't know when or if I'll have the chance to eat.

"I fucking hate him," I mumble to myself before pushing away the plate with the remaining handful of fries still left.

My belly full, at least I can be happy about one thing. While I'm still being held hostage by a monster, I'm not hungry anymore.

That attempt at seeing the brighter side of the worst thing that's ever happened to me succeeds for about thirty seconds before I go back to feeling nothing but pure hate. Closing my eyes, I let myself fantasize about killing him. If I thought I could break a glass without him hearing it, I'd wait until he's asleep and sneak into his room to slit his throat. No, I don't have a way to escape this place, but at least he'd be dead.

After today, I'll take not being hungry and him paying for what he did, even if it means I suffer the consequences. I've never killed anyone or anything, though. I don't know if I'm even capable of that.

I read somewhere that hate makes everything

impossible. Whoever said that was wrong. Hate makes one thing possible.

Hurting the one who hurt you.

Hate makes that more than possible. It makes it necessary.

CHAPTER TEN

ing

A STUPID SHOW ABOUT COPS OR SOME GROUP OF special agents plays on the TV in front of me, but try as I might, I can't get into it. The one character talks like some kind of fucking teenage punk ass, making me want to throw my beer bottle at the screen.

I know it's nothing to do with him or any of the other characters that's making me hate everything tonight. My problem sits a room away. Fucking woman! I should have just left her in the hands of that asshole that first night. Instead, I had to pull the whole white knight act and when I don't have a choice but to do something like what I had to this morning, suddenly I'm the bad guy equal to the likes of Tap.

Fuck all of them. I should have known she wouldn't understand why I did what I did. Maybe she would prefer to be holed up with Tap in his place. I doubt she'd get to sleep on his couch or have the chance to eat dinner he made her. She'd be lucky if she didn't get tied to the fucking wall in his filthy bathroom with the added bonus of being forced to sit in her own shit and piss.

She has no idea how bad it would be for her if Tap had gotten his hands on her. I've seen that guy beat a girl so badly we had to rush her to the hospital so she didn't die. The motherfucker basically caved her skull in. He gets off on hurting women and likes to brag about how many he's raped. Sophie wouldn't fare any better with him.

My mind snaps out of its haze about Sophie as the teenage asshole on the TV says something ridiculous to make himself sound like a badass. Stupid show.

While I search the blanket and sheets for the remote, I can't help but wonder why she can't see that I did that this morning to protect her. As if anyone would want to put on his own personal sex show for a bunch of guys. Like I'm some goddamned porn star.

The look of complete disgust on her face when she said she'd been sick all morning after what happened refuses to leave my brain. After I came in her mouth, she puked. I made her physically sick.

I run my hand through my hair and wince as my stomach churns. I'll be lucky if I don't puke up that whole hamburger from dinner if I don't stop thinking about this.

A noise from the living room catches my attention, and I hear her footsteps as she walks across the floor before closing the door to the bathroom. Is she taking a shower? I listen for the sound of water running but hear nothing.

Why the fuck do I care what the hell she's doing?

A few minutes pass as I stew over how much I hate this whole goddamned situation, and suddenly, I sit up in bed. Can she use anything in the bathroom to hurt herself or come at me to hurt me? I mentally run through everything I can remember I have in there. No razor blades since I ran out a few days ago. No scissors. No glass. All the glasses are in the kitchen.

Then I look over on the nightstand for the painkillers for my leg. Fuck! They're gone.

I race through the apartment to the bathroom and grab the doorknob. She locked it.

"Sophie! Open this door!"

She doesn't answer. I press my ear to the door to hear what she's doing, but there's nothing. Silence.

Did she escape out of the window? We're on the second floor. She'd break her neck climbing down to the ground.

I bang my fist against the door as my mind races about what she's up to in there. Did she OD on the painkillers?

"Sophie, open this fucking door! Now!" I bellow.

But still she doesn't answer.

Fuck! Dreading I'm going to find her lifeless body in God knows what shape, I kick the door down and stumble in, crashing onto the floor. Stunned, I look up and see her sitting in the bathtub. She's hunched over clutching her knees to her chest and staring at me with pure hate in her eyes.

My heart struggles to stop racing, but the way she looks at me makes it skip a beat. Never before has anyone glared at me like that.

"Sophie."

She doesn't answer and turns her head, dismissing me.

"Are you okay? Did you take something?"

I impatiently wait for her to answer, trying to see if she's breathing normally by watching her body. Finally, after so long I wonder if she ever intends on answering me, she turns to look at me again. Now the hate in her eyes is gone, replaced by sadness that makes my chest ache.

In a small voice, she answers me. "I didn't take your pills, if that's what you mean. Leave me alone."

"I didn't see the bottle on the nightstand and thought…"

Her eyes narrow as I let my words fall silent. "You thought I'd swallowed the rest of them. I put the bottle in your drawer when you fell asleep last night because I kept knocking it off the nightstand and I didn't want to wake you."

She doesn't say it, but in her eyes I see she's thinking, "And a lot of good being nice to you did for me, you fucker."

I don't know what to say. I stand there staring at her sitting in the tub and want to make her understand why I did what I did, but nothing I think to say sounds right.

Avoiding meeting her gaze, I finally mumble, "I wanted to make sure you weren't hurt."

My concern falls flat, and she doesn't answer, so I walk out, leaving the door ajar, and head back to my room. The problem is even knowing she didn't OD can't make me stop thinking about how sad she looked and how I felt inside when I saw her sitting there in the tub looking so pathetic.

For a half hour, I listen to hear her footsteps as she walks back to the couch, but she doesn't leave the bathroom. I should just let her stay there, but I can't.

I don't know why. I just can't.

When I return to the bathroom, she's still sitting in the tub, so I reach in to lift her out and I'm startled at how ice cold the water is. Hooking my arm under her legs and my other arm around her back, I pick her up as she protests.

"Put me down. I don't want you touching me. I hate you," she says in a sad voice.

I ignore her and brace myself for her hand to connect with my face while I carry her through the living room. "You can hate me out here. You can't spend the night in the bathtub."

She looks at me in confusion as I march past the couch on my way to my room. I place her on the bed and then open the nightstand drawer to take out the bottle of painkillers.

"I don't want to kill myself," she growls as she scrambles to cover herself with the sheet.

"Then this won't be a problem then." As I stuff the

bottle into my pocket, I add, "You can sleep in the bed tonight."

"No. I don't want to. I don't want to be anywhere near you," she snaps, glaring up at me again.

"Well, then you're in luck because I'll be on the couch."

"This bed smells like you," she says, practically spitting the words out in disgust.

"Then change the sheets," I answer sharply and point over toward my left. "Bottom drawer of the dresser the TV's on."

She mumbles something as I'm leaving the room, but I don't hear it and don't ask her to repeat it. I'm tired of fighting with her.

A few minutes later, I settle in on the couch and wish I had decided when I moved into this place to put the TV out here. Sitting alone in the darkness isn't exactly my thing. Leaning back, I stretch out and close my eyes as all the objects in the apartment Sophie can use to attack me run through my mind.

Knives in the kitchen drawer. Cast iron pots in the cabinets. Those scissors I worried about before that I keep near the silverware.

Thank God I'm a light sleeper.

Memories of how she looked this morning on her knees in front of me with my cock in her mouth swim around in my brain, making sleep impossible. I had to do that. There was no other choice. If I didn't make my claim irrevocable like that, Tap would spend every minute of the time she's here challenging me for her.

How can she not see that?

My cock gets hard as the memory loops through my head, the most pleasure I've let myself enjoy in ages. In truth, thinking about it gives me more than the actual act, which was nothing more than one man enforcing his power over another. Nothing about that came anywhere near sexy.

I had no choice. Even if she never understands, it doesn't change that.

After nearly an hour of thinking about her, I begin to drift off, exhausted from the events of this entire day. Just as I'm about to fall into sleep, I sense her next to me.

My eyes fly open, and there she is standing next to the couch, staring at me with that look of defeat that made my chest hurt before in the bathroom. The dim light coming from the bedroom glints off the edge of the knife hanging by her side.

"I prayed for my uncle and his men to come here today and kill all of you," she says softly.

"Maybe it will happen tomorrow. I don't believe in God, but you never know."

All the while, I watch for her hand to move upwards and aim the knife at my heart. But she stands almost perfectly still just staring at me with the purest hurt I've ever seen in someone's eyes.

"What are you going to do with me?" she asks after a long silence.

I take a deep breath in and let it out slowly, hoping with each second that the air from inside my lungs takes everything else from me and I can feel hollow instead of feeling like I'm swallowing all the hurt in her dark eyes. I can't afford to let these emotions she brings out in me take me over.

"I'm going to let you sleep in my bed and make sure Tap and the rest of them don't get their hands on you."

My answer doesn't change anything. She still has nothing but hurt in her eyes, and I still can't get my emotions under control when it comes to her.

"Why? Why are you doing any of that? You obviously think nothing more of me than they do after what you did this morning."

For the first time, I have an answer to her question. It makes no sense, but it's the only answer I have. "Because you're mine."

She screws her face into a look of confusion. "Yours? I'll never forgive you for what you did, King."

"Then you'll be unhappy, but you'll still be mine."

I wait for her to respond to me, but she only glares at me for a moment longer before storming back to the bedroom. The door slams closed, leaving me alone in the dark with my thoughts about her once more.

Closing my eyes, I let my memories of this morning come alive again, the vivid image of her staring up at me as I fed her my cock making me hard again. The feel of her soft lips against my skin as she took all of me into her mouth stirs something in me that's lay dormant ever since I came to this place.

That won't be the last time her mouth is on me. Willing or not, I'll have her as mine. Completely.

Lost in the ecstasy of my memories, I glide my hand over my stomach to my cock and grip it in my hand. I don't know why Sophie affects me like she does, and at this moment, I don't fucking care. I want to feel something other than the usual emptiness that rules my days filled with hurting others for Duke and the need that's become nearly constant since Sophie came into my world.

A creaking noise from the floor tears me out of my fantasy, and a second later, I open my eyes and see the flash of her knife in front of me as she takes her first swipe at me. She doesn't know how to wield a weapon, even a kitchen knife, and misses me completely.

I won't give her another chance to hit her mark.

Grabbing her wrists, I squeeze her right arm tightly and she cries out in agony. The knife falls, and the blade hits with a clank off the wood floor. Left without her weapon, she tries to pull her arms from my hold, but it's no use.

Now she's pissed me off.

"You wanted to play, little girl. Let's play."

"Let go of me! You're hurting me!"

I pull her down on top of me so her pussy is pressing against my still-hard cock. She squirms in an attempt to get away from me, but it only makes me more excited.

"Feel that? You keep struggling, you're going to make me come for a second time today," I say with a chuckle.

"Fuck you!" she screams before spitting in my face.

It drips down my cheek as I stare up at her in

surprise. I knew she was feisty, but I didn't expect that kind of bravery. Good. I like strong women.

"Little girl, I'm in the mood for playing, but if you want it rough, I can oblige you that too."

Her eyes flash rage as she shakes her head above me and tries to yank her hands free from mine. "You're a pig! I hate you!"

Lifting my hips, I press my cock to the front of her shorts and feel she's wet. So she doesn't hate me as much as she claims. Good.

"Your mouth says you hate me, but I can feel how wet this has made you. You can't wait to feel those sterling silver studs on my cock when I fuck you, can you?"

She tugs her arms, but she can't get away just yet. Frustrated, she whines, "I do hate you! I want nothing to do with you."

I look down my body and see her breasts pressed to my chest. I can feel how hard her nipples are, another clue that she's lying.

"You don't hate me, but that's okay. I'm not against a hate fuck from time to time. I bet you'll be a scratcher, raking those fingernails down my back, while I pound into you."

Sophie spits at me again and tries to maneuver her hand so she can scratch my face, but even though she has the better position, she's no match for me, even in her supposed rage.

"I won't let you do that to me. We're not surrounded by those all those bastards with guns now.

It's just you and me here, and I'll fight you until either you die or I do," she snaps.

Her threat only serves to arouse me more, and I flip her over onto her back, taking away the last shred of any advantage she may have had. Pressing her hands above her head, I watch as she struggles against my hold, enjoying the fire in her.

My hard cock juts out of my shorts, the only remnant from those moments a few minutes before when I fantasized about how good she felt sucking me off. Looking down into her eyes, I smile.

"You caught me in a compromising position, little one. I normally wouldn't be whipping my cock out right before a woman comes at me to slit my throat. Not that you could. You're not very good with knives."

Something about what I say takes all the fight out of her, and I feel her resistance against my hold ebb away. I doubt she's willing to give in, so I stay on alert for whatever she plans to spring on me next. She may not be much of a fighter, but she's brave and smart.

"I'm never going to stop trying to kill you," she says softly, her gaze fixed on my face with an intensity that surprises me.

"You can try, but I'm the least of your concerns in this place. Someday, you'll see that."

Sophia shakes her head, and with a frown, says, "I'll never see you as anyone but the person you are. You're a villain just like all those scumbags who watched you act like a big man this morning. I bet they were proud of you, weren't they? Did they make you King Dick for today?"

I know she's serious, but the way she phrases that makes me laugh in her face. "I think I'm always able to claim that name. Or at least part of me is."

My amusement at something so serious to her upsets her, and she catches me off guard, yanking her wrist from my hold. A split second later, she slaps her hand against my cheek hard, stinging my skin. Instinctively, I pull my arm back and curl my fingers into a tight fist.

But the threat of my hitting her doesn't upset Sophie. She's tougher than that.

"Nice. You start the morning off forcing a woman to suck your cock and then you end your day by punching her," she says with as much disgust as she can muster. "You're a real Prince Charming, King."

My arm shakes as I hold my fist back, ready to let it fly. I don't want to hit this woman. Why does she insist on pushing her luck?

CHAPTER ELEVEN

*ophie*

Even as I wait for the inevitable pain that will come from King's fist slamming into my face, I can't stop myself from wishing this morning hadn't happened between us. Being in a place filled with people who terrify me, I liked believing at least he might protect me.

How can I think that now?

"Something tells me this isn't the first time a man has wanted to smack the hell out of you, little one," he says in a low voice that sends a chill through me.

"Just do it so you can be the first man to do that to me, too. Today's your day for firsts with me."

He wants to do it. I can tell by the way his arm shakes that he's holding himself back. I can't imagine why. After all that he's done to me already, punching me would be nothing.

Opening his mouth to say something, he remains silent for a long moment before pressing his lips together. He lowers his arm to his side and shakes his head.

"Do you think you'd be able to say things like this with Tap or any others in that room this morning? And do you think they'd let you get away with hitting them and not beating the hell out of you?"

Although I know the answer to both questions is no, I refuse to give him the satisfaction of letting him think he did something heroic earlier. "I have no idea. You're all monsters, so I can't say."

"I thought you were smart, Sophie, but I'm beginning to believe you're not. The best you could hope for with any of them is they didn't kill you because of that smart mouth of yours. I did what I did to make sure they all knew you're mine. I wanted to make sure I could keep you safe."

"By forcing your cock down my throat?" I ask, unable to keep the words inside my mouth.

King hangs his head and sighs, like hearing the truth of what he did bothers him. I can't imagine why. All he had to do was stand there and enjoy himself. He wasn't the one being dehumanized and treated like a sex slave.

Seconds tick by while I wait for him to answer my question, but instead, he releases my arm and climbs off the couch. I watch as he picks up the knife and simply walks away, leaving me lying there hating that he has the freedom to just walk away and not answer for what he's done.

I want to follow him and make him say something. He shouldn't be able to get away with not responding.

For a minute, I stew on the couch, even more disgusted that he's taken the bed back. I spent time changing the sheets so they wouldn't smell like him, and now he's in there stinking them up with his scent.

By the time I get to his room, I'm ready for a fight. No, he's not the first man to ever hit me. Well, not the first male, anyway. I didn't lie when I said he had the distinction of being the first man to hit me. Kenny Jordan hitting me in the seventh grade doesn't count.

I fling open the door to see him standing next to the bed facing me. I don't want to look below his shoulders, in case he hasn't fixed himself and he's still hanging out, but I can't stop myself. My gaze drops to his crotch, which is thankfully covered by his black boxer briefs, and then I quickly raise it again to focus on his face.

I hate that I was so curious about that part of him.

"It's rude to not answer a question you've been asked."

"I think it's also considered rude to ogle a guy's junk, but maybe that's not what you were doing when you looked down my body," he replies with a smile that tells me he's enjoying this.

But he shouldn't be. I asked him a serious question. I want a serious answer.

"Maybe if you didn't lay around with it just hanging out."

His smile fades and he sighs like he's bored with our conversation. "What do you want?"

All of a sudden, I can't ask him the question I need to. It's almost as if the sight of him like this makes me feel foolish for needing some explanation for what he did. I know the answer already.

"You said I could have the bed. I already changed the sheets so it doesn't smell like you."

"Has anyone ever told you how charming you are, Sophie? You have a real way about you that makes a person feel good, you know that?"

"So now it's my duty to make you feel good? Does this responsibility go both ways?" I ask, my anger returning.

His dark eyes sparkle, and he flashes me a smile that's nothing less than sexy. "If you want me to make you feel good, I'm going to have to share the bed with you."

And that little comment makes me feel like I want to explode.

"Do you think that's funny? After what happened this morning, now you think you should joke around about anything having to do with sex?" I ask, my voice on the verge of cracking I'm so upset.

As soon as I stop speaking, I see I may have pushed things too far. King takes three large steps and stops right in front of me mere inches away from my face. I fight the urge to look away when he stares down into my eyes but says nothing. The silence unnerves me, but I want him to see I'm not afraid of him.

"None of this is fucking funny. Not the fact that I had to do what I did so none of those other guys would do worse, especially Tap, who gets off hurting pretty things like you. Not the part about being hated in my own home for doing what I could to protect you. And definitely not the fact that if I do fall asleep, I'm liable to be attacked by some knife-wielding madwoman who probably won't kill me but might slice the top inch of my skin off. No, Sophie, none of this is funny to me."

His warm breath drifts across my face when he exhales after each sentence, each puff of air smelling like beer. I look up at him and wait for him to continue, but he falls silent right after saying my name.

At least he didn't call me little one.

"Well, none of this is great for me either."

"Then maybe we can call a truce."

I don't want to admit it, but I'm not against that idea. I just need to hear him say something else first before I can promise not to try to kill him in his sleep.

But I won't beg for an apology, just like I won't beg for anything else. Not from King or anyone else in this world.

When I don't agree to his suggestion of a truce, he sighs and says, "Sophie, I swear I did what I did to keep you safe."

He doesn't say I'm sorry, but it's the closest I'm going to get. I'll take it.

Even if I don't believe it.

"Fine. I promise not to try to kill you while you sleep."

"How thoughtful."

"And I'll go back to sleeping on the couch, if you want your bed back."

For a moment, he seems to consider my offer but then shakes his head. "No, you can have it. I said you could, so it's yours."

"What about your leg? Shouldn't you keep it elevated or something?"

He smiles, and it lights up his face. "Is it that you want me to sleep in the bed with you, little one? Afraid of the dark?"

"Why do you have to call me that? Why not just say Sophie?" I ask in frustration that every time we get close to being almost nice to one another he has to do something like this.

"Are you afraid of the dark, Sophie?" he asks so seriously that I wonder if he's still joking with me.

"No, but what if your boss shows up and sees us not in the bed together? Won't he think Tap can have the right to say he should be with me?"

"That's surprisingly shrewd. Okay, we'll both sleep in here."

When he turns to walk back toward the bed, I can't stop myself when my gaze roams over his body. This won't be the first time King and I sleep in the same place, but he was hurt before and I didn't have to worry about him trying anything. Now he's not, and I know he's feeling well enough to get hard.

And what he said before about getting wet around him wasn't wrong. I don't know why or how, but just being near him makes me think of things I shouldn't even consider.

"HE HAS NO IDEA...NO NEED...I'VE GOT THINGS under control..."

I wake up and King's mumbling next to me. I listen to see if he's speaking to me, but he seems to still be asleep.

"I'll let you know when. Don't worry. I got her..."

After a few moments, I figure he's talking in his sleep, so I roll over and put the pillow over my head until he stops a minute later. Wide awake, I hear a noise that sounds like it's coming from the living room. I lay there frozen in terror and wait to see if I hear it again. It sounded like footsteps. Is there someone else in the apartment?

Turning toward King, I nudge his shoulder. "I think there's someone out in the living room."

His eyes open, and he looks over at me. In the moonlight, I see he's angry I've woken him. "What?"

Pointing toward the bedroom door, I repeat what I said. "I think there's someone out there."

He scrubs the sleep from his face and rolls out of bed. Staggering toward the door, he looks back at me and shakes his head. "I think you're losing your mind, you know that."

When he reaches the door, he turns around and stares at me for a long moment. "This better not be some stupid attempt to overpower me, Sophie. If it is, I swear to God..."

Just as I'm sure he's about to threaten me with something worse than being held against my will, the sound of someone's footsteps outside the bedroom comes through loud and clear. He hears it too and spins away from me to throw the door open. On his way out of the room, he grabs the knife he took from me off the dresser and then he's swallowed up by the darkness of the hallway.

"Who's there?" he asks in a booming voice that terrifies me. I've never heard him sound like that.

I wait to hear what will happen next, but there's nothing but silence, except for the sound of his footsteps as he marches through the apartment. He returns to the bedroom, and I exhale, realizing I've been holding my breath the entire time he's been gone.

He's frowning, so I quickly say, "I'm not crazy. I heard something out there."

As he climbs into bed, he mumbles, "I didn't see anything."

Sitting up, I watch him turn away from me and hate how he's dismissing this. I heard something. I know I did.

"So you think I just made it all up?"

King looks back over his shoulder at me with a look of disgust. "No. Now, go to sleep."

But I can't let this go.

"I didn't make this up. I bet you think I grabbed something while you were out of the room and I'm just lying in wait here, don't you?"

He stares back at me for a few more seconds before he rolls over and faces me. "I do now."

"Are you kidding? Do you think I'd be that stupid to say that if I did?" I ask in utter shock that he truly believes this whole noise thing was a ruse to give me the chance to set him up.

Without saying another word, King reaches under the covers and begins searching the bed. His hands graze my leg, sending a rush of something completely strange coursing through me. I instantly move away from him, unsure what I'm feeling.

"I can't believe you're doing this! This is insane!" I say, protesting a bit too much as I struggle to get my emotions under control.

King looks up at me with suspicion in his eyes and wrinkles his forehead. "You know, just for future reference, you might want to act innocent if you really are innocent."

"What the hell do you mean by that?" I ask, unsure what he's talking about.

Does he know I reacted to his touch a minute ago? How? Did I make a face, or worse, did I let out a sigh? Oh, God. I probably did and just didn't realize it.

He seems confused too, which makes me wonder what's going on. "I mean you're not acting innocent, Sophie. I'm not sure how much clearer you need me to make that."

His hands begin searching the sheets and blanket, once more grazing my thigh as he rummages through the covers to find whatever he thinks I've hidden in them. Again, my body reacts, but this time I know exactly what that feeling is.

Need.

As he busies himself with locating some concealed weapon, I pull my knees up to my chest in an effort to make sure he can't reach me. When he finds nothing, he lays back and looks over at me like he still thinks I'm up to something.

He has no idea how much I wish I was at this moment.

"So I guess you didn't send me out of the room just to hide something you can use to try to kill me."

Still clutching my knees, I don't try to hide my irritation with him. "I told you I didn't. I'm not stupid."

His gaze rolls down over my body, starting first at my head and then slowly moving toward my feet. "Then why are you sitting over there like that?"

"Like what? Like a person unjustly accused of a crime?" I snap as he sits up beside me.

"No, like the exact opposite." He reaches out to feel near my legs and adds, "Something tells me you're sitting like that for a reason."

I push my legs out to stop him, but it doesn't take more than a second for him to see I'm not hiding anything other than the effect he's having on me. As soon as his hand brushes my hip, a tiny moan escapes my lips like some involuntary cry for him my body lets out against my brain's orders.

It stops him dead, and for a long moment, I can't look away, even as humiliation covers me. That sparkle I've seen before in his eyes appears again, followed by that wicked smile he wears when he knows he's gotten to me.

The only problem is this time the way he's gotten to me isn't okay. It's not right for me to feel any desire for him. Not after what he did.

He doesn't say a word, but he doesn't have to. It's probably written all over my face how much I want him. I wish he would say something so I could at least try to answer him with a believable lie.

But he doesn't. Instead, he slides his arm around my body and faster than I can push him away, he pulls me to him, crushing my breasts to his broad chest. His hold on me makes escaping impossible, though I squirm for a moment before it's obvious I really don't want to be anywhere else but right there next to him.

The moonlight breaks up the darkness, making it impossible not to see the need filling his eyes. It frightens me, and although it should repulse me, it doesn't. I hate that I want him as badly as I do. I don't understand why he makes me feel this way. I silently tell myself this might help me escape, but I know that's not the truth. That's not why I want to feel him between my legs. That's not why I want to taste his lips and listen to him moan my name as he fucks me.

If only he'd say something, I'd be able to return us to the verbal sparring from a few minutes ago. This silence as he stares at me but doesn't move a muscle is like sweet torture. I can see in his eyes he wants me like I want him, so why doesn't he do something?

I open my mouth to speak, hoping to move us from this sexual limbo to either more or less, but before I can say a word, he presses his lips to mine in a hard kiss that takes my breath away. His tongue snakes into my mouth and glides over mine, making me crave more.

More of his mouth. More of his tongue. More of his body against mine.

More of him.

Stuffing my hands into his hair that's too long for my taste, I close my fingers around it and love how soft it is against my skin as he holds me hard to him. His teeth nip at my tongue, startling me, and he leans back and smiles.

"Like a little pain with your pleasure, Sophie?"

His question sends fear rushing through me. Nearly twice the size of me, King could crush me, if he chose. What if his idea of a little pain isn't as little as I can handle?

When I don't answer, he adds, "I promised I wouldn't hurt you, little one. This kind of pain is the kind you'll like."

As his hands roughly push my T-shirt over my head and then move down to my shorts, I don't know if I'm scared or excited about what's about to happen next. All I know is I want to feel those metal studs and that cock of his inside me again.

CHAPTER TWELVE

ophie

KING TUGS MY SHORTS OFF IN ONE SWIFT movement, taking my underwear along with them so I'm suddenly completely bared to him. His eyes roam over my body, and I can't help but think he looks like a ravenous beast sizing up his next delicious meal.

Pushing me back onto the bed, he settles in between my legs and runs his fingertip up through my pussy to my clit. It glides easily because I'm so wet, which doesn't escape his notice.

With a smile, he looks down at me and runs his tongue over his bottom lip. "Someone's ready."

The way he says that makes me feel like he's always known I'd be ready for him. I want to protest —to tell him I hate that I want him—but I can't muster up the words to lie. I do want him. I want to feel him inside me, letting me feel what it's like to be fucked by him and those metal studs when he's deep inside me.

I reach out and run my hand over his cock. It's rock hard and as ready as I am.

Yet he doesn't move to take his clothes off. Instead, he runs his hands across my breasts and down my ribs until they come to rest on my hips. I watch in rapt attention, waiting for him to be naked like me, but he's got other ideas.

Pushing my thighs open wide, he slides down until his mouth hovers over between my legs. His warm breath dances over my bare skin, and then a second later, I feel the first touch of his tongue on me. It sends a jolt of electricity racing through every inch of my body, and I let out a tiny cry that sounds like a needy plea for more.

He presses his mouth to me and hums. "Little one, you taste so fucking good."

I grip the sheet tightly in my hands as my eyes roll back in my head when he sucks my clit into his mouth and bites down just hard enough to make it feel like skyrockets are exploding inside me. Oh, God, is this what he meant by a little pain? No one has ever bitten me there, and if anyone had ever mentioned it, I would have pushed them away in horror.

But with every second that passes, I can't get enough of his teeth pressing against me like this.

When he slides his finger inside, he releases his hold on my clit, flicking his tongue over it just once and driving me crazy for more. I look down my body to see him staring up at me with a devilish look in his eyes, like he knows he controls me completely.

"I told you the pain would be the kind you like," he says in a low voice that resonates against my tender skin. "Want more?"

"Yes," I whimper, practically begging for him to make me feel that way again.

I wait for his mouth to give me what I want, but instead, I feel him slide a second finger inside me, stretching my body to accommodate them. I'm as wet as I've ever been, but I can barely handle the pressure they produce as he thrusts them hard into me.

Tilting my hips to give him easier access, I feel my release begin to uncoil inside me. But that's not possible. I've never come from being fingered.

My brain seems to shut down, and then I feel King's mouth on my pussy again, sending me over the age into the abyss of ecstasy. His tongue creates waves of pleasure that add to my orgasm, making me lose control like never before in my life.

King rides each wave, his fingers fucking me while his mouth pushes me to higher and higher heights. My fingernails dig into my palms through the sheet, tiny stabs of pain that ground me as every other part of me soars.

And then his fingers and mouth disappear from my body, leaving me desperate for more. I open my eyes, reeling from my orgasm, and see him strip off his boxer briefs. He turns back toward me and smiles wickedly, as if he's got more in store for me.

"Up on your knees, little one," he orders before

flipping me over onto my stomach. He stuffs his hand into my hair and yanks me back hard, bringing tears to my eyes. I cry out, but it's cut short when I feel the tip of his cock and those piercings nudge my opening. I hold my breath and close my eyes, and then King tugs roughly at my hair for a second time.

Leaning forward, he grazes his lips against my ear and speaks the words that make me run wet. "I'm going to fuck you so hard, and you're going to beg for it even harder."

A mixture of fear and desire tears through me, but there's not enough time for me to think before he pushes his hips forward and buries his cock completely. The feel of him so large inside me takes my breath away, making my head spin.

He begins to thrust in and out, those metal studs gliding against my tender skin inside me. They leave trails of pleasure that push out through my body, making me yearn for more. I moan with each time he enters me and miss the feel of him filling me when he pulls back.

King tugs my hair, sending waves of pain across my scalp, and in my ear he whispers, "You're so tight, little one. Feel me stretching your cunt with each time I pump into you?"

I try to answer yes, but the word is lost in a moan as he savagely thrusts into me and then stills himself when he fills me up. Jesus, this man fucks like a beast, just as I imagined, and with every inch of his cock inside me, I still want more.

His hand slips from my hair and slides down to

around my neck even as neither of us move another muscle in our bodies, remaining perfectly still and joined completely. I arch my back, tilting my head back as he tightens his hold on my throat.

I should be frightened. This man controls the very air I breathe, but all I feel is need. If only he'd start to fuck me again...if only he'd slide his hand down to my pussy...if only he'd speak again and send me over the edge.

And then, as if he's reading my mind, he moans low in my ear, "What do you want, little one? Say it."

This time I can answer. "Please, fuck me. Hard. Give me what I need."

A sound like a growl comes from him, and he sinks his teeth into my earlobe. "Oh, baby. Be careful what you ask for."

Turning my head, I look into his eyes and whimper, "Fuck me. Make me forget all the bad of this place."

He doesn't say anything, but I see in his eyes he understands. I don't know if this place is horrible for him too, but for tonight, it can be something else. Even if it's just a chance to lose ourselves in each other's bodies, that's enough.

I feel him pull away from me, and then a second later, he pushes forward and touches somewhere deep inside no other man has ever reached. Over and over, he pounds into me as he presses his fingertips against my neck, and then one last time he fills me before my body unravels around him.

"Milk my cock. Fuck, your cunt feels so good, Sophie."

He pushes into me once more before I feel him come, and then we both fall still as he fills me up one last time. His hand releases its hold on my neck, but I miss the feel of his possessive touch instantly. When he eases out of me, a chill runs over my back, and a moment later, the time we've shared is over.

Exhausted, I collapse onto the bed and close my eyes, unsure what will happen when he returns. I don't know how he acts, though, because I'm so tired that I fall asleep. When I open my eyes, it's morning and I only see the back of him as he walks out of the bedroom. I hear the click of the lock on the front door, and then I'm alone again.

I stretch my legs and feel an ache in the pit of my stomach. He didn't even say goodbye when he left. His ability to fuck me and then ignore me the very next morning makes me wish I didn't give in to my desire.

What did I think he'd be like? He's holding me against my will here. No matter how heroic he's painted himself to be in his own mind, I know better.

At least I should have.

Feeling foolish, I walk into the bathroom to take a shower. His scent clings to every inch of my body, and I want to rid myself of it. I can't forget what I am to him and how much I want to find a way to escape this place.

THE APARTMENT DOOR OPENS, AND BEFORE ME, TWO

men flank King with each one holding him up. Bruised and bloodied, he staggers in with their help. As they pass me, I'm shocked at how bad he looks.

No one says a word to me, and they all walk toward the bedroom. I don't know if I'm supposed to wait in the living room or go in to help him. As I try to figure out the right thing to do, the two men march past me and slam the front door behind them.

The sound of King's moaning hits my ears, and I look in to see him sprawled out across the bed. I creep over toward him and quietly ask, "What happened?"

Opening his eyes, he smiles and shakes his head. "Just a normal day at the office." He pushes himself up with a low groan, but when he tries to stand, he falls back onto the bed.

"You look terrible. Do you want me to get you a damp cloth for the blood?" I ask as it rolls onto the bed sheet from a gash on his cheek.

"No. Help me up," he says, grabbing onto my forearm and nearly dragging me down on top of him.

I steady myself on my feet and pull him off the bed. He sways left and right, almost knocking me over, but after a few seconds, we're both able to stand up straight.

"Is this because of Tap? Did he do this to you?" I ask as he leans on me to take his first step.

King laughs and then lets out another painful sounding groan. "No. This was a bunch of motherfuckers who ambushed us on a job the boss sent us on. Help me into the bathroom."

We walk across the apartment, step after each

shaky step with me doing the job it took two men before, but finally we reach our goal and he grabs onto the door so he doesn't collapse onto the floor.

"I'll start a bath. It will make you feel better resting in the hot water."

I leave him clutching the doorframe to turn on the water, but by the time I turn around, he's found his way over to the sink. White-knuckled, he holds onto the porcelain and leans forward to look at himself in the mirror.

"Fucking-A. Those bastards got us good," he says and then lets out a heavy sigh.

"Sit down on the edge of the tub and I'll help you get your shirt off. Then you can take the rest off and get into the bath," I say as I gently turn him around toward the bathtub.

He sits down and looks up at me so I can finally get a good look at his injuries. His left eye is swollen shut, and the right one is so bloody I can barely see its unique color. A gash along his left cheekbone oozes blood and looks like it might need stitches.

"You're almost unrecognizable."

"Some might say that's a good thing," he says with a smile that shows me at least he didn't lose any teeth in this ambush that got him.

"I'm going to take your shirt off, so I need you to lift your arms, okay?"

Easing it over his head, I toss it into the corner and turn back toward him to see his chest is bloody too. I quickly search his torso for any injuries, but I can't find any.

"Were you cut anywhere but your face? Where's all this blood coming from?"

King hangs his head and sighs. "Angelo. He didn't make it. I tried to help him, but there were too many of them."

Sadness clings to each word, and even covered in blood, his expression shows how much the loss of his friend affects him. I don't know if I've ever met this Angelo person or if he was one of the men in that office, but my humanity and King's emotions make rejoicing about the loss of him impossible. I want to be hard, but clearly, I'm not cut out for that part of this world.

"Let me clean you up a little so you're not sitting in bloody water," I say as I grab a washcloth and dampen it.

"Thanks."

I drag the cloth over his skin and wipe the remnants of his friend's blood off his muscular chest and shoulders. It only takes a few seconds to make the white washcloth deep red, so I rinse it out in the sink as King sits gripping the edge of the tub.

"This won't take much longer," I mumble as the reality of what I'm cleaning makes me want to burst into tears.

Another man's blood. A dead man's blood.

Finally, I get it all off his skin and rinse the cloth of as much of the blood as I can. Forcing a smile, I avoid meeting his gaze and say in my best happy voice, "That's better. Now let's put something on that gash in your cheek or all that work I just did will be for nothing."

"I think I have something that will work," he says, lifting his chin toward the vanity mirror.

He doesn't let go of the tub to help me as I pull open the cabinet door, and a quick glance at the contents on the shelves shows me he's got bandages and tape that will work fine.

I clean off the skin around his injury and cover it with a large bandage before taping it to his cheek. "My guess is you're going to need stitches, but this will do for now."

Needing to push away my feelings and unable to keep pretending none of this bothers me, I turn away and check the bath water. It's hot, but it will do him good to ease his pain.

"This should help a little. I'll leave you alone so you can relax."

I step around him to leave, but he stops me by grabbing my arm. "I need your help with my pants."

As much as I need to escape this room before my emotions spiral out of control, I have to help him. Barely able to push the memory of the last time I had to kneel before him, I crouch down and tug his pant leg while above me he unzips his pants. The sound stops me for a moment, and I freeze there as he pulls his foot out.

We repeat this with his left leg, and I toss his pants over on top of his shirt on the floor in the corner while he removes his boxer briefs and socks. As ridiculous as it seems after last night, I turn away so I don't see his naked body.

"Not sure what this modesty is all about, but I can't make it into the tub without your help."

I wince at that truth and take a deep breath, letting it out slowly as I turn around to face him. Focused on his battered face, I nod and take my position next to him to help.

"Okay. Just go slow. I don't think I could keep you up if you start falling."

As he hobbles into the tub, I hold him up so he can safely get in. He lifts one foot and then the other, and I can't help but be amazed at how someone so strong can be made so vulnerable.

"I'll leave you to your bath. Call me if you need anything."

When I reach the door, behind me he says in a low voice, "Please stay."

For a moment, I consider running away from that room so full of the evidence of King's horrible world. I don't want to think of Angelo dying or King being knifed or anything else that did this to him. My hand grips the doorknob as all of this runs through my mind, but the sound of pain in King's voice stops me.

When I turn around, he's staring up at me looking so beaten that I'm taken aback at the sight. I don't know how I'm going to keep my emotions from rushing out of me, but I can't leave.

"Okay. Do you need help?" I ask, unsure where to stand or what he wants me to do.

As if my answer does something for him, he leans

back against the tub and closes his eyes. "No. I just want you here."

I take a step toward him and stop. Those two guys who helped him into the apartment probably didn't lock the door when they left. I might be able to get away.

But then as I'm standing there considering what I'll encounter after I make it down the stairs, he moans and something about the sound of him in so much pain and seeing him look so bad hits me deep inside. I should leave. I should risk it because I might never get another chance.

I take another step toward the tub and crouch down next to it. Water beads on his tanned chest, and I can't help but remember the feel of his skin against mine last night.

Reaching for the soap, I lather up the bar in my hands and gently begin washing his arm. Dried blood comes off with just a little rubbing, leaving his skin clean. I lather up my hands again and touch his chest, feeling his taut muscles.

King opens his eyes and groans as I slowly move my palms against his side. "Careful. I think I've got a couple busted ribs."

I wince at the thought of how much pain he must feel from broken ribs and return to focusing on his chest. Slowly, I make my way down to his abs and wash off the blood that's dried on his skin there.

As much as I don't want to look between his legs, it's impossible not to. I don't know if it's because I'm a completely perverted person or because of what we did together last night, but I glance at his cock and see he's nearly hard.

"You have a wonderful effect on me," King says softly and chuckles.

My cheeks grow warm, and I turn to see him grinning. "I'm getting the feeling you're not as hurt as I first thought."

King shakes his head and groans. "You have no idea, little one. My body feels like someone's used it to go twelve rounds. I might have to live in this tub for a while because I'm pretty sure I won't be able to move any time soon."

"And yet, you're well enough to get hard. How does that work?"

"That works, dear Sophie, because it has a mind of its own."

I don't know how much I believe that, but I'm not sure I want to keep talking about his cock at the moment. I already feel like something's wrong with me because I keep glancing at it. Thank God King can barely see out of one eye.

"One of these days, you're going to have to tell me about the boys you've spent your time dating."

"Why?"

"Because there must be something very wrong with all of them if you know so little about how men work. It doesn't matter what kind of shape I'm in. If you're around, I'm hard or getting there. Any man who doesn't feel that when you're nearby is either gay or a fool."

I think he means this as a compliment, in a strange

way, and I can't help but smile at his assessment of my former boyfriends. "I don't think any of the guys I dated liked other men."

"Then they were fools."

The way he says that so definitively makes me wonder how he can be so sure of that. "I don't know. One guy was a physics major, so I don't think anyone would say he was a fool."

"Well, if he didn't get excited when you were next to him, then maybe he had some kind of other problem. All I know is if you're nearby, I'm ready to go, no matter what shape I'm in."

"Maybe you're just oversexed. Ever think of that?"

He slides his hand down his body and wraps his hand around his hard cock. It's a purely masculine move that I can't deny thrills me. There's no shame, no shyness about displaying it in all its glory. Even in his large hand, his cock is thick and sensual with those two silver balls on each side of the top of it.

"I'm a red-blooded American male with a healthy sex drive. Nothing wrong with that."

As he talks, his hand slowly moves up and down the shaft from his balls to those piercings. Curious, I finally work up the nerve to ask him why he got them.

"Did it hurt when you did that? Got pierced, I mean," I say, stumbling over my words.

He thinks about my question for a few moments and sighs. "A little. Nothing too bad."

I wish I could ask more questions since I've never seen anything like that in my life, but I don't want to sound naïve or stupid, so I don't say anything else about those metal studs that I find fascinating.

"I think you like the way they look, don't you, little one?" he asks seductively as he continues to stroke his cock.

"I think I like it better when you call me by my name," I say, deflecting so maybe I can get control of the conversation back.

But he doesn't let me.

Closing his eyes, he moans low and deep. "You didn't seem to mind my nickname last night."

I'm thankful he can't see the blush that I'm sure is making my face bright red. Just thinking about last night makes me weak in the knees, among other places on my body.

"Do you want any of those painkillers the doctor gave you for your leg? I can get you a glass of water to take some," I offer, happy to change the subject.

King slowly shakes his head but keeps his eyes closed. "No drugs."

"Okay. Then you just relax. Call me if you want me to run more hot water for you. I think if you keep it warm it will make you feel better."

I stand and he looks up at me, his eyes narrowed in pain. I wish he would consider taking something, especially if he has bruised or fractured ribs.

Then he speaks, and I know the look on his face isn't because of his injuries.

"You can't wait to get away from me, can you? They probably left the door open, but make sure you keep away from the likes of Tap or you'll end up in worse shape than me," he bites out.

His anger toward me comes off him in waves I can practically see, and I don't want to try to say I haven't thought of that because I can't lie that well. I turn to leave, and the last thing I see is the look in his eyes that I swear seems like betrayal or hurt.

I walk to the front door and check it. Unlocked. There's nothing to stop me, so I open the door and peek out. Not a soul in sight.

Finally, my chance to escape this place.

CHAPTER THIRTEEN

ing

THE SILENCE IN THE APARTMENT TELLS ME SHE'S gone. I stand in the doorway to the bathroom and listen for any sign of Sophie but hear nothing. Maybe she's in the bedroom sleeping. Maybe she's in the kitchen.

I close my eyes as stabbing pain in my ribs makes it hard to breathe. She's not here.

By the time I make it to my bed, I barely have enough strength to care where the fuck she is. Still, I hope she finds a way off the estate. If not, all that's in store for her is a world of hurt, likely at the hands of that asshole Tap, assuming the dogs don't get her first. Duke will finally give her over to him once he realizes I couldn't stop her from running.

Silly girl. If only she'd been patient.

Even lifting my cell to my ear hurts, so I quickly lower my arm and squeeze the phone between my head and shoulder after calling the doctor. "Cam, when you can, come up. I need your help with a gash on my cheek and maybe a rib or two."

"Okay, King. I'll be a while. Marsh is pretty ripped up. Don't take any painkillers yet, though. It's better if you're awake for me."

I stare up at the white ceiling and groan as pain tears through me again. "No pills. Got it. Not that I was planning on moving from this bed anytime soon. Just come in. The door's unlocked."

"I'll be there as soon as I can."

He ends the call, so I turn my head and let the phone drop into the sheets next to me. Over on the dresser, the bottle of painkillers sits there calling out to me like some kind of goddamned siren. That's the last thing I need right now. Whatever my ribs feel like doesn't matter. If Sophie gets caught, I'm going to need to be on my game when Duke calls me down to his office to ask just how she fucking had the chance to go roaming around the estate.

Not that anything I say is going to matter at that point. Just the fact that she had the chance to get away from me says it all. He'll give her to Tap after this. Why wouldn't he? Her escape is proof I can't control her, and I can't argue with that.

Somewhere in the pain from my ribs pinching at my ability to take in a full breath of air another kind of hurt presses down on me. It makes my chest ache. I know what that fucker will do to her. She won't make it out of this place alive if he has anything to say about it, no matter what Duke plans to use her for.

I did what I could. If only she'd been patient for just a little while longer.

The sound of the front door opening makes my eyes fly open, and my heart pounds against my chest as I wait to see if she returned. If no one saw her, we might be okay.

One second passes, followed by another, and I begin to wonder if my ears are playing tricks on me and I didn't really hear the door open. Am I delusional because of the pain?

I watch for any sight of her appearing in the bedroom doorway, but I see no one. Unable to wait, I call out, "Who's there?"

Cam walks into the room a few moments later as he stuffs his phone into his jacket pocket. "Sorry about that, King. Someone texted me just as I walked in, and I had to answer back right then and there. I didn't mean to startle you."

Waving off his explanation, I force a laugh that makes me feel like my fucking ribs are stabbing my insides to come out. "No problem. I just didn't know if that motherfucker Tap had somehow gotten lost and walked into the wrong apartment."

The doctor sets his black bag down on the bed beside me and smiles in a way that tells me he knows far more about all of us than he lets on. Cam's older — maybe forty or forty-five — and doesn't tend to get involved in company bullshit. He just tends to our wounds when he can. He's an actual doctor, so he has a practice somewhere I think, but Duke relies on him to handle the scrapes and bruises the bunch of us end up getting doing our kind of work.

"How's the leg feeling?" he asks, glancing over at me as he rummages through his bag looking for something.

I shrug. I haven't thought about my leg for at least a day or so. I guess I was too busy thinking about something else.

Someone else.

"It's fine. I'm just not going to let Stills do your job anymore," I joke.

Cam rolls his eyes at me and laughs. "I think that's a good idea." Changing the subject, he nods toward my cheek. "So what do we have going on under this bandage?"

"Think my leg but not as bad. I don't think it needs stitches," I answer as I unpeel the tape from my skin and lift the bandage to expose the gash that runs along my cheekbone.

His eyes run the full length of the cut before he nods. "Nice job. You're right. I can use steri strips instead of stitches. You've had so many of these injuries you're starting to know as much as I do."

"Well, I'm a quick learner."

He gets to work closing the wound and applying the bandages while I lay there and try to get a full breath of air into my lungs. I fail and wince as the pain stabs at me once more.

"You cleaned this up nicely. I'm impressed, King. Normally, you're a mess with this kind of thing."

I take this opportunity to mention Sophie and hope she hasn't been caught roaming around the grounds already. "The girl helped. You know me. I'd leave the damn thing all bloody and fucked up, but she kept insisting on cleaning it up so it doesn't get infected."

My intention had been to bring her up so Cam might say something to Duke since I know he gives him a full report whenever he tends to any of us. Unfortunately, I didn't think further than that, and now Cam's looking around for any sign of her, which I should have thought of.

He doesn't ask about her, but I have to keep the façade up, so I add, "I think the whole thing made her sort of sick to her stomach. You know how females are. She's hiding out in the bathroom, probably puking her guts up."

Leaning back to admire his handiwork on my cheek, he smiles. "Well, I can understand that. Taking care of wounds isn't for everyone. This looks good now, and I don't expect it to be any problem for you."

I look up at him and smile. "No scar I can make up a story for when I'm old and gray?"

"You already have a lot of those, but I'd hazard a guess that this might not be one you can add to your collection. So, what else did they get? I'm assuming you're not breathing like that because you like me."

"One of those fuckers got me right in the ribs. Fuck, man, I thought he sent a couple of them shooting right out my fucking back it hurt so much."

Cam nods, giving me a sly smile. "And the payback for that was your usual?"

"He's not going to be crushing anyone's ribs ever again, so yeah, my usual," I say proudly, happy to report that fuck with the size thirteen shitkickers got what he had coming to him.

The doctor offers me his hand and then pulls me up off the bed as a thousand spikes of red-hot pain shoot through my torso. "Fuck! That hurts. There's got to be at least a couple that are bad this time," I say through gritted teeth.

"Let me check," he says as he moves his hands to my sides and then begins to press against my skin. "I'm not sure anything's broken, but they could be badly bruised. I'm thinking we need some X-rays, though, to be sure."

I shake my head and wave off his suggestion. "I don't need X-rays. It's not like you're going to be able to do anything different if we find out they're broken and not only bruised. I'll be fine."

Cam twists his expression into the usual look of disapproval he wears any time I tell him I don't want to bother with his tests. They don't change anything anyway. It's not like he can set broken ribs. They just need to heal on their own.

"You know, if it's a bad break, you can have internal damage. You don't want to mess up any organs."

"I'll be fine."

"Just promise me you'll make sure you take deep breaths so you don't get pneumonia. If so, I'll be sure to tell Duke that you're only out of commission for a few days to give you a chance to heal a little."

Taking a deep breath hasn't been easy up to now, so I'm guessing it's going to hurt for a while. I don't want the doctor telling Duke I'm out of commission at all, though, so I need to show him I'm all good right here and now.

I tilt my head back to look at him and inhale deeply through my nose. The pain threatens to make my eyes tear, but I force myself to smile through the unbelievable agony this single breath is dealing me.

After I let it out, I say, "See? All good. The worst thing was the gash on my face, and that didn't even need stitches. I'll be at his office the same time I am any other day I work."

Cam rolls his eyes. "Okay, but at least rest for tonight. I'll give you something to sleep."

He tries to hand me another bottle of pills, but I push them away. "I don't need anything. Thanks."

For a long moment, he stares at me, like he's sizing up how likely it is I feel as good as I claim. Finally, he closes his bag and nods. "I swear you're made of steel, King. You have my number. Call if you need anything. I'll check back with you about the cheek in a couple days."

"Thanks, Cam. Do me a favor and lock the door on your way out. I don't need any wayward sons of bitches wandering into my place while I'm trying to get some sleep."

"Gotcha. Remember, call me if you need anything, especially those pills you wouldn't take," Cam says with a smile that makes me think he knows I'm in a metric shit ton of pain but won't call me on it.

I watch him leave, and before he even reaches the front door, I collapse back onto the bed. If I didn't have to worry about the effect of painkillers on my ability to hold my own with the likes of Tap, I'd swallow a bunch of them because just taking that single breath in made me feel like someone was ripping my body apart with pliers.

Closing my eyes, I pray to a god I don't believe in that I can get some sleep. Anything that will let me forget about this pain for even a little while.

Pounding on my front door rips me out of a sound sleep, and without thinking, I sit up in bed, only to feel like a vice is crushing my body. I fall back onto the bed nearly in tears at how bad this feels. Holy fuck!

"King! You in there?" I hear someone yell, and I remember I told Cam to lock the door on his way out.

What seemed like a great idea at the time is way less fucking spectacular now as I struggle to get myself out of bed. After far more effort than I ever thought I'd need to get to the floor, I walk through the apartment and throw the front door open, already pissed off at whoever it is banging the fuck out of it.

One of the guys I work with stands there with his fist at the ready to pound again. Nico's surprised expression probably matches the one I had on when I first woke up a few seconds ago. Taller and bigger than most of Duke's guys, he looks like he spends every minute of the day at the gym. He also has a streak of meanness running through him that rivals Tap's, but he's not a psychopath.

"King, you have to get up. The boss wants you."

"I am up, man," I snap, already disgusted with this conversation. "What time is it?"

Nico shrugs. "I don't know. Right around one, I think."

One o'clock in the morning? Why the fuck does Duke need me at this time of night? Then it dawns on me. Sophie. She got herself fucking caught, and now on top of feeling like a fucking truck ran me over, I get to watch him hand her over to Tap.

Fucking great.

"Any idea why he needs me now?" I ask, pretending to not know just in case it's something else.

"In his office. Now. That's all he said," Nico says, repeating our boss's words verbatim, I'm sure.

"Fine. I'll be right there," I answer as I slam the door in his face.

Fifteen minutes later, I'm dressed as well as I'm going to be considering my ribs threw up a roadblock every time I tried to put a T-shirt on. I don't usually wear button down shirts, but in my current state, it's all I could manage.

As I walk through the living room, I glance over at the empty couch where Sophie usually sat. My stomach tightens at the thought of what Duke is so eager to discuss since I'm pretty sure it's nothing good and has everything to do with her.

Closing the front door behind me, I take one last look back at the couch. "Serves her right. Stupid girl."

By the time I reach the hallway outside of Duke's office, I've screwed my face into its usual I don't fucking care expression I put on any time I have to be around him. Busted ribs can't change that look or he'll know I give a damn about what's going on with her.

I walk in ready to see Tap holding Sophie and her dark eyes full of fear silently pleading with me to save her, but there's no one there but Duke. Seated behind his desk, he looks worried.

But why if this meeting has nothing to do with Sophie? There's no way he'd just hand her over to Tap without rubbing my face in it. Duke's never that nice.

He studies me for a minute before he extends his arm to offer me a seat in front of his desk. "Relax. Take a load off, King. I'm guessing I woke you up."

As much as I don't want to sit because standing hurts so much less, I take the seat he offers and nod. "Needed a little sleep after today's action."

His eyes move up and down like he's examining me for some defect. "I hope you feel better than you look. I've seen shit warmed over that looked better than you do at this moment, although the dress shirt makes you seem a little less roughed up."

"I feel like shit, but don't worry. I'll be fine tomorrow. A little more sleep and I'll be good."

He believes my act and easily moves on to the reason he dragged me down here in the middle of the night. "Okay, then down to business. I think I have a rat in my midst."

My heart slams into my chest, and I worry how much my whole body hurts at that moment is so obvious that he's going to decide not to continue telling me about his suspicions. I need for him to trust me, so I fight every instinct inside me to wince as my ribs send waves of pain radiating through my torso.

I have to keep cool, so I casually ask the logical question anyone would. "Why?"

"That ambush today. Somebody knew what you three were there for. Somebody other than the buyers."

Nodding, I pretend like I'm thinking of what he's suggesting. "We did go in there expecting only three of them. Then, out of nowhere, it's like double that many came at us from all sides. Angelo got the worst of it because he was closest to where they came from. Poor guy."

Duke sighs deeply, like the loss of one of his men bothers him. "Well, I don't think he was the rat, unfortunately, so my problem still exists."

So much for caring.

"One of the new guys?" I ask, quickly wondering who he suspects. "Personally, I'd be looking at Tap."

At my mention of that asshole, Duke throws his head back and laughs. "That's because you two don't get along. Men shouldn't let women come between them. There's enough pussy in this world to go around for everyone."

"I hated him long before she came along. He's too apt to go rogue. He's all about him, and everyone else can go fuck themselves. People get hurt, or worse, killed that way."

I watch for his reaction since I know he likes Tap.

Even more, I wonder if Duke already knows Sophie has run off. I've already decided I'll claim she hurts him more than helps him since Tap should have never taken her in the first place.

"He's proven himself almost as much as you have, so for now, Tap isn't my rat," Duke says sharply, effectively ending our discussion of him.

All the better. Talking about that fuck only makes me want to crush something, preferably him.

We sit there silently as he thinks about who his rat can be and I think about how thankful I am Sophie didn't escape until after what went down at the buy meeting yesterday. If she'd left earlier, Duke would think she got word to her uncle and the shit show that greeted the three of us was his way of retaliating.

Curious, I break the silence between the two of us and ask about that very idea. "Any chance her uncle had a part in what went down yesterday? Tap did take his niece."

"Maybe, but with her still with you, I don't see how. Any chance she got your phone and called him?"

I chuckle and shake my head. "She and I aren't close. She's basically my slave. I take what I want from her, and she cooks my meals and keeps my place clean. I guess she's more like a housekeeper-cook-whore."

My description of Sophie's part in my life amuses him, and he lets out a deep belly laugh. "I should get one of them. Kill three birds with one stone."

We laugh together, and he adds, "You know, Tap reminds me every damn day that she should be his."

"Well, he's wrong, and anyway, he'd just abuse the hell out of her. He probably wouldn't even fuck her. Complete waste of fucking pussy, if you ask me. You'd end up sending her back looking like goddamned hamburger meat if he got a hold of her."

Duke shakes his head. "All of this over some cunt. I wish he had never grabbed her at all. I've heard nothing from her uncle about her either, which makes me wonder. I don't like wondering, King. You know that."

"Leave it to Tap to grab some useless bitch. She's probably the daughter of the one brother or sister her uncle doesn't like," I say with a forced chuckle. "Just another reason he shouldn't have her."

My jab at Tap falls flat, and Duke quickly moves the conversation back to his rat problem. "Well, I want you to keep your eyes open from now on. We need to find the rat among us, King."

"Okay. I'll pay close attention to what everyone's up to."

Not that I think what happened with that ambush was because of a rat. If anything, it happened because of how sloppy Duke tends to be with his business instead of one of us turning on him.

"Let me know if you see anything suspicious. But for tonight, you need to get some more sleep. Take tomorrow off. I need to deal with Angelo and his family, so nothing's going on tomorrow. Stay in bed and rest up. I'll see you two days from now."

I'm not unhappy with getting time off to nurse my

ribs, so I stand up and give him a smile as I carefully turn to leave. "If you insist."

As I'm walking toward the door, Duke says, "And don't spend your whole time fucking that girl. By the looks of you, what you need is sleep, not pussy."

I turn my head and give him one last look. "No worries on that. I'm beat."

His office door closes behind me, and I can finally let out a sigh of relief. If Sophie hasn't been caught yet, maybe she did find a way to escape. She's smart. If any woman can find their way off this estate, it would be her.

I can only hope that's the case and she hasn't been grabbed by Tap for good this time.

CHAPTER FOURTEEN

*ophie*

My heart races as I struggle to catch my breath. For three hours, I've tried to find a place to make a run for it. Mostly, I've run from bush to bush and prayed to God those terrible dogs King talked about won't really devour me if they catch up to me.

I scan the grounds in front of me for any sign of where the estate ends. All I see are trees. Shouldn't there be some evidence of a wall or fence or something? Is it possible that all those things King told me about guards and rabid dogs were lies?

Stepping out from behind a large hedge, I think I see a break in the tree line. Clouds obscure the moon, making it far darker than last night when there was enough moonlight pouring in through his bedroom window. I just need to take a chance. I can't stay crawling among bushes and hedges until morning or they'll surely find me.

No guards have passed by the entire time I've been out here, so I take a deep breath and make a break for that hole in the trees. The feel of the damp grass brushing against my feet and ankles as I run toward my goal makes me realize how long it's been since I was free. Free to run. Free to leave that apartment. Free to do anything.

I see where I want to run to and my hope soars that after hours of hesitating, I've finally got a chance to make it off this goddamned estate and back to my life. With each time my feet hit the ground, I rejoice, sure I'll be free tonight.

And then just as I believe that with all my heart, I hear a man's voice shouting in the distance. "Hey! Who are you? Get back here!"

With every fiber of my being, I silently answer him. "No fucking way, pal!"

But then I hear him yell to a second man, and suddenly, all my hope disappears. The hole in the trees shows me there's a stone wall. I'm trapped.

I look around like a frightened animal, desperate for a way out and finding none. My mind races. I can't let that man get me. He'll take me to that boss of King's, and he'll give me to Tap.

No! I'd rather die.

Turning back toward the apartment buildings, I run as fast as I can, sprinting like I've never done before. At best, I'm a jogger, but that won't be enough to outrun the guard rushing across the grass toward me.

I hear him get closer as panic rises in me. I can't let him catch me! I have to get back to King's apartment!

My thighs burn, as if the muscles in each one want to explode out through the skin. Adrenaline pumps through me, thankfully, making it possible for me to keep going. In the distance, maybe a little over a hundred yards in front of me, I see the stairs that lead up to King's. If only I can get back there, I'll be safe.

But my feet can't move fast enough to beat the man getting closer and closer with each step. He keeps yelling, but my heartbeat pounding in my ears makes it impossible to hear exactly what he's saying.

Not that it matters. Nothing he has to say to me is anything good. He's like everyone else here, no doubt. Cruel and vicious.

Not everyone.

As the thought of King fills my mind, I reach the stairs and my foot slips off the first one. My shin bashes off the metal step, and I cry out in pain, but there's no time for that. I have to reach his apartment or this guard will take me away to someplace far worse.

I hear his heavy breathing right behind me as I fight for that last bit of strength to climb those stairs to my only safety on this entire estate. My eyes fill with tears from the pain in my legs and the fear that I won't make it in time, but I look up and through the blurriness, I see King standing at his apartment door.

"King! Wait!" I yell to him as he opens the door to go inside.

Don't shut me out here with this man! Please!

"Stop! Get back here!" the man behind me barks.

My foot lands on the top step just as I feel the guard's hot breath on the back of my neck. He almost caught me. King stands staring at me, and for a moment, I'm not sure he's going to save me.

Gapsing, the guard says, "I caught this woman running toward the back of the property. I need to take her to Duke right away."

King looks at me with utter disgust and shakes his head at the man. "No need to bother him. She's mine. I sent her out on an errand and she must have fucked up. Leave it to this one. Stupid cunt. I told you to go to the kitchen in the main house. Can't you do anything right?"

I don't know what to make of the revulsion in his voice. Is he just talking like this for the guard's benefit so he doesn't take me, or does he really think so little of me? Either way, his words sting.

I search his expression for any hint of the kindness I've seen in him before, but I find none of it now. All I see is rage.

He grabs me by the hair and pushes me toward the door. "I got this. Have a good night, man."

Behind me, the man starts to say something, but King forces me into the apartment and slams the door closed before he can finish. I wait for him to say something, but all he does is release his hold on my hair.

Now that I'm alone with him, I'm suddenly terrified. He pushes me away from him like he can't stand to be near me and walks away without saying a word.

He slams the bathroom door shut, leaving me standing alone in the living room. What will he do when he comes out? Will he hit me? He's never been violent with me when we've been alone, but the way he looked at me outside makes me wonder. I've never seen him so angry. He looked more like Tap than himself out there.

God, why did I try to escape? I didn't even try to figure out how the place was laid out beforehand. I had no plan, and once I got even a few yards away from the apartment buildings, it was so dark that I couldn't see where I was going.

I run through my reaction once that guard saw me and hate how stupid I was. I heard him yell, and what did I do? I ran around like a scared mouse in a maze, foolishly thinking I could outrun him. If King's apartment building hadn't been as close as it was, that man would have caught up with me.

The bathroom door opens with a creak, startling me, and my heart beats wildly as I brace for what he's going to do to me. Will he just scream at me and berate me for being so foolish, or will he hit me? He's going to make me pay for my mistake. Just the way he spoke to me in front of that guard tells me that.

As all of these ideas race through my mind, he walks by me without even glancing over toward where I sit. His mouth is set in a thin, straight line. Neither a smile nor a frown, it's a look of tightness that frightens me.

I wait for him to bark my name or order me to follow him, but there's nothing but silence. It terrifies me, and I sit frozen in place on the couch for the moment when he decides to finally say the words he's holding inside.

After nearly five minutes, I can't wait any longer and slowly make my way to his room. I don't want to hear him yell at me, but even worse is waiting for what's about to come next. Stopping in the doorway, I don't know what to say.

He's standing in just a pair of jeans next to the bed, the glow from the nightstand light illuminating his shirtless back. He doesn't look beaten and broken like he had in the bathtub hours ago.

Now he looks powerful and strong, his emotions caged for the moment but like someone I should fear.

He doesn't turn around when I step into the room. Maybe he doesn't want me there. I'm not sure I should want him to turn around, but not knowing what will happen next bothers me too much.

My foot makes the floor creak, but he doesn't flinch. I wait a few more seconds and clear my throat, but still, he doesn't turn around.

Finally, it's too much. I can't stop myself from saying something.

"I…I know I made a mistake. It was stupid of me. I'm sorry."

Even now, he doesn't respond or turn around, and suddenly I feel defensive. "It's not like you care about me, King. I'm nothing to you. You showed that out there with that guard."

Suddenly, he spins around to face me and I see in his expression he's even angrier that I thought. Then he begins to speak, and my stomach drops.

I've pushed him too far.

"You obviously want me to treat you like I did outside. I've let you sleep in my bed. I made sure you were fed and comfortable, but still you tried to run away."

I wait for him to call me by his nickname for me or my name, but he just stops talking. I thought I hated hearing him say little one, but now I miss it, strangely.

He slowly walks toward me, and with each step I see the rage in his eyes. When he stops just inches away from me, he stares down at me and shakes his head. "You know, my boss is probably going to give you to Tap now because your running away is proof I can't control you. I can promise you none of your sulky apologies are going to help you with that fuck."

The way he looks at me so full of hate forces me to look away. "I'm sorry. I just wanted to go home."

"I tried to protect you, Sophie. Now you'll be at the mercy of someone who likes hurting people."

King caresses my cheek with his fingertips, and I turn to look at him as his hand slides down to encircle my neck. Slowly, he squeezes it and says, "Maybe that's what you like, little one. You like it when men treat you rough?"

I swallow hard, frightened by him now. Shaking

my head, I feel his hand continue to tighten around my throat.

"No."

His hand doesn't leave me, his fingertips pressing into my skin just below my ears, and he leans down so his lips are close to mine. My heartbeat races as my emotions unspool inside me.

"I can smell the fear coming off you, but just like that first day, there's something even more delicious underneath. What's that, little one?"

I don't know how to answer because I know he's right. I'm terrified, but being this close to him makes me want him more than I've ever wanted a man in my life.

"Maybe I should give you a taste of what it's going to be like for you once Tap gets his hands on your body," he whispers against my lips.

"Please don't let him take me, King," I whisper back, barely able to hold back my tears.

Leaning back, he grins like this is funny to him. "I'll get to hear all about it since he loves to brag about how rough he likes it. We had to take some poor little thing to the hospital so she didn't die after he got through with her. Ready for that, Sophie?"

"You promised me you'd protect me," I say, shaken by the reality that he's going to just hand me over to that pig.

King's eyes open in rage, and he pushes me up against the wall. They're filled with a wildness I've never seen in him until now.

"You decided to take advantage of my weakness,

ABBI COOK

little one. Now you'll suffer the consequences of that choice, and I can guarantee you Tap won't treat you like I did."

I feel his hard cock press against my hip. He's enjoying seeing me terrified.

Suddenly, my own anger explodes inside me, and I spit in his face. "Fuck you! You're the same as him if you let him take me!"

I wait for his rage to match mine, but he merely smiles at me as he wipes his chin. "Let's see then."

He grips my shoulders, and before I know it, spins me around and pins me to the wall. His forearm presses against my shoulders, immobilizing me. Unable to move my upper body, I try to turn my hips away, but he pushes against my ass to hold me still.

"Thought you'd get to have some control, little one? Think again. Just wait until that asshole ties you up or chains you to the wall so he can fuck you. I'll do my best to show you, though."

"King, please…I'm sorry," I cry to the wall in front of me.

I feel his hand tug my shorts and underwear down off my legs, and then he jams his knee between my thighs to open them. The next thing I feel is his hard cock against my ass.

"Mmmm…that's the delicious scent I smelled."

He moves his hand around my hip and runs his finger through my pussy. I hate that I'm drenched and he knows how much I want him, but just one touch on my clit makes me moan softly.

I prepare for him to push hard into me, each

second that passes more terrifying than the last, but instead, he spins me around to face him. In his eyes, the anger and hate is gone now, replaced by pure need. His hands tear at my shirt and bra, ripping them from my body as I shake in fear that his rage will reappear at any second.

For a moment, our eyes meet, and then he kisses me hard, his tongue sliding into my mouth to tease me and make me remember what he's capable of doing with it. A mixture of fear and longing courses through my body, and I cling to his neck, desperate to feel his body against mine.

My head swims from the most intense kiss I've ever experienced, and I rake my fingernails over the back of his neck. He growls my name near my ear, sending a rush of need through me.

"Sophie…"

The way he says it, like it means something to him, makes holding back my tears impossible. Being with him hasn't been perfect by any means, but now that I'm losing that, I can't control my emotions.

He lifts me off the floor, and a second later, he lowers me onto his cock. The feel of those metal studs is cool against the delicate skin between my legs, and as he slides his cock into me, they touch nerve endings that make it nearly impossible to think of anything but how much I want this.

When he's completely nested inside me, King stops and looks down at me. "Fuck, little one. You feel so good."

Before I can form words to tell him how good he

feels inside me, he rears his hips back and slams into my body hard. He's thick and long and every thrust into me takes my breath away.

He fucks like an animal, moaning and grunting low and deep into my ear. His left hand holds me by the ass while his right hand tugs my hair. A mixture of pain and pleasure rolls over me, ratcheting up my need for him even more.

"Do you feel my piercings every time my cock fills your cunt, little one?" he groans and then pumps hard into me balls deep.

"God…yes…" I answer as I push my heels into his lower back to keep him inside me.

"You belong to me."

"But Tap…"

King leans back and wraps his hand around my neck. Shaking his head, he looks deep into my eyes. "You're mine. He touches you, and I'll kill him."

His mouth crushes against mine, and he goes back to fucking me like every thrust is meant to tattoo him onto my body. My release comes over me like a wave of pure ecstasy, and I come hard, clinging to him as the orgasm he's given me rocks my body.

My thighs quiver against his sides, and a few seconds later, he pushes into me one final time before flooding my body with all he has. Drenched in sweat and exhausted, the two of us sag against one another.

Breathing raggedly, he whispers in my ear, "You're safe. I promise. Just promise you won't run away again, Sophie."

I hate being in this place more than I can explain. I

want to be free again. I want to return to my home and my life.

But when I look up at him, I see care in his eyes I've never seen before in them.

So I say the words I know should be a lie. They aren't, though.

"I promise. I won't try it again."

He slides out of me, leaving me feeling empty and missing him. Lowering me to the floor, he pulls me to him and presses a kiss to the top of my head.

My cheek against his chest, I listen to his heartbeat still racing from our time together as the reality of what I've done sinks in for real, finally. "What's going to happen, King? Your boss is going to find out from that guard that I tried to get away."

"Shhh. Don't worry. I'll take care of it."

"But that man is going to tell him what I did."

King tilts my head back and leans down to kiss me softly on the lips. "I told you I'd take care of it. I won't let anyone hurt you, Sophie."

The way he says that, like it's something definite he has complete control over, makes me want to believe he'll be able to keep his word and protect me. The very idea of Tap terrifies me more than I even want King to know. But if his boss wants to take me away, how can he stop him?

I open my mouth to ask that very question, but I decide to believe in King. Whatever this is between the two of us, he's never shown me he can't be trusted.

Even if I've shown him the opposite.

He winces and sits on the edge of the bed in obvious pain. I'd forgotten how hurt he was until now.

"We shouldn't have done that. Now your ribs are going to hurt more."

Turning to look at me, he smiles sweetly. "I knew what my ribs would feel like after. I still wanted you."

"I don't understand you. You're hurt, and yet you do things that will make you feel bad. That makes no sense."

He chuckles and shrugs like what I said is funny to him. "But it feels so good while I'm fucking you, so why wouldn't I take some pain for that pleasure?"

"There are other ways to feel that way that might not have caused you so much pain."

"Not the same," he says, shaking his head. "I'd take being inside you over your hand or even your mouth any day of the week."

I'm not sure what to say to that as I feel my cheeks start to get warm from a blush. Looking away toward the floor, I mumble, "I guess that's a compliment."

His fingertip touches under my chin, and he gently turns my head so I face him. "It's definitely a compliment, especially considering I think I have at least a couple fractured ribs."

"I don't understand men," I say with a sigh.

Wincing, he takes a deep breath in as pain washes over his face. He lets it out slowly, and then answers in a strained tone, "There's not much to understand. We like to eat, drink, sleep, fuck, and fight, not necessarily in that order. Even the worst of us don't have needs that go past those five categories."

"So why did you want to take me from Tap? Because you wanted to fuck me? I don't fit into any of those other categories."

All of a sudden, King turns distant. It's like a gulf has formed between us, even though he sits right next to me. My heart sinks to hear his voice sound emotionless too when he says, "He owed me, so I took you. Simple."

Simple? How can taking a human being to pay a debt be simple? I can't explain it, but the way he dismisses any other reason for wanting to take me from Tap hurts my feelings. How can I expect him to protect me when I mean so little to him?

"Please promise me no matter what happens that you won't let him get me. I know I'm just a repayment of a debt he owes you, but my life depends on it."

And just like that, King looks at me and all that intensity I see when we're together and he's deep inside me rushes back into his eyes.

"You're not just a repayment of a debt, Sophie." He stops for a long moment and then continues, "You're mine. I told you that. I won't let him touch you."

Mine. He says that like it means something more than just that I'm the person he keeps here in his apartment.

I want to ask what mine means to him, but it sounds childish and naïve, so I hold back and instead ask another question almost as important. "What about your boss?" I say, worried the answer to that question might not be the same.

"He has no interest in taking you from me. You don't have to worry. Trust me."

"I don't have a choice, do I?"

He doesn't respond for a moment, but then he shakes his head and I see the hint of a frown. "No, you don't."

We sit in silence as he slowly breathes in and out until I finally say, "I'm not sorry for wanting to be free, but I am sorry I may have caused you more trouble."

In a quiet voice, he says, "I don't blame you for trying to escape, Sophie."

"You just blame me for being stupid about it?"

King shakes his head again. "I just need you to believe me, okay? I won't let anyone hurt you. I swear."

He gets up and slowly walks out of the bedroom, leaving me sitting there naked on the edge of his bed wondering why I do believe him. He's no less vicious than any of the other men I've seen at this place, yet something about him makes me think he'll do as he promises.

I want to hate him. I want to leave this place and never think about him or anyone here again. But I don't know if I'll ever forget King.

All I know is I will leave this place someday. With or without his help, I will escape. That's the only sure thing I can cling to, and I can never let that thought leave my brain.

CHAPTER FIFTEEN

ing

MY EYES FLY OPEN, AND I LOOK DOWN IN HORROR at my side expecting to see someone with a sharp knife rooting around inside my gut. Barely awake, I see nothing, but then a second later, I instinctively take in a deep breath of air into my lungs and cry out in agony.

"Fuck!"

Beside me, Sophie stirs but doesn't wake up, and I hold onto the side of the bed as I wait out this current wave of pain washing over me. A minute passes and then finally it subsides, so I let the air out of my lungs slowly, terrified that pain will return while I stare up at the ceiling and try to think of anything to get my mind off how fucking bad this hurts.

One hell of a way to wake up. Misery, the breakfast of champions.

Turning my head, I look over and watch Sophie as she sleeps. Her mouth turned down into a frown, her bottom lip juts out into a pout. It's cute in a strange way since the only other times I've ever seen anyone look like that is when babies sleep.

Closing my eyes, I silently wonder what the fuck is wrong with me. She shouldn't be here. I should have left her out on the couch. She would have been perfectly fine out there. The damn thing's as comfortable as this bed, for Christ's sake. Millions of people sleep on couches every night.

I stop beating myself up long enough to look over at her again. Why she's here doesn't take a rocket scientist to figure it out. That doesn't explain what's wrong with me, though. I know better than to let anyone in, most of all some woman. Females get guys like me killed. They get in the way. They fuck up our thinking.

Women like Sophie bring out things in us that make doing the job impossible.

I know all of that, and still she'll stay with me in this bed. She belongs here with me. And yet, a tiny voice in the back of my mind whispers this is a mistake we'll both pay for in the end.

"Why are you staring at me like that? Did I kick you or something in my sleep?"

Her question tears me out of my daydreaming about our eventual demise, and I shake my head. "No.

At least I don't think you did. I woke up with a sharp pain in my side, so maybe you did."

With a wince, regret washes over her. "I'm sorry. I didn't do it on purpose. I guess I move around a lot when I sleep."

In truth, I have no idea if that's true. Until I woke up in utter agony, I hadn't felt a thing since I drifted off to sleep last night. In fact, I can't remember the last time I slept so well.

"It's okay. I'll be fine."

Remembering what Cam said about getting pneumonia if I don't keep my lungs in shape, I take a shallow breath in and hold it there, waiting for the pain to come rushing back any second. When it doesn't, I let it out slowly and try another, slightly deeper inhale. Better to feel pain now than be laid up in bed for weeks while my place is taken by the likes of Tap.

As if she can read my mind, Sophie asks, "Why do you do what you do with your boss?"

"Do what I do? What do you mean?" I ask as I let that deeper breath out of my lungs with relief. No red-hot, searing pain yet.

She doesn't answer for a long moment, and when I look over at her to see why she's hesitating, she looks uncomfortable. "I'm not actually sure what you do, but you work for that Duke guy, right?"

"Yep."

"So, what do you do for him? Like why were you in my neighborhood that night?" she asks as she props her head up on her hand and then waits for my answer.

My boss's warning not to have pillow talk with her echoes in my head, but I push it away. It can't hurt to tell her what I do. Who's she going to blab to?

"I do a lot of things, but that night we were there to collect money from someone who owed Duke."

She listens to my answer and quickly asks, "For what?"

"What did he owe him money for?" I ask in return, knowing what she means but unsure how much further I want to go into what I do in this world.

Too clever for my little game, she smiles. "Yes. What did he buy that he had to pay you guys for?"

I know what she thinks. Drugs. Maybe guns. Not that either of those answers would be incorrect most of the time when it comes to the people Duke deals with, but in this case, neither is right.

"He didn't buy anything. It wasn't that kind of debt," I say, explaining nothing and only muddying the conversation.

Sophie's eyebrows draw in toward her nose, making her look only slightly less beautiful. Clearly frustrated, she sighs. "You know what I'm asking. If you don't want to tell me, don't, but why answer in the first place?"

Something about her exasperation makes me chuckle, but no sooner do I start, so does the pain in my side. She sees me cringe and quickly sits up.

"It's okay. You don't have to answer. I'm sorry I asked."

"I'm not angry, Sophie. My ribs just gave me a shot of pain when I chuckled. I can answer your question."

"Only if you want to," she says shyly, looking down at me while she stays away from me.

"He owed him money because he borrowed money. Loan sharking," I explain even as I wonder why she hasn't laid back down.

Does she think I'm going to lash out at her?

"Oh."

"You sound disappointed," I say, smiling. "What did you think I'd say?"

Sophie hesitates for a moment and then looks down toward her legs. "I thought you were going to say he bought someone...like me, I mean."

"No, Duke doesn't sell people," I answer before touching her knee.

Looking up at me, she studies my face for a few seconds and shakes her head. "He only takes them? What's the end game of that?"

"He doesn't even do that. Tap took it upon himself to grab you. We were just supposed to go get money," I explain, but at my mention of his name, she moves her leg so I'm not touching her anymore.

Suddenly quiet, she avoids looking at me. Everything in her body language says just hearing Tap's name now bothers her. Why, though?

"Sophie, I told you I'll keep you safe. You can believe me. I won't let Tap or anyone else get their hands on you."

"You said a lot of things last night."

Between the pain that ebbs and flows through my body and the great sex last night, I'm not sure I can pinpoint what she's referring to. What did I say that has her so worried?

"I meant what I said about not letting him or anyone else hurt you. I promise."

Lifting her head, she looks down at me with such innocence in her eyes that I almost don't recognize her. "You said I was yours last night. Did you mean that?"

I look up into her big brown eyes and nod. "Yes."

"What does that mean?"

"It means no one else can touch you. That's what it means."

But that isn't what she wants to know. And just like that, she backs me into a corner I shouldn't have been anywhere close to.

"Is that it?" she asks in a voice barely above a whisper.

She bites her lower lip anxiously as I consider what to tell her. It's not it. And that's the worst part of all of this. I don't know when or how I let this happen, but she got under my skin.

For a man like me in a world like this, nothing could be worse.

Reaching out for her, I pull Sophie down and kiss her with every bit of need inside me. Nobody else will ever touch her again. If they do, I'll kill them.

And I don't care what that does to put me in danger.

Her soft lips search for my tongue, sucking it into

her mouth and teasing me. Lifting her head, she smiles playfully.

"You should really rest those ribs."

I pull back the sheet and show her I've already dismissed that idea. With a gentle tug on my hard cock, I shrug.

"Too late for that. Come here."

My hand pulls her head back down, and I kiss her hard, needing the feel of her lips on mine. She's so soft compared to everything else that surrounds me in this world we're trapped in. I crave that mouth, and as much as having her suck my cock at this moment sounds like pure ecstasy, I have a better idea.

She mews against my hold, so I slide my hand down and lift her onto me. She's wet and ready, just like I need her to be. "Somebody woke up in a good mood this morning," I say against her lips.

"I would have said I was still sleepy until you kissed me, to be honest."

That's a lie, and she knows it as well as I do. I can see it in her eyes, even though she's brave enough to keep her gaze fixed on me after she says those words.

Shaking my head, I smile up at her. "No, you weren't."

With a quizzical look, she asks, "What do you mean?"

All this talking when I could be inside her makes me wish I hadn't mentioned her good mood, but now that she's taken the conversation and her lie this far, I'm going to push her a little more for the truth.

I push her hips down so she's pressed against my

cock. My ribs make moving next to impossible, so Sophie's going to have to do all the hard work today.

"You laid there trying to fall asleep last night, but you couldn't. You tossed and turned thinking about how I said you were mine, and you wanted to know what that means. Then you woke up and it was the first thing on your mind, so when you had the opportunity, you asked about it. You weren't sleep. You were curious, little one."

My claim is met with silence, and I study her face as she tries to think of something to say. Her cheeks grow pink with each passing moment, a tell-tale sign I'm right.

Finally, her mouth turns down into that pout like when she's sleeping, her bottom lip jutting out and making me want to suck it into my mouth. "How do you know I didn't toss and turn before I fell asleep because I'm torn about wanting to be with you and wanting to be away from this place?"

There's more truth than bluff in that statement too, but just hearing her talk about leaving irritates me, even if I do know somewhere deep inside that the sooner she gets away from here the better.

But it can't be until the time is right.

Stuffing my hand into her hair, I tug her head down so her face is level to mine and stare into her eyes. "Patience, Sophie. Don't do anything stupid again, or I won't be able to protect you."

Her eyes grow wide with fear. "I-I won't. I promise."

"Good. For now, we're both stuck in this place

with very few choices, so we might as well take advantage of the fact that I'm hard and you're wet."

Sophie looks down between us and then back up at me. "That deep breath you took in looked like it hurt. Don't you think this is going to make things worse?"

Typical woman.

"One, this never makes things worse. Never in the history of the world has good sex made things worse. But you're not wrong about me being a little laid up, so you're going to be doing the hard work this morning, Miss Sophie," I explain.

Her eyebrows shoot up into her forehead at hearing my new nickname for her. "Miss Sophie? What happened to little one?"

"I thought you hated little one," I tease as I run my hands down over her body and grab her hips.

"I thought I did, too, but Miss Sophie sounds like a kindergarten teacher."

A hint of her pout returns, so I say, "Well, as hot as fucking an innocent kindergarten teacher sounds, you seem to dislike it, so I'll go back to little one. Happy?"

I don't give her a chance to answer before I lift her off me and push myself up against the headboard. In a seated position, I stretch my legs and she hovers above my cock, teasing me with what's to come. At the first touch of the head to her pussy, she sighs, and as much as I want to lift my hips and bury myself balls deep inside her, the memory of the pain from just one breath this morning stops me.

Instead, I push her down onto me and achieve the

same perfect goal. A few seconds later, she's filled with my cock and lets out a tiny moan.

But I want to hear her scream this morning.

"Let me see you ride me, little one. I want to watch you come for me."

On cue, she rolls her hips, and the top of my head nearly blows off she feels so fucking good. She's dripping wet, but still her cunt fits me like a glove.

"Is this hurting you?" she asks sweetly, her body moving up and down my shaft while I hold her hips to keep her from going too fast.

I shake my head and grin. "Hurting is the last thing this is doing to me."

That she cares charms me, but I don't want sweet or kind this morning. I want rough and hard, and when I hear her scream my name, that's when I'll be satisfied. Me coming will be good, of course, but her yelling while she rides my cock and creams all over me is what I want.

Arching her back, Sophie's body undulates like she wants to feel every inch of me fuck her. I reach up and cup her breasts in my hands, squeezing her hard nipples between my thumbs and forefingers. A single pinch makes her squeal, and she starts to bounce up and down on my cock.

"See? I told you a little pain would be nice," I groan before giving her tits another hard squeeze.

She swipes her lower lip with the tip of her tongue and smiles down at me. "I've never liked anyone doing that to me."

"That isn't what I saw. It's too bad I don't have a

mirror behind this bed so you could have seen how much you liked when I gave each of them a pinch."

Leaning down, she kisses me before rolling her hips again to take my cock deep inside her. "I didn't say I didn't like it with you."

"Well, if that's the case, I've got something even better you're going to love."

A look of confusion settles into her face, and for a moment, she stops riding me. She doesn't have to worry. Like I told her, she'll like this kind of pain.

I cup her right breast in my palm and lift it to my mouth. It's heavy in my hand, and her nipple is the perfect shade of deep pink. Flicking my tongue over it, I taste her skin and love the way it hits my taste buds. Like soap and water, she's clean in my mouth.

When I hear her start to moan, I close my teeth around her skin and bite down. Not too much, but hard enough that she's surprised.

"You bit me!"

I look up at her and nod. "Uh-huh. And you loved it."

She doesn't answer, but I know by the way her cunt squeezed around my cock when I nipped her breast that it made her want more. I take her into my mouth and suck even harder than I bit to inch up her pain even more.

Her response tells me my little one enjoys things a little rougher. Tugging my hair, she holds me to her and rocks her hips back and forward, riding my cock for all she's got. I sink my teeth into her tender flesh again, making her moan even louder now, and I know it won't be long before I hear what I've been waiting for.

I let her nipple pop out of my mouth and move to the other one, pinching it hard before I suck it deeply into my mouth. Sophie pulls hard on my hair and squeals again, and then I bite down.

"Oh, my God! Oh…King…harder!"

My hands slide down to her hips and squeeze her skin, forcing her to ride me as fast as she can. My cock slams into her pussy as my teeth nip hard on her tits, and the combination makes her cunt nearly strangle my shaft inside her.

And then, she explodes, just like I wanted and screams as her release tears through her. "King, oh fuck! Don't stop!"

There's literally no better feeling than hearing a woman scream your name at the moment she comes all over your cock.

Sophie collapses on top of me, landing on my chest. Pain radiates through my torso, but a second later, I come inside her, pushing everything bad away for at least a few moments.

As much as I don't want to, I gently lift her off me to ease the pressure on my busted ribs. She looks down at me with confusion in her eyes, and then they grow wide when she realizes what just happened.

"Oh, King! I'm so sorry. I forgot about your ribs," she says as she quickly rolls off my hips onto the bed beside me.

"I'm okay. I just can't handle anything more on me right now."

We lay there silently for a few minutes as I try to coax some air in and out of my lungs, and even hurting like someone used me as a punching bag, it's the most relaxed I've been in longer than I can even remember. Next to me, Sophie watches as I struggle for that breath.

Gently touching my arm, she says, "I really am sorry. I didn't mean to crush you like that."

I can't help but chuckle at her use of the word crush. Looking over at her, I smile. "You're a little thing, so it's okay. I'll be fine."

"You say that all the time. Are you really fine?"

Without a thought to lie, I shake my head. "My ribs are fucking killing me, if I'm being honest."

She gives my arm a sympathetic squeeze and then shakes her head. "That's not what I mean. I want to know if you're really fine with all of this."

All of this. She has no idea what that means, and I can't tell her. My existence is full of secrets and falsehoods, and not just the ones that relate to her.

So I lie, like I do to everyone around me.

"You mean doing what I do? I'm fine with it."

Her dark eyes open wide, like she can't believe that. "Really? Hurting others and working for a man like your boss?"

"Some men are bad men. In fact, I'd wager that most men are bad men. You should probably keep that in mind."

My answer silences her, so I figure I'll turn the tables and get her to talk about her life. "I suspect we should be hearing from your uncle any time now. Are you two close?"

It's a serious question, but she reacts with a big smile that lights up her face and makes her look more beautiful than I've seen her yet. A tiny laugh escapes her, and she shakes her head as she answers, "That moron Tap couldn't have grabbed anyone less likely to get my Uncle Victor's attention. My father and my uncle barely speak. He never approved of what he did with his life, so my father stopped talking to him when I was a little girl. I doubt my family even bothered to tell my Uncle Victor I'm missing."

Even though it hurts to laugh, I can't stifle a chuckle at how stupid that asshole was to choose Sophie. He thought he was going to strike some huge blow at her uncle's organization. What a fucking idiot.

That Sophie's father never liked what his brother did for a living makes me think he'd hate to see his daughter lying there naked in bed with the likes of me. It wouldn't matter what my motives are or how well I'd tried to treat her and keep her from harm.

I didn't lie to her when I said I was a bad man. I have no choice. This is who I am.

CHAPTER SIXTEEN

ophie

"WHAT DID YOU DO BEFORE YOU BECAME A BAD man?" I ask, needing to know the man who takes care of me is more than just a villain.

King shakes his head and shrugs. "Nothing. I guess I was a bad kid who grew up to be a bad man. I don't know why you have such a hard time believing that. Was your uncle something before he became a bad man?"

I don't have an answer for that. My Uncle Victor last appeared in my life at my third birthday party. I barely have any recollection of it, but from the pictures I've seen of that day, he'd become that bad man King talks of by then. There I sat at a picnic table in my backyard blowing out the candles on my birthday cake in my frilly pink dress with a big white bow in my hair and my mother standing beside me smiling in that stunning way she always did when she was truly happy. And behind us a few feet away, my father and his brother stood glaring at one another, my father pointing his finger in my uncle's face, and my Uncle Victor staring back with hate in his eyes.

"I don't think people are born bad, King. You had to be something else before you took this job," I say, more curious now than before.

His dark eyes look flat, not like when we're together and every time I look into them I can't help but get lost in them. Now he seems so different from that man.

"You want me to be something honorable, but other than taking you off Tap and trying to make sure you eat and have somewhere to sleep, there's no honor inside me."

Why he insists on downplaying the good he's shown me I don't know, but I shake my head, not buying this bad guy thing anymore. "So you're saying you and Tap are pretty much the same? How can you expect me to believe that?"

I expect my mention of Tap to upset him like it usually does, but this time, he rolls his eyes and smiles. "He's an asshole, so no, we aren't the same. He's also a moron, like you said, so again, not the same at all. His version of bad fucks things up. Mine gets things done."

Watching him speak, I can't help but like to see him light like this, so I joke, "Bad man. Is this what you put on your tax returns for the IRS? Like I had to say I was a student last year. Do you write in bad man or is there a more technical term for what your job is?"

My question makes his mouth drop open for a few seconds. "You're funny, Sophie."

"I get my sense of humor from my mother. I also got my nursing skills from her, too," I say proudly.

Suddenly, I miss her and my family, the life I had, more than I can handle. I don't know what makes it hurt so much now, but I begin to tear up just thinking how worried they must be about me.

Maybe if King would let me call them or if he could get a message to them that I'm okay. He wouldn't have to tell anyone where I am. Just that I'm alive and miss them.

"My family is probably worried sick about me, King. If only I could call them so they could hear my voice and know I'm okay. Can I call them, please?"

He shoots down my request before the words are out of my mouth, shaking his head and frowning. "No. It can't happen."

Just hearing those words and knowing how much my mother and father must be hurting not knowing if I'm alive or dead crushes me. Why did he dismiss that so quickly?

"Their hearts are breaking, King. They think their daughter is dead. I've been missing for a week now. Just something to let them know I'm okay. You promised you wouldn't let anyone hurt me. Now all I want you to do is let me tell them I'm still alive and safe."

"I'm sorry, Sophie. You can't."

"What if you somehow sent them a message? Could you do that? It doesn't have to be anything long or involved, and you wouldn't have to show your face. Just a slip of paper stuck in their mailbox that would tell them their daughter is still alive. That's all I'm asking for, King. Please."

He closes his eyes, and I expect him to refuse me yet again, but finally after nearly a minute of waiting for him to say something, he looks at me and that sparkle appears in his eyes again. "Give me the address before I leave tomorrow morning. I'll see what I can do."

My heart leaps at his words! Just knowing my family will know I'm okay and that they don't have to worry about me being dead in a ditch somewhere makes me happier than I ever imagined I'd be in this place.

Inching over toward him, I kiss him softly. "Thank you, King. See, I knew you weren't just a bad man."

"Not a word about this to anyone. Understand me?" he says with such intensity in his voice that it frightens me. "No one can ever know, Sophie."

I press my face into the space between his jaw and his shoulder and sigh against his warm skin. "No one will know. I promise. No one will ever know you did this for me."

As much as he claims he's a bad man, I see hints of goodness in him. I'm no fool, though. I know who he has to be in this place. He has a role to play. But under that façade of cruelty is something kinder.

KING STOPS AT THE FRONT DOOR AND TURNS around to look at me seated on the couch. "I'll be back later."

"Thank you for taking that to my parents. It means the world to me."

He looks like he wants to say something else, but he turns and leaves, locking the door from the outside as he always does. We spent the past day together in bed, sometimes talking and other times fucking, and now we have to return to what we've always been.

Captor and captive.

Not that either role fits us well anymore. As much as he wants me to believe he's that bad man he claims he is, I've seen glimmers of sweetness from him that prove otherwise. The very fact that he's willing to get a message to my parents to let them know I'm okay shows that.

And even though I am locked in this apartment while he's gone during the day, when we're together in this place, I'm as free as I've ever been in life, except for the fact that I can't leave. He doesn't hurt me, I'm fed, and I even get to sleep in his bed.

But whatever we may want to feel about this, we're both trapped in some way in this world. He may get to move around more than I do and have more freedom, but he must do what his boss tells him to do and be that bad man he's so sure he is.

I think of all these things as I shower off the day I spent in bed with him. From somewhere I didn't know still existed in me, I feel guilt bubble up and make me question if I should do as I swore I would after that morning and kill him in his sleep. I hated him then.

The natural question after I admit that is why don't I hate him now? Because I don't. I'm not sure I could, to be honest.

That fact makes me stop what I'm doing, and I stand perfectly still under the water as it rolls down over my head and makes me clean again. As much as I should hate him, or at least should want to hate him, I don't hate King. Does that make me some pathetic creature, or worse, does it mean I've deluded myself into thinking any of this is normal or okay?

I don't know the answers to these questions. If someone asked me how I'd behave in a situation like this before that Tap bastard grabbed me off my street, I probably would have proudly tilted my chin up and pronounced I'd fight tooth and nail, savagely doing everything to find a way to escape.

The truth turns out to be far different. I've never given up believing I'll get away from this place. With or without King's help, I will. I believe that in my very marrow. But until I do, I'm stuck here, held hostage in a place filled with vicious creatures who have no problem going after one another like wild animals and who would treat me just as badly, if not worse.

Someone stronger than I am might not have given in to King. I think I might have believed I could be that kind of woman until this. Again, the truth is very different.

I know better than to lie to myself about him,

though. He may well be that bad man he says he is. Or maybe he's the man who does sweet things like feed me hamburgers and fries and let me sleep in his bed.

Perhaps the truth is neither one of us is who we thought we'd be before we were thrown into these circumstances. I can't say. All I know is he's promised to keep me safe, and as much as I wanted to hate him after that morning in his boss's office, he has.

And because of him, I'm still alive and my family will soon know I'm okay. They won't have to live each day wondering if that's the day I'll be found dead. For that and many other reasons, I don't hate King.

I step out of the shower and wrap myself in a towel, and out of the corner of my eye, I catch a glimpse of myself in the mirror. Cleared of steam since I stayed in there until the water ran cold, it shows me the reflection of a woman who's been without makeup for a week.

Since I began wearing makeup at thirteen, I've never been without it for that long. Even that night when I went out for a run, I had makeup on my face.

But now as I stare at the woman looking back at me, I see someone I barely notice. Natural Sophie seems bland, like a washed-out version of a woman who's been called beautiful before by men and women. Her eyes don't pop without shadow, and her cheekbones don't impress without highlighter and contouring. Her lips don't seduce without a sexy red shade or glossiness that makes a man want to kiss them.

I don't know this me.

My eyes scan around my head and I wince at how my hair looks after a week without a dryer and straightener. Smiling, I realize I am what every boyfriend has ever called me in the middle of a heated argument.

"You are high maintenance, Sophie," I say to my reflection, chuckling at how stunning this is to me.

A sound like the front door opening tears me from my embarrassment of realizing what I've been all these years, so I quickly smooth my hair from my forehead and screw a smile onto my face. Not that King hasn't seen me looking much worse, but old habits are hard to shake.

The bathroom door flies open, startling me, and before I know it, Tap comes storming in. Stunned and terrified, I try to scream but nothing comes out at first. His big, round eyes flash pure rage, and he grabs my arm, squeezing his fingers hard into my skin.

"Let go of me!" I scream, finally able to get my voice to work. "King! King, help!"

"He can't help you this time, bitch!" Tap barks before yanking me toward the doorway.

"You're hurting me! Let go of me!" I scream as loudly as I can so anyone nearby can hear me. "King! Tap's got me! Help! Someone help!"

From out of nowhere, Tap's fist hits my face, and everything turns to black.

MY EYES SLOWLY OPEN, BUT ALL I SEE IS DARKNESS. Unsure of where I am or what's happened to me, I lift my right hand to touch my cheek to relieve some of the pain there and feel a metal cuff around my wrist. Raising my left hand, I feel the same cold metal press against my skin.

Wide awake now, I wiggle my legs and find no cuffs or chains attached to them. I lift my arms to my sides again and guess the chains are about three feet long. They're attached to the floor, so I can't stand.

The ground beneath me feels cool against my skin. Concrete, I guess.

That fucking Tap took me from King and brought me here, chaining me up like some kind of wild animal. Then a horrible thought crosses my mind. Did King give me to him for some reason?

No. He wouldn't do that. I can't believe he'd do that after promising me he'd protect me.

Then a second terrifying thought comes to me. Did his boss find out he sent my family a message to tell them I'm okay and King's being punished by Tap taking me? Or worse, did his boss kill him for betraying him with that note?

Tears well in my eyes as all my hope from the past week disappears in the darkness around me. The only person protecting me is nowhere to be found. I'm alone, chained to a concrete floor in a foreign place. I don't even know if I'm on the estate anymore. Does King even know I'm gone?

Pulling my arms into my sides, I curl up on the hard concrete and let the tears come. I want to scream, but I have no fight left in me. I have nothing left in me now.

That message King was supposed to leave for my parents has turned out to be a lie. I'm not okay, and I'm afraid I'm never going to be okay again.

Worst of all, I'm afraid the man who has me now is going to be the one who ends my life.

Footsteps coming down the stairs make my mind go blank. One step. Another. A third and a fourth. Then silence.

"Ready to play, bitch?"

Every inch of my body shakes in terror, and Tap takes the final step onto the basement floor. I swivel my head left and right to sense where he is and anticipate where his fist will come from. The last time it came from my left side. Will it be the same this time?

"You didn't answer me," he says angrily. "Ready to play? Because this time I'm going to make you feel things you've never felt before in your life."

I turn toward the right and feel his hot breath on the top of my head. My legs are free, so I kick them out to hit him, but a second later, he sits down hard on my thighs, forcing my calves to press against the concrete beneath me.

"You think you can kick me, bitch? No wonder that asshole likes you so much. He's stupid too."

"Please don't do this," I beg, knowing I'm wasting my breath with this man. There is no kindness in him.

"Oh, I'm going to do this and from today on, everyone will know what you are, fucking cunt," he snaps, spitting at me as he speaks.

I feel the first press of the point of his knife against my forearm and freak out, flailing my arms as much as my chains let me. I catch my fingernails on his skin and claw as viciously as I can.

"Fucking bitch!" he bellows and then slams his fist into my eye.

My cries explode into the darkness around me when he drags his blade over my skin. Each cut stings more than the last, but by the time he finishes with my right arm, I feel nothing but blood dripping off me.

Pushing my arm away, he grabs my left one and begins carving into my flesh. I cry out, but I feel myself fading away. As my eyes close, I feel nothing.

CHAPTER SEVENTEEN

ing

KROGER GROANS IN HIS SLEEP WHILE I SAIL INTO the parking space and slam my foot onto the brakes, sending him flying forward into the dashboard. I'm fucking on edge this afternoon knowing what I have to do, and it's become impossible to hide it.

"What the fuck, man?" he snaps as he sits back in the seat and looks around. "Where the hell are we?"

I open the car door and mumble, "I have to get a few things. I'll be back in a few minutes."

Right before the door slams shut, he yells, "A grocery store? What are you getting in there? Get me an orange juice!"

As I head toward the front doors of the store, I mumble to myself that he should get his own goddamned orange juice and stuff my hand into my front pocket to feel the note for Sophie's parents. My stomach twists into a tight knot with each step across the parking lot. She said her mother would be here helping elderly people get their groceries between four and six.

Sophie described her as nearly her twin, just older with hair that's a few inches shorter, so as I march through the store, I look for her mother's version of the face that's become something I look forward to each morning when I wake up and each night when I come home.

My palms grow sweatier with each aisle I search. Dozens of women around the age I guess Sophie's mother would be seem to be shopping today, but one after another they aren't her.

I head down the cereal aisle and let my gaze pass over the colorful boxes filled with breakfast for children. Somehow I doubt she's here, but then I see a woman standing in front of the oatmeal boxes with a hunched over elderly woman leaning on a cane. I stop dead, stunned at how much Sophie's mother looks like her daughter. Same color hair, same body type, same gentle smile.

"You love apples and cinnamon, so let's get a box of that, Carol. It's easy to make, too, so you can even microwave it in the morning," she says as she places the oatmeal in the cart next to them.

The elderly woman nods her grey head and grabs a second box. "Better get two then. I like having enough in the house, just in case," she says in a wispy, grandmotherly voice.

"Mrs. Varens?" I say quietly.

Sophie's mother looks over at me and smiles just like her daughter. A strange man walks up to her in a store, and she's more than willing to just talk to him. Like mother, like daughter.

"Yes?" she asks, her gaze searching my face for some clue to who I am and how I know her name.

I pull the note out of my pocket and hand it to her without saying another word. I don't know what I'd say even if I could. I'm the man who's keeping her daughter hostage.

She's confused, but I don't stay around to answer any questions. I hear her let out a sob as I leave the cereal aisle and hurry toward the front door. By the time she realizes what she knows about her daughter, I'm in the parking lot.

Kroger's still sitting in the passenger seat, and I slide in behind the wheel and drop the car into drive to get the hell out of there. As I put my foot to the floor, he says, "Where the hell is my orange juice?"

"They were out."

He starts complaining about never getting what he wants anymore, but I'm not listening. I try to focus on where I'm driving, but all I can think of is the look on Sophie's mother's face when I handed her that piece of paper and the sound of her cry as she read the words on it.

Until that moment, keeping Sophie didn't feel wrong. I was doing the right thing when I took her away from Tap. I was treating her well when I fed her and let her sleep in the bed.

But the second I saw her mother's face and heard her sadness, all of that vanished. Now, it's impossible to avoid the truth.

Although I'm not a monster like Tap, I'm no hero.

"Can we at least stop at a store on the way back to the estate? I'm fucking parched over here," Kroger says, still complaining.

It tears me out of my thoughts, and I throw him a look of disgust at the whining sound of his voice. "Whatever. Yeah. If you see one, just let me know."

We ride along in silence back to the estate, my mind filled with the truth about Sophie I don't want to admit but can't avoid. The expression on her mother's face won't let me. When I park the car in front of the garage where we all keep our cars, Kroger jumps out and slams the door behind him.

"What's wrong with you, King? It's like your head is stuck up your ass or something. I told you two times about stores on our way here, but you kept going. What the fuck, man?" he says when I catch up with him right before we go through the back door of the house.

Christ, he's irritating me today!

"Still with the goddamned orange juice thing?" I snap as I walk into Duke's office.

"I'm fucking thirsty. Since when is that a fucking crime?" he barks back before sitting down in one of the chairs in front of the boss's desk.

Duke stares at the two of us, clearly confused why we've brought our bullshit argument to him. Sitting back in his leather chair, he folds his arms across his chest and shakes his head.

"Why are we talking about a crime involving orange juice? I would have thought you two would be better than knocking over a fruit stand," he says with a chuckle.

Kroger turns around and throws me a look of disgust. Scowling, he explains, "We didn't do a fruit stand. I just told King to stop at a store because I wanted a fucking orange juice and he drove by every one of them. Every damn one!"

Done with bitching me out for the second time about the juice, he turns back to face Duke and adds, "It's like he's been out of it all day."

Looking past him, Duke focuses his attention on me now. "Is something wrong, King? It's not like you to not be on your game out there. That kind of thing gets people hurt."

I know full well what being distracted can do to someone in our business. I don't need him or Kroger giving me chapter and verse on how to do my damn job.

But I also don't need to get on the boss's bad side either, so I swallow my aggravation and paste a smile on my face. "No need to worry. I'm all over the game here and there and everywhere. Sorry, dude. I guess I just didn't hear you because I was focused on all the traffic. My bad, man."

For a few seconds, neither man says anything, but then in his usual, decent way, Kroger waves it all away and laughs. "It's no big deal. I was just thirsty."

Duke cocks an eyebrow at both of us, shaking his head. "You two sound like an old married couple. Maybe I should pair you with new guys so you don't have to spend so much time around one another."

I don't say anything, but all I can think is the last thing I need is someone new, or worse, someone else like Tap. Kroger complains sometimes and he's a little too passive for me most of the time, but I'd take working with him over that asshole any day.

While I keep my thoughts to myself, Kroger lets his opinion out loud and clear, surprising me. "Duke, we work well together. The whole orange juice bullshit was just that. Bullshit. All of us have a good thing going, except for Tap. Put him into the mix and it all goes to hell."

"Another one with a problem with Tap? Is this your doing, King?" Duke asks, clearly angry.

"Not a word from me," I quickly say, wanting nothing to do with anything about Tap.

"No, boss. King's got nothing to do with this. This is all me, Duke. He's unpredictable. That's even worse than being distracted, if you ask me. Like grabbing that girl last week. You know that's going to be nothing but trouble for you when her uncle retaliates, and then we'll all be in it."

As Kroger talks, Duke's expression grows darker and darker until he puts his hand up to stop him. "You must be reading my mind today, son." Looking over Kroger's head, he says directly to me, "I finally heard from her uncle this afternoon. Seems he just found out about his niece being taken. He's not happy, and I don't blame him, but I don't need this blowing up into some drawn out thing. Victor Varens and I have had our problems, for sure. We've kept on our own sides of this business by respecting one another, for the most part, and this little issue endangers that arrangement."

"She's been taken care of, boss. I promise you that. You can send her back today, and she'll have nothing but nice things to say about her time with me," I say with a smile.

"Then let's get this done. I'll let her uncle know she's safe and sound and she can come home tonight. I'll tell him it was all a mistake on Tap's part. Better to smooth this situation over than create a problem that we don't need."

"I agree. I'll get her ready now, and text me where you want me to take her," I say as I move to leave as soon as I can.

"Thanks, King. I knew I could rely on you to handle this."

I practically run across the grass to reach the apartment and give Sophie the news I know will thrill her. I imagine her face when she hears she's going home. Those big brown eyes of hers will be as wide as saucers, and she'll give me one of those beautiful smiles that light up her whole face.

Taking the stairs two at a time, I don't even care about the pain in my ribs now. I throw the front door open and rush in expecting to see her sitting on the couch.

But she's not there.

Maybe she's in the bedroom. Hurrying through the

apartment, I fling the bedroom door open, but she's not there either.

"Sophie! Where are you?" I yell as I spin around to walk toward the kitchen.

I check there and don't find her. Something's wrong. I race to the bathroom and find it empty. Is it possible she risked everything and climbed out the window? It's two stories up. She would have had to find a way to shimmy down the side of the building.

She promised she wouldn't do anything stupid. I was sure she understood it was only a matter of time before I figured out a way to get her back home. She knew she had to be patient.

But a quick check of the window shows it's still locked from the inside. She didn't leave that way.

Confused, I look around the bathroom and see a towel on the floor. I didn't leave one there, and Sophie's never done that before. Lifting it up, I feel it's still damp.

Maybe she brought her clothes in when she took a shower.

Still unsure about all of this, I walk out to the living room and see her shoes next to the couch where she's left them since she came here. Something is very wrong. Even if she brought clothes into the bathroom and left the towel on the floor, she wouldn't leave without her shoes.

But how the hell did she get out? The door locks from the outside. Someone had to come in to let her out.

Or to take her.

Tap. That motherfucker! How did he get in? The only two people who have a key to my apartment are me and Duke.

My mind races at the thought that my boss just spent the last ten minutes talking about Sophie and how she needs to go back home while the whole time he knew Tap had her. I can't believe that. It makes no sense.

The problem is Tap couldn't get into my place without Duke's key.

Maybe he picked the lock. I don't know. None of this makes any fucking sense. I don't care how it happened. I need to find Sophie right now.

I break into a full sprint and run across the estate to the building where Tap lives. His apartment is on the bottom floor, and I bang on the door until my fists ache. No answer. I look in through his front window, but I see no evidence she's in there.

Where the fuck would he have taken her?

My legs feel like the muscles might explode out through the skin as I run full speed to Duke's office. Every second she's gone she's in danger. I just need to make him see that without letting him know the true reason why I'm worried.

Kroger is still in his office talking with him when I burst in, slamming the door off the wall as I rush in. Shaking my head, I catch my breath and tell him what's happened.

"She's gone. Tap fucking took her. I know it. And he's going to rough her up, if he hasn't done it already. That deal with her uncle is going to go up in flames if we don't find her before he screws everything up."

Duke stands up and pushes his chair out behind him, sending it crashing into the wall. "What the fuck is it with this girl? Does she have some kind of pussy that shoots out fucking money like an ATM, for God's sake? I told him he couldn't have her last night. Have you all lost your damn minds? This is why women are nothing but fucking trouble!"

My heart races, but I try to remain cool so Duke doesn't know how terrified I am that Sophie at that very moment might be in real danger because of that asshole Tap. "We need to find her, and he's not at his apartment. Anywhere else he'd be?"

"I sent him out on his own today since no one else wants to be paired with him lately. Maybe you guys are right. We'll go to his place and check it out on our own."

Kroger jumps up to join us, and we walk over to Tap's building far too fucking slowly for my taste. I can't let anyone see how worried I am, though, so even as I want to tear across the lawn and kick his fucking front door in myself, I play it cool.

"You know, the only way he could get into my place is with your key since the two of us are the only ones who have one," I mention as casually as possible when we stop at Tap's front door.

Duke narrows his eyes and look over at me. "I want to say he can pick the lock, but either choice isn't good."

Once he opens the door, I march in and begin

looking for any clue that she's there. His place is set up like mine, so in seconds, I've checked every square inch of his home without finding her there.

Duke and Kroger wait for me in the living room, and I return to see them standing there disgusted.

"She's not here."

Dirty glasses and empty beer bottles cover the coffee table, and the couch has dozens of take-out bags filled with garbage piled on it. Tap lives like a pig. Not surprising.

Under his breath, Duke mumbles, "This place is a goddamned mess."

I have to shrug, like I'm as disgusted as they are by the way he lives, while all the while fear for what's happened to Sophie fills me. I don't give a fuck about what his living room looks like.

"Where else would he have to take her to?" I ask, struggling to keep my voice calm.

Duke shakes his head. "I don't know."

The three of us silently stand in the middle of Tap's filthy living room as my mind races with how I'm going to find Sophie before he does anything to her, and then I hear a tiny cry that sounds like it's coming from the back of his apartment. I checked back there in his bedroom, though. She's not there.

"Did you hear that?" I ask, straining to hear that sound again.

Kroger and Duke both shake their heads. But I know I heard something. Looking around, I search for a closet door but see none.

"This is set up just like my place. Was your apartment set up like this, Kroger?"

He nods and then says, "Except since I was on the ground floor, I had to walk down into the basement to do my laundry. You guys who live on the second floor get to have your washer and dryer in your apartment."

I hear the faint sound again and my heart slams into my chest. "Where was the door to the basement in your place?"

Kroger points toward the kitchen a room away. "Right next to the refrigerator."

I hurry to the next room and see a door right where he said his was located. I nearly rip it off the hinges when I open it, and a second later, I hear that sound again, but this time it's loud and clear and I know exactly who it is.

Sophie.

"I found her! She's down in the basement."

By the time I get down the stairs, her sobs fill my ears. It's pitch black, but I follow the sound and find her chained to the floor, curled up naked and terrified.

Crouching down, I gently push her hair back off her face and try to see her, but it's too dark. She shakes uncontrollably when I touch her, probably thinking I'm that asshole Tap.

"It's me, Sophie. I'm here. I'm going to get you out of here and take you home," I whisper.

"King? Is it really you?" she asks, her tone pleading for me to save her.

A light hanging above our heads flickers on so I can see her, and I have to stop myself from cursing out that fucker Tap. Black and blue bruises dot her chest and legs, and there's a cut on her cheek from where he punched her. Bloody cuts on her forearms show she's been tortured too.

Duke and Kroger begin to walk down the wood stairs to where we are, but I stop them. "I need a bolt cutter to get these chains off her. That son of a bitch has her chained to the goddamned floor!"

"I'll get one. Hang on!"

Duke continues to come down the stairs, and when he gets to where I wait with Sophie, I hear him groan. "Jesus Christ. Is she okay?"

I shake my head in utter disgust. "No. Look at her. She's been here for hours sitting in her own piss, for fuck's sake. She's bruised up and down her arms and legs, and he hit her so hard he ripped open her face, and the fuck carved into her goddamned skin. How the hell are you supposed to send her back looking like this?"

Even as I say that, I know I should temper myself so I don't sound like a possessive boyfriend, but I don't care. That asshole did this to her, and Duke should have known better than to let Tap go off on his own.

Duke pats my shoulder, as if that's going to help anything. "I'll get Cam over here to fix her up. He'll be at your place waiting for you."

Regret hangs off his every word, but it's too little, too late. He quickly walks back upstairs, leaving me to take care of Sophie, but that's just how it should be.

ophie

KING'S TOUCH SHOULD CALM ME, BUT I CAN'T STOP shaking. I can tell he's trying so hard to be gentle. It's not who he is, but he's doing his best. I want to tell him it's not as bad as he thinks, that Tap didn't bother to rape me because he was having too much fun torturing me, but every time I open my mouth to explain what happened, the words get stuck in my throat. All that comes out are sobs.

I have no more tears left. King probably thinks I'm in shock because I'm not crying, that I don't know what's going on. But I do. He found me, just like I prayed to God he would. All these hours chained to this concrete floor made me question everything, except King. I never doubted if he was still alive, he'd come and take me from this horrible place.

The only thing I didn't know was if he'd get to me in time before Tap killed me.

"Sophie, I'm going to get you out of these chains and then we'll go back home. You're safe. I promise."

Instead of making me feel safe, his words make panic race through me. He sounds frightened, something I've never heard in King's voice.

"It's bad, isn't it?"

"No. You're going to be fine."

He smooths my hair and shakes his head, but his smile doesn't go all the way up to his eyes. He's lying.

I watch where his gaze falls to my cheek before he winces ever so slightly. He's trying not to scare me, but it's not working.

"You said he did something to my cheek. Why do you keep looking at me like that? How bad is it?"

God, I hate how weak my voice makes me sound. Like a victim.

"It's going to be fine. We'll be like twins with matching wounds, especially if the doctor only uses butterflies on you too. Don't worry. Cam's okay. He'll fix you up."

King smiles again, but this time it's real. I can tell by the way it lights up his entire face, especially his eyes. They sparkle like chocolatey emeralds when he's genuinely happy.

"Promise?"

"I promise. I haven't let you down yet, have I?" he says just as someone walks down the stairs to join us.

Covering me, he yells at them, "Who's there?"

"It's just me, King. I got the bolt cutters you need."

I can't see the man, but he sounds kind, and when he hears his voice, King relaxes, leaning away from me. Looking around him, I see the man and remember him from that first night when Tap grabbed me off the street near my house.

"Thanks, Kroger."

Embarrassed that this person can see all of me, I curl up in a ball the best I can. King sees me do this and says to him, "Hey, do me a favor and go upstairs and watch, just in case Tap comes back. I don't need him coming down here and trying anything. And get me a towel, too."

As Kroger runs back up the stairs, King turns back to face me. "Sorry about that. He's a good guy, but I didn't think about how he shouldn't be here while you're like this. My mind is occupied with other things."

"What? What are you thinking about?" I ask, afraid he'll tell the truth and it will be that seeing me like this makes him sick to his stomach.

He ignores my question and points at my left arm. "Lift up your arm so I can get these chains off you."

"The cuts. He drew something on my arms."

King's gaze drops and I see him cringe. I can't look, though. Squeezing my eyes shut, I shake my head.

"Sophie, I need you to let me take these things off you."

I do as he orders, and a few seconds later, I'm free. My arms drop to my sides like heavy weights that threaten to crush me. King pulls me to him and holds my body against his, even as I try to fight him.

"I'm filthy. Don't touch me. You'll get covered in all of it too."

Squeezing me tightly to him, he shakes his head. "Shhh. You were there for me when I looked like someone used me for a punching bag. Now I'm here for you. You're safe, Sophie. I promise. I promise."

His words lull me into a calm I didn't think I'd ever feel again, and in his arms, I believe that he'll keep me safe. "I want to get out of this place, King. Please get me out of here."

Against the top of my head, he whispers, "I'm just waiting for Kroger to get back here with the towel. No need to have you showing off the goods to everyone on the estate."

He's trying to cheer me up, but when I lean back to look up at his expression, I see his attempt at lightening the mood didn't work on him either. In his face, all I see is a mixture of rage and sadness, each one fighting to overwhelm him as he stares down at me and pretends like none of this bothers him.

Footsteps on the stairs tear us out of a quiet moment, and I shrink behind King while he covers me. "You got that towel, Kroger? I want to get her out of here before that asshole gets back."

"Yeah, here it is. I had to look through like three cabinets. Tap lives like a fucking pig. This was the only clean one I could find."

A second later, King wraps it around my body and once more tries to smile to make me think everything is going to be okay. "Let's get the hell out of here. When we get back to the apartment, Cam will be there and then you can take a long bath and soak in the hot water like you told me to. You were right. It worked, so now I'm telling you to do the same."

Turning his head, he yells behind him, "Kroger, watch the stairs."

I slowly stand from my concrete prison, but my legs give out before I can get my balance. King catches me in his arms, and when I try to stand again, he shakes his head, stopping me.

"Don't. I'll carry you."

He moves to scoop me up into his arms, but I push his hands away before he can touch my legs. "No! I'm covered in—you don't want to get it all over you."

Laughing, he ignores my protests and lifts me into his arms anyway. "A little piss isn't going to be a big deal. I've been covered in blood and brains more times than I want to remember, so this isn't going to be anything worse."

As he turns to walk toward the stairs, I bury my face in that warm space between his neck and shoulder. His skin smells like only King does. I can't place why it's different, but it's quintessentially him.

Masculine. Strong. Protective.

I don't want to think about how I smell or what I feel like against his skin. It will only make me cringe. How he can ignore the scent of piss baffles me since before I filled my nose with the smell of him, that's all I could breathe in.

Step by step, he takes me out of Tap's basement

prison until we reach the upstairs that looks just like King's apartment. I didn't see this when he brought me there, and now I just want to spit on everything I see as we leave this place.

Kroger holds the front door open, and when King takes that first step out into the night air, all I can think of is how fresh it feels against my skin now that I'm free. I know that's not really true. I'm still not back in my home, safe and sound in my own bed, but in some ways, I am free.

King walks slowly back toward his apartment, each step solidly landing on the grass. His eyes narrowed to slits, he appears angrier now than he looked back in Tap's basement. He's nothing less than seething, but I don't understand the change in him. If anything, shouldn't he be happy now that I'm out of that terrible place?

Then a thought rips through me. Is it possible he thinks I did something to make this happen?

Looking up at him, I say, "I didn't let him in, King. I wasn't trying to get away either. I swear to you I didn't do that. He had a way in on his own."

He doesn't immediately answer, but I watch as his expression softens. Without meeting my gaze, he nods and says quietly, "I know you didn't, Sophie."

And in those five words, I hear what I need. Like I believe in him, he believes in me.

THE DOCTOR SMILES DOWN AT ME AND NODS AS HE

gently presses the last butterfly bandage to my face. "There you go. Not bad at all, right?"

I try to smile back at him, but it feels all lopsided because my cheek hurts. "Thank you."

"You'll be fine. I don't expect a scar there, so that's good. I think you'll be back to new in no time. The cuts on your arms aren't deep, but we'll have to see. King said he'll put the bandages on them."

He turns to talk to King, and I sit on the edge of the bed clutching that disgusting green towel from that asshole's apartment and wishing the doctor would leave so King and I can be alone. After a minute, the doctor turns his focus back to me and pats me on the shoulder.

"If you need anything, have King call me and I'll get here as soon as I can."

They walk out of the bedroom, leaving me alone, so I tighten the towel around me again and follow them out. King thanks him at the door, and then closes it.

"Your cheek will be fine. Cam does good work."

But he doesn't look at me when he says that and doesn't mention the cuts on my arms.

"Come on. Let's get you cleaned up."

I walk behind him, wanting to reach out to hold his hand or touch his arm. Anything to feel some connection to him.

"Maybe a quick shower will be a good idea instead of a bath. Wash up, and then you can soak in the tub for as long as you want in clean bath water," he says as he turns on the water.

Tossing that disgusting green towel over into the corner, I look at his arms covered in dirt from me. "What about you? You're filthy too."

He waves away my concern and steps back to hold open the door to the shower. "I'll be fine, Sophie."

Something's wrong. His voice is so flat. What happened to the man who couldn't think of anything else when I was around, especially when I stood naked in front of him?

"Why are you acting like this? Why does it look like you don't even want to be near me, like I sicken you right now?"

He looks away toward the shower door handle that's suddenly become such an important focus for him and shrugs. "I'm not acting like anything. I just thought a shower would be good. Get all that piss and blood and dirt off you."

My emotions begin to unwind inside me, threatening to explode into something I don't know if I can handle right now. Taking a step toward him, I touch his chest, and he flinches.

"Why are you acting like this? I barely touch you and it's like you hate the feel of me near you."

I wait for him to answer, to say something to prove to me I'm wrong, but instead, he just shakes his head and lets go of that damn door handle. "I'll be out in the kitchen if you need anything. Just yell."

The bathroom door slams behind him, and then I'm alone. I feel like someone hollowed me out, leaving just this outside shell that repulses him now. Looking down, I see the bruises on my legs. Are they the problem? Is it the injury on my cheek? I touch it gently and tears fill my eyes.

Or is it the cuts on my forearms?

For the first time, I see what Tap did to me. On my left arm, he carved SLUT and BITCH into my skin. Tears well in my eyes, and I look on my right arm to see one word sliced into me.

CUNT

I can't stop myself from crying. Tap cut into me the three words he used to describe me. That's all I was to another human being.

The sound of footsteps coming toward the bathroom makes my heart skip a beat, but then there's nothing but silence. Is King waiting outside the door? Why won't he come in?

When I don't see the door open, I step into the shower and let out a heavy sigh as the water washes away all the dirt and piss on the back of my legs. Lathering the bar of soap in my hand, I scrub my skin to ensure it's all gone as I get lost in my thoughts of what's happened between King and me.

I didn't ask for Tap to do what he did today. King said he knew I didn't try to run away, so why can't he even look at me now? If he doesn't blame me, why is he acting like this?

The bathroom door opens, and I hold my breath as I wait for him to say something. I hear the sound of clothes rustling, but still he stays silent. Did he bring me new clothes to wear?

"King?"

He steps into the shower before turning his back to

me. I stand there stunned but unsure what will happen next.

"What are you doing?"

Still he says nothing, not even turning to look at me when I talk to him.

I watch as the water hits his head and rolls down his tanned back, running over his taut muscles on its way over his body. He stands perfectly still, not looking for soap to wash his hands and arms that my dirty legs touched, and making not a single noise.

"Why won't you look at me now? Am I so revolting after what happened that I make you sick? He didn't rape me. He barely touched me, except to hit me."

For the first time, he looks back at me and shakes his head. Pain like I've never seen before in him fills his eyes.

"I don't blame you, Sophie."

"Then why are you acting like you do?"

Again, he shakes his head, and when he answers me, that pain in his eyes comes out in his words. "I don't mean to act that way. I'm just not the right person for you now. You need someone kind and gentle after all you've been through. That's not me."

"Then why did you come in here?"

Turning away from me, he says in a low voice, "I didn't want you to be alone. I didn't want to be alone."

I take a step toward him and reach out to brush my fingertips over his shoulder. He doesn't pull away this time, so I take another step so my body presses against his. A heavy sigh leaves him, and he leans back against me. His skin is hot and smooth against mine, alive like I wish I was.

He's so strong while I'm weak. His anger proves that. I don't have the power to be angry about what Tap did. Maybe that's why he doesn't want to be around me now. I don't seem enraged enough at what happened.

If I could be, I would.

Pressing my cheek to his back, I confess that truth to him. "I wish I could be like you. If I was, I could be angry."

"You should be angry," he says, his words resonating through his body.

"I don't have the power to be that, King. Weak people get to be every emotion but angry. We can be sad, but we can't be angry. I lost that power when he took me."

King turns in my hold and faces me. He gazes down at me, and for the first time, he looks like the man who's taken care of me while I've been here.

"You're not weak, Sophie."

"No, you're not weak. I have no power here."

He hangs his head and sighs. "I've tried to make this as safe as possible. I'm sorry this happened. All of it. He never should have grabbed you that night in the first place."

Every word he speaks sounds so full of regret that I can't stop myself from taking him in my arms and holding him to me. I know what kind of man he is, but more than that, I know what he's done for me.

King wraps his strong arms around my shoulders,

enveloping me in his hold that overpowers mine, and I close my eyes as a feeling of safety washes over me. He possesses all the power, but in some way there as he stands with me, I feel stronger.

"What's going to happen now?" I ask in a small voice, almost afraid to hear the answer.

His embrace tightens around me, and he answers, "You'll go home. I promise. As soon as I can arrange it, you'll leave here and forget this place."

I look up at him, stunned by what he said. "Home? How did you—?"

He pushes my wet hair off my face and smiles down at me. "Your uncle finally got in touch with my boss. Probably because of that note I gave your mother today. You were supposed to be back home already, but that asshole screwed everything up. I'm going to have a hard time convincing Duke to send you back with all these bruises and that gash in your cheek, but I'll find a way."

And just like that with one mention of my mother finally knowing I'm alive, I begin to cry again. "Did she look sad? I know she probably seemed okay because that's the kind of person she is. She never shows what she's really feeling."

"She looked like you," he says in a faraway voice. "So much like you I was surprised."

"Was she happy when she read the note?" I ask, my heart practically bursting at the thought of my mother finally knowing the truth.

"I didn't stick around to see. The last thing I need

is to be nabbed by Victor Varens's guys in the Stop N Shop, Sophie."

He's right, but I wish he could tell me how she reacted. My mother's a strong woman, though. She probably didn't outwardly show much emotion, even if inside she was jumping for joy.

"Hey, look at me."

Tilting my head back, I force a smile. "It's okay. I understand. I didn't expect you to risk yourself."

"I walked away, but I think she was overjoyed to find out you're okay."

I lay my head on his chest and feel all my worries ebb out of me. "Thank you for doing that, King. It means the world to me that you helped me let my family know I'm okay and they don't have to worry."

He gently strokes his hand over the back of my head, and I have a hard time believing this is the same man I once swore to hate for the rest of my life. "Soon you'll be home and all of this will just be a memory."

I hear those words, and part of me is so happy I can't put my feelings into words. But another part of me can't imagine how I'm ever going to forget King.

CHAPTER NINETEEN

King

SOMEWHERE IN THE BACK OF MY MIND, I KNOW THIS is the last night Sophie and I will ever be together. I know it's the right thing to do to send her home. She never deserved to be dragged into this world. She's too sweet, too soft.

I know this and still my chest feels like someone's carving my heart out of me with a dull knife.

She dries off and looks around the bathroom for her clothes. "I forgot to bring my things in. I'm not even sure where I left them this morning."

Pulling the T-shirt I brought in for her off the shelf, I hand it to her. "Wear this. You've been in those clothes ever since you got here. For tonight, you can wear one of my shirts."

"Oh. Okay."

As I dry off, Sophie turns her back to me and slips the shirt over her head. It falls to the middle of her thighs, and when she spins around to show me, I can't help but laugh at how tiny she looks in it.

"It's like a shirt made for a giant," she says with a giggle before lifting the sleeve to her nose. "It smells like you."

I knot the towel around my hips. Curious, I look at her and ask, "What does it smells like me mean?"

Sophie shrugs like it's nothing, but then a shy smile lights up her face and her cheeks turn an adorable shade of light pink. "I don't know. It just smells like you."

As sweet as that sounds, the second my gaze falls on her cut up arms, my rage pushes every other feeling out of me.

"Sit down on the side of the tub. I need to wrap up your arms."

I look up to see her smile fade as she does as I say. My hands begin to shake I'm so full of anger that Tap hurt her like that. I turn away and grab the gauze pads and tape from the vanity, knocking the antibiotic cream into the sink as I stand there fighting the urge to rush over to Tap's and kill him.

"They don't really hurt anymore."

Nodding, I avoid meeting her gaze as I crouch down in front of her. "I need to put some of this ointment on so your arms don't get infected. It won't hurt, but it'll be cold."

My hand hovers over the arm with the words SLUT and BITCH carved into it, and when she doesn't respond, I look up and see her force a smile. Fuck, I hate this. I'm not what she needs at this moment, but I'm all she's got.

The cream drops onto her skin, making her jump, but I can't focus on anything but this task because if I let myself feel anything right now, I'll spin right the fuck out of control. I hear her take a deep breath when I gently wrap the pad around her forearm, but I don't lift my head to look at her. I don't want to see the pain in her eyes as I cover those words.

I tape up the gauze on her right arm and then repeat it all on the left one, my hands shaking as I say nothing because I can't find the words to say. If she's permanently scarred from this…

Standing, I toss the antibiotic ointment and tape into the sink and mumble, "Those will be fine. Don't worry."

It takes everything inside me not to throw the bathroom door open I'm so fucking angry, but I don't want her to see that. Her footsteps stop behind me as I walk toward the bedroom, and I turn around to see her standing near the coffee table. Looking down toward her legs, she tugs on the bottom of my T-shirt.

"Aren't you coming to sleep in the bed?"

"I wasn't sure I should."

She won't look at me. I put this doubt in her mind. If only I could have been the gentle soul she needs instead of a man who runs mainly on rage and hate. She isn't sure she's anything more than my captive again because of me. I can't let our time end like this.

"Come here, Sophie."

She slowly walks over to me and stops without looking up. "It's okay if we go back to the way it was when I got here."

Lifting her chin with my finger, I shake my head and smile. "No. You'll sleep in there with me."

"I just thought…you seemed to be awkward about things."

What I felt awkward about is nothing she should worry about. It wasn't awkwardness either. It was pure rage, but I didn't mean to let her see that. She doesn't deserve to suffer because of what that asshole did to her.

He's the only one who'll suffer.

"You belong in there with me, Sophie."

She stares up at me, her dark eyes wide. "But I figured since you didn't want to do anything in the shower and you wouldn't even look at me when you put the bandages on my arms…"

"I told you I'd never let anyone hurt you. I didn't live up to that promise, and for that, I can't forgive him. Or me. You're my responsibility, and I should have protected you. I'm sorry for today, little one."

Her brown eyes fill with tears, and taking a step toward me, she reaches for my hand. "You have no blame for today, King. Neither of us do. But I'm okay. I never doubted you'd come for me. I'm stronger than I look."

She has no idea how strong she truly is. I've never met a woman like her, and the very idea that this is the last night I'll ever have with her makes me wish things could be different, even as I know they can't.

Sophie and I belong in two different worlds. She's as good as I am bad, as kind as I am brutal. But for one final night, we'll bridge those two worlds.

"No matter how strong you are, you should have never had to deal with any of this," I say as I lead her to my bedroom.

Behind me, she says in a tiny voice I barely hear, "I promised myself I'd hate you forever for what you did."

Turning to look back at her, I get the feeling she has more to say, so I don't tell her I hated that I had to do that. What would it matter anyway? I did what I did, and like with everything else I've done in my life, I'll have to pay the price for that someday.

"I understand why you did it, though," she says in that same tiny voice. Looking away, she adds, "I'm not sure why I didn't go on hating you, to be honest. Maybe it's this place, or maybe it's you, but I don't know if things would have happened between us if I wasn't here like I am."

The way she avoids using the actual word makes me smile. I glance down at our hands still joined together and then up at her.

"You're a captive. Hostage. Whichever you like. You don't have to be afraid to say what this is. I've never had any delusions that this is anything but two people who never wanted to be part of Tap's fucked up plan getting stuck together."

Hurt settles into her expression. I didn't want her to take that to mean what it sounded like.

Shaking her head, she says, "Please don't think I hate you now. That isn't what I meant at all."

Fuck. Suddenly, neither one of us seems to be able to say what we really mean.

I feel her fingers tighten around my hand, but I ease it from her hold and shrug. "You'd have every right to hate me and everyone here. You never should have ended up here in the first place."

"Would you think I'm crazy if I said I'm not sorry it happened?"

Throwing my head back, I let out a full laugh. "Yes."

Sophie's sense of humor has made me laugh out loud before, but as I sit down on the bed, I notice she hasn't moved. Her face shows she didn't intend for that to be funny.

"Why do you seem so different tonight? If it's not because of what Tap did, then what is it? First, you can barely stand me touching you in the bathroom, and now when I tell you that I'm not sorry I got to be here with you, your response is to laugh at me. Why are you being like this?"

As if her question makes something explode inside me, I snap, "Like what? Like someone who's about to lose the only...What do you want from me, Sophie? What are you expecting me to act like?"

My outburst surprises her, and she steps back away from the bed. At first, she doesn't know what to say and just stares at me with a look that's a mixture of confusion and hurt. She opens her mouth to say something, but closes it, like she doesn't want to let whatever's inside her out.

But I want to hear it. I want everything from her tonight. The good. The bad. Whatever she has left, I want. It's all I'll have of her once she's gone.

"Say it, Sophie. Whatever it is, say it."

"I'm not just what these words say on my skin."

It's a question as much as a statement, a quiet plea for me to be the person she needs after all she's been through. Staring up at her, my chest hurts from all the anger coursing through me and how much I wish I wasn't who I am.

I stand and take the few steps toward her until my body nearly touches hers. She doesn't look up at me, and I wrap my arms around her so all she can feel is me protecting her like I'm supposed to.

And then the tears I knew needed to come out finally start. As she sobs against my chest, I say nothing because nothing's good enough. She needs actions, not hollow words from the likes of me.

Her body trembles against mine, and with each sob, I hold her tightly to me.

Against my skin, she whispers, "I hate that I'm crying."

She shouldn't hate crying. She should hate me. She should hate everyone at this fucking place.

I smooth my hand down over her dark hair and press a kiss to the top of her head. "You're going to be okay, Sophie. You're strong."

Looking up at me, her mouth turns down into a frown that makes me wish I didn't say whatever is making her so unhappy. I want to see that cute little pout or that smile of hers that lights up everything around her. Not this frown.

"I think there's something wrong with me because I'm going to miss you, King. I don't know what to do with that. And then you act like you're going to miss me, and all I can think is how unlucky we both are."

She stops talking and takes a deep breath. For a moment, she tries to give me a smile but fails. Stepping away from me, she leaves me standing there wishing so many things at that moment but most of all wishing she was still in my arms.

"At least if one person is lucky, the one with that person gets to enjoy some benefits from that luck, but if neither person is lucky, like us, then no one can be happy."

I walk around her and sit on the edge of the bed. She turns to face me, and I reach out and run my fingers along the bottom of my T-shirt that hangs to the middle of her thighs while I think about what she said about luck. I'd never thought of it like that, but she's right. We're not lucky, and neither one of us will be happy after tonight.

But for one night more, we can find all the happiness there is to be had for us here.

Looking up at her, I try to hide how much I'm going to miss Sophie. "Come here."

As she climbs onto my lap, I slide my arms around her body and pull her close to me. I want to commit the way she feels to my memory, to impress it onto my mind so I can't forget when she's gone and I'm alone in this bed once again.

"All I can think is why did this happen? If we weren't supposed to ever have a chance to be happy together, why would the universe bring us together like this?" she whispers into my ear.

I tilt my head back and look up into those brown eyes so full of sadness. "I don't know. Maybe all the happiness we get is tonight and the other times we've had here."

"That's not fair. Why would two people find their way to one another only to have it end so soon?"

And right there, right in those words, the difference between our two worlds couldn't be more obvious. To Sophie, we found our way to one another, like somehow we were meant to be. To me, she was forced from her life and into mine.

I like the tenderness in her idea of us, though. I'll miss that the most about having her here with me. For a short time, she brought something kind and sweet to my life. As much as I can't help but be hard and brutal, having a gentle soul waiting here for me each day made me wish things were different.

But they aren't.

"We only have this night, Sophie," I say, cradling her beautiful face in my hands. She closes her eyes, and I add, "No regrets."

And just like that, the frown turns into that pout I love.

"One more night, and then what?" she asks,

forcing me to admit the truth out loud for the first time tonight.

"And then you'll go home to your life and not be foolish enough to run alone at night, even in a safe neighborhood. You'll ask your uncle to send one of his guys over to your house to make sure you have locks that keep bad men out."

"And I'll wish I didn't meet you in this place surrounded by these people," she says, finishing my thought with her own.

I kiss that sexy pouty mouth and pull her hard to me, wanting to keep her as close as I can until I have to give her up. My tongue slips between her lips and teases hers as thoughts of everything I want to do to her fill my mind. I want her to leave me with no doubts how I felt about her. Never again will she wonder if any man had ever been so consumed with her that he wondered how he'd live without her when she was gone.

Her hands roam over my skin, exciting every inch of me she touches. It's like my body knows this may be its last real chance to feel truly alive. Not that farce it's experienced for so many years but real emotions and real reactions that only a woman can bring out in a man like me.

Sophie breaks our kiss, tearing her mouth from mine, and leans back away from me. I open my eyes to see her shaking her head.

"This isn't fair," she says, fighting back tears.

"Life isn't fair."

"I hate this."

Pulling her to me, I kiss her with everything I have inside me and whisper against her lips, "I love this. And I love how from this point on, you're always going to know that in a world full of people, I couldn't think of anything else but being inside you whenever you were around."

"I don't want to think about how I'll be when you're not around, King. For tonight, the entire world exists here, in this bedroom between just the two of us."

"Then no more regrets," I say before I lay back onto the bed and pull her down on top of me.

She rolls her hips and her pussy glides over the front of the towel covering my hard on. With a giggle, she looks down between us and shakes her head.

"How is that towel still on you?"

I shrug and lift her off me just enough to slide it from around me. "It's not anymore, so feel free to go back to what you were doing before."

"You mean this?" she asks and then sits up on my hips to glide her wet pussy over my now uncovered cock.

"Exactly that," I say, pressing my hands into her hips and holding her still. "But I think that's enough foreplay."

Sophie slides her tongue over her bottom lip and bites it as I angle my hips and sink deep into her ready cunt. She's hot and wet, and it only takes seconds for me to get lost in how fucking good she feels around me.

"Oooh, God…" she moans, dragging her nails

down over my chest. "I almost don't want to move it feels so good."

Flipping her over onto her back, I plunge into her and smile. "Now you don't have a choice."

Her heels press into the small of my back, pushing hard to keep me where I am inside her, but I buck against them and pull out of her needy cunt. Sophie grabs my neck and tugs me down, kissing me hard.

"Fuck me," she moans against my lips. "Make it so I can never forget you, King."

And that's all it takes to kick my body into overdrive. I thrust my hips forward and slam into her, desperate to mark every inch of that perfect cunt as mine. She cries out like it hurts, but I see all over her face how much she wants it even harder.

That timid hostage who wondered if she liked a little pain with her pleasure doesn't have to wonder anymore. She loves it hard, and I love giving it to her exactly that way.

I plunge into her until there's nothing left between us. I want to fuck away the reality that in just a few short hours, she'll be leaving me. I want to forget how much that makes me hate everything in this goddamned world but her. I want her to feel every part of me and know it's hers, every inch of who I am she possesses in a way I never believed possible.

She may never hear those words from me, but I want her to know she became my entire world for the short time she was in my life.

Her fingernails create streaks of pain across my back, tearing into me with every push of my cock into her. "I want to mark you like you've marked me," she sobs as she scratches down my spine. "I want whoever there is after me to know I was here with you so you don't forget."

I watch her fight back tears and fuck her with everything that exists inside me. All the rage. All the hate. All the love, only for her.

"There's no forgetting you, Sophie," I groan out just before I come inside her.

Dragging her fingernails down the front of me, she digs them into the skin on my hips and holds me still inside her. My cock twitches with each shot of cum into her, but the rest of my body doesn't move.

Her release follows a few seconds later, and she becomes more beautiful in those moments beneath me when she surrenders all she is to all I am. I watch her, filling my eyes with every tiny movement her mouth makes and how her brown eyes so wide when she looks up at me seem to beg for just a few more minutes of this perfect time between us.

I collapse on top of her, and our drenched bodies press against one another as we struggle to catch our breath. My back stings from the tiny cuts her nails made when a drop of sweat trickles into them, the pain searing the memory of this last time with Sophie into me. I lay perfectly still with my eyes closed hoping to feel it again, but after a few minutes, it's gone.

Sophie runs her hand down over the back of my head and lets it come to rest on the nape of my neck. Her touch is soft, like already she's not completely there with me anymore.

But then she presses her lips to my ear in a kiss and whispers a single plea that tells me I haven't lost her yet.

"Please don't forget me."

I hold her to me, her heartbeat pounding against my chest, as I try to imagine how I could do that. I don't know how she did it, but she got under my skin. What started as a flash of decency I wasn't sure still existed inside me anymore since I began working for Duke morphed into a way to protect an innocent from a psychotic asshole and then it turned into something much more.

"Never."

As much as I wish she wouldn't forget me, I know better. Sophie will return to a world full of school and parties with guys who have no idea how incredible she is. One day, she'll find one of them interesting enough to give him a chance, and with every day he makes her smile, she'll forget another moment we spent together.

It's only natural. If so much of her time here hadn't been the worst thing she'd ever experienced, maybe a trace of what we were together could exist in her mind, but to forget the bad, she'll have to give up the good too.

And then one day, all of this will disappear from her memory.

But as much as her future offers her that chance, mine doesn't. I'll return to the life I chose years ago when I didn't have any other choice. The part of me that fell for her will fade away, replaced with the hardness required to do what I do.

We all have our roles to play. Sometimes, though, we step out of them for even a short time and get a taste of what another life is like.

IN THE BRIGHT SUNLIGHT, I SQUINT WHILE I DRIVE Sophie toward her house in that suburban neighborhood I have no business being in this morning. A heavy feeling hangs between us, but neither of us say a word the entire way there. Just thirty minutes from the estate, it's like I'm driving to another world entirely, one where I don't belong in the stark light of day.

My only knowledge of this place is Carney's house, so I drive there and can't help but notice how perfect it seems as his wife sits on the front porch drinking her morning coffee with one of her neighbors. Does she have any idea of the trouble her husband routinely hovers so close to? One look at her and how happy she looks tells me no, she doesn't.

Is it all for the better that she remains ignorant, or should I pity her for being in the dark about the man she's devoted herself to? I don't know, and as I look away from that idyllic scene at Carney's house, I realize I've never thought that about anyone else.

"Drive one street over. It's a brown house with white shutters and a little yard."

Turning to look at Sophie, I nod. Brown house. Little yard. Will she someday be like Carney's wife sitting on the front porch with a cup of coffee talking to the neighbor while her husband gambles their life savings away or is forced to go to someone like Duke for a loan to hide that nasty habit of his from her?

I hate that future for Sophie.

As I stop the car in front of her house, I can only glance over at it before that future seems to materialize right before my eyes. Grabbing her arm, I hang onto one last moment with her before she leaves my life forever.

"Don't let yourself be fooled by any guy who seems good. We're all bad men, Sophie. Some just show it more than others."

One last time, she gives me one of her gentle smiles that lights up her face. "Then I guess I got lucky finding the one bad man who's not so bad, after all."

She leans over and kisses me softly before opening the car door. "Remember, you promised to not forget me, King. And even though you haven't asked me to do that, I won't forget you either."

I watch as she runs into her house, slamming the door behind her and leaving our time together with me.

With one last glance at that brown house with the white shutters, I pull away and start back toward the world I live in. "Don't worry, Sophie. I won't forget you."

By the time I get back to the estate, all the good she brought out in me has receded to a dark corner inside me and I'm once again the same man

233

I've always been. I walk into Duke's office to let him know Sophie's back home safe and sound, but instead of finding my boss, Tap and Marsh are sitting in the chairs in front of his desk waiting for him.

"Where's Duke?" I ask Marsh, even though Tap spins around to throw me a nasty look.

"He'll be down in a few minutes," Marsh answers without turning around.

"Fine."

I turn to leave and Tap is on me before I take two steps toward the door. He sneaks a few shots in to my kidneys, but when I get him face-to-face, whatever advantage he had disappears. I quickly look at his hands for his usual weapon of choice but see no knife.

Too bad because I came ready for him today.

My switchblade is out of my pocket and in front of him before he knows what happened. For all that he did to Sophie, and for all the hate I have inside me for that, it's time he paid with blood. I don't give a fuck that he's Duke's favorite anymore.

All I care about is revenge. Sophie couldn't strike back at him, but I can for her. And now he's going to find out what happens when you take a shot at the king and miss.

For the first time since I've known him, fear fills his eyes at the sight of the light glinting off the blade in my hand. "How's it feel, asshole? You've been playing with those fucking toys of yours all this time, and the one day you need even one of them on you, here you are without it."

"What the fuck is this about?" he asks in a squeaky voice that shows how terrified he is.

I point the tip of the knife toward his face and laugh. "It's about having to deal with you every fucking time I don't want to. It's about you being a fucking asshole who makes my life more difficult. But most of all, it's about you taking what was fucking mine."

Tap lifts his hands like he's surrendering to me, but it's no use. There's no chance for a reprieve this time.

"I didn't touch her. Not that way anyway. Why the fuck do you care so much anyway?"

"Because she was mine. I made that perfectly clear to you, and still you thought you could come into my home and snatch her from where she belonged."

I take a step toward him as he backs up closer to the corner of the room. "Not such a big man when you're not the one with the knife, are you?"

When I woke up this morning next to Sophie, loving the feel of her body pressed close to mine in the bed we shared, I didn't plan to strike against Tap. I was lost in the ecstasy of being with the one person who gave me a reason to smile.

That all changed when she slammed the car door behind her and ran back to her life.

From that point on, the desire to avenge Sophie pushed out everything, except for the memory of her smile when she tried to tell me I'm not the bad man I know I am. Tap couldn't be allowed to continue to walk around without suffering the punishment he was due.

My mind filled with pure rage for what he did to her, I slash at him with surgical precision. He lifts his hands to protect himself, but he's too slow and the blade slices through his skin from ear to ear.

For a long moment, everything falls silent in the room, except for the desperate sound of him gasping for air. His hands clutch at his neck, but it's no use. There's no stopping the blood as it pours out of him, spurting like a geyser from the gash that goes far too deep.

He can't speak anymore. No more cocky bullshit coming out of his mouth. No more threats to wreak havoc on the world because he wants to.

I watch him slide to the floor, his round eyes bulging out of their sockets in shock that it was me who did this to him. On the other side of the room, Marsh stands watching it all but saying nothing. Older and smarter, he knows better.

When Tap takes his final breath, I turn to look at Marsh and nod. More satisfaction than I thought I'd get from killing that fucker courses through me.

"When you take a shot at the king, you better kill him or he's going to kill you."

"Fuck, man. Something tells me we all read that situation with the girl wrong."

After I wipe Tap's blood on my pants, I put my blade away and smile at Marsh. "Something tells me you're right."

He stares at me in shock, but his eyes grow wide when I pull my gun from my waistband and aim for the center of the old fuck's forehead. One shot is all it takes. No chance for reprieve. No chance to say a single word that can change my mind. Nothing. Marsh drops to the floor with a thud, and then it's over.

I walk out into the hallway and head up to where Duke unknowingly waits for me. My job at this fucking place is officially over as of today.

CHAPTER TWENTY

ophie

FOR NEARLY FIVE WEEKS, MY MOTHER HAS HOVERED over me like she's afraid if she leaves me alone for more than a few minutes at a time, I'll disappear. She doesn't have to worry. I don't know how I know that, but I do.

Five weeks feels like forever, but then again, so did ten days with King.

I've tried to forget everything about that time, except when the two of us were alone in that apartment of his that I hated until I was leaving and then I missed it. I stay inside my little house with my mother keeping a close eye on me, but sometimes late at night I wish I was back in that place, as odd as that may seem.

Staring out the front window, I find myself looking

for that black car I associate with him. Has he driven by since that day five weeks ago when he let me go and I ran away wondering if I'd ever forget him?

I wonder what he does with his days now. Does his life change with the seasons like so many people's do? Has he been cooped up in that apartment of his in the heat wave that's settled in over the northeast in the past few weeks?

I glance out at the flowers I planted back in the spring that dot my front yard now, and I notice someone's walked over one since the last time I looked. Has he come to check on me late at night and kicked his boots through them, inadvertently stomping on a daisy on his way to the porch to look in through the front window where I now sit?

No. That's never happened. He left that day to go back to his world just like I went back to mine.

"Sophie, honey, what are you wearing tonight?" my mother asks from the dining room.

I look over at her sitting at the table with her cup of tea and cranberry scone and shrug. "I don't know. It's not a black tie affair or anything like that, is it?"

My tiny attempt at humor seems to confuse her. "Well, no. It's nothing like that. I just think you should wear something nice since it's the first time you're going to see your uncle in over ten years."

"I'm a little surprised Daddy even wants to go to this, to be honest, Mom. They haven't talked for so long I thought they'd never speak again."

My observation makes her nod, like it's something she's thought about and can finally agree with me on.

But it's nothing but the truth. However, since my mother is convinced it was my uncle's influence that brought me home to them, she's persuaded my father it's time to mend his relationship with my Uncle Victor.

"I think it's a good thing they finally are talking again."

What my father wants to do or what he thinks about the whole situation remains a mystery to me. I haven't brought it up to him, and he hasn't mentioned it to me. The two of us seem perfectly happy not to discuss what happened to me at all, in fact.

My reasons are simple. I can't talk about it without having the truth of what I experienced with King show all over my face. I don't know his reasons for sure, but I suspect they have to do with the utter fear that what he's hated all his life finally touched his child and he doesn't know how to deal with that yet.

The truth of that time at Duke's estate is something neither of my parents know, and as much as I try to keep it alive in my mind, I'm happy to not talk about it with them. My uncle came to see me right after I returned home, but he didn't ask what happened either. No doubt, he thinks he's the reason behind why I was let go.

But they're all wrong. King is the one who gave me back my life. No one else. Not Duke. Not that asshole Tap. Not my uncle.

King.

And for that, I'll always owe him more than he can ever know. I may never have a chance to repay him, but I hope he knows how much I can't forget the time we spent together.

My mother clears her throat, tearing me out of my thoughts and back to our conversation about what I should wear tonight to my uncle's for a party he's throwing to celebrate my return and his renewed relationship with his brother. I have no idea what dress I'll choose, so I toss the question back to her.

"I don't know. Any suggestions?" I ask, loving how excited she instantly gets at being asked her opinion.

"Oh, I think the black dress you wore to Candy's engagement party last year would be lovely. Don't you?" she asks, her eyes wide with anticipation as she waits to hear if I agree with her.

It's actually a very good choice, so I smile and answer, "I do. Black sheath dress it is."

MY HEAD SWIVELS LEFT AND RIGHT TO TAKE IN ALL the sights of my uncle's mansion. Priceless works of art hang on the walls of the entryway, some sculpture that looks vaguely sexual with two figures intertwined stands in a niche in the wall that looks like it was created just for the piece, and a marble table in the center of the room that I guess cost a small fortune directs visitors past an enormous vase. And this is just the room to pass through to get to the rest of the house.

I turn to my mother as a maid dressed in a black and white uniform greets us and whisper, "I didn't know Uncle Victor was this…"

My sentence drifts off to nothing as I try to find the right word. Rich isn't enough to convey how much money he seems to have. Just coming up the circular driveway to this enormous home told me that. Wealthy seems inadequate to describe this place too.

Before I can find the right word, my mother chuckles in my ear and says, "Loaded?"

I look at her and smile at how cute she can be sometimes. "Yeah. Did you know?"

As she's shaking her head no, my father joins us, and I hear him mumble in disgust, "So, I guess what they always say is wrong. Crime does pay."

My mother and I both throw him a look that tells him we really don't want a scene tonight. All I can think about once he says that, though, is that picture of my birthday party with my father and uncle glaring at one another in the background while my mother and I are all smiles for the camera.

From a room off to the left of the entryway, my uncle walks in to join us and I'm instantly surprised at how out of place he seems among all the artwork and expensive furniture. Dressed in a pair of black dress pants and a pale blue dress shirt, he looks more like a middle manager at some company than some big crime boss. His hair is short and not slicked back, like I expected it to look, and he seems younger than I imagined he'd be since he's my father's older brother.

"Isabella, I'm so happy you came," he says full of charm as he leans forward to kiss my mother on the cheek. "You're as beautiful as you were when I saw you last all those years ago."

My mother blushes like she always does when someone compliments her. "It's very good to see you again, Victor. Thank you for inviting us and for all you've done for us."

I hear my father groan as I wait for the fireworks to start. I had hoped we'd get through more of this night than just walking through the front door.

Turning to look at my father, my uncle smiles and it seems genuine. Extending his hand to shake my father's, he says, "The long lost prodigal brother back once more. It's good to see you again, Joey."

No one ever calls my father Joey. He bristles when anyone refers to him as Joe. My father is very much a Joseph. Always has been and always will be. This night is starting off on all the wrong feet.

Out of the corner of my eye, I see my mother's face contort into an expression of panic. She reaches out for his hand and gives it a squeeze I know is meant to let him know she really wants him to play nice with his brother. When I look at my father, though, his expression says the last thing he wants to be is nice at this moment.

"Victor."

And that's it. In the flattest tone possible, my father lets his brother know how his opinion about him hasn't changed in the least, even if he believes he had a part in rescuing me just over one month ago.

Thankfully, my uncle doesn't seem offended when he turns to face me. "And Sophie, my beautiful niece. What a lovely young woman you've grown up to be."

His gaze focuses on my cheek where the cut had

been when he saw me right after I returned home. As I have since the day I returned, I wear long sleeves to cover the scars from what Tap did to my arms, so he has no idea to look there. When he realizes no scar has been left on my face as evidence of my time at the hands of one of his rivals, his smile grows broader.

"I'm so happy to see you're in such good shape after all you've been through," he says as he leans forward to kiss the spot just below on my cheek.

"Hi, Uncle Victor. Thank you for having us here tonight. This place is stunning. I didn't realize you had such a beautiful home."

My flattery strikes just the right note with him, and he beams his approval for my compliments. Taking me by the arm, he says to my parents, "You two take a seat in the living room. I want to spend a few minutes with my niece."

Once we're out of earshot, he says, "Let me show you around. I rarely get to show off my house like this. I hope you'll humor an old man."

I look back at my parents and see the two warring sides of their love for me. My mother looks as pleased as punch, like I've just been chosen Miss America, and my father looks panicked, like I've just been carried off by a shark.

"I'm so happy I was able to help with that situation, Sophie. As soon as I heard Duke's men had gotten hold of you, I let him know there would be hell to pay if you weren't returned home immediately. Thankfully, you weren't there even a few hours more or you would have been caught in the middle of a nightmare."

Confused by what he means, I look at him as he shows off some priceless tapestry hanging in the hallway to his study. "A nightmare? Worse than being grabbed off the street at night?"

My question stops him, and he looks at me strangely, like he can't believe what I said. "Well, that was terrible, of course, but being trapped in the middle of a massacre would have been a true nightmare, Sophie. You're very lucky I got you out of there when I did."

Massacre? The word sends chills down my spine, and suddenly I feel like I'm going to be sick. Was King in the massacre? Is he dead?

I can't ask my uncle, but I have to know. My head begins to pound as my stomach roils at the thought that he's gone.

"Can I have a glass of water? I'm not feeling so good right now."

My uncle smiles and begins to lead me back down the hallway to the living room where my parents wait for us. Patting my hand, he says, "I understand. I shouldn't have mentioned it. I'm sorry about that. But I wanted you to know how fortunate you were to get out of there when you did."

Desperate for some shred of information to cling to, I ask as casually as I can, "So you mean all those people are dead?"

Oh, God. Just saying that makes me feel like I'm going to black out. King can't be dead. It's not possible. Maybe he was still in the car driving back from my house when that all happened. It was a long drive back to the estate.

But if that's the case, why hasn't he tried to contact me now that he's no longer working for Duke? Wouldn't he want to see me if he could?

By the time we get back to the living room, my head is spinning and I don't know if I can pretend to be okay for the next few hours here. I want to be at home where I can cry for the man I thought I'd see again. I didn't know how or when, but I thought we'd be together again somehow.

"Sophie, what's wrong? You look as pale as a ghost!" my mother cries out as she rushes to my side to help me onto the couch.

"I'm fine, Mom. I just felt a little lightheaded. It's my first time out since I'm home, so maybe that's it. I think if I can just have some water I'll be okay."

A woman seems to appear out of nowhere with a glass of water for me, so I thank her and quickly down a ladylike gulp, hoping it helps my stomach settle. If only I knew the answer to the question I asked my uncle, I might feel better.

After a few minutes of my parents worrying too much about me, my uncle returns and sits down next to me. Needing to know anything he can tell me about what happened at the estate, I quietly ask, "Did all those people die?"

"From what I've heard, yes."

My mother begins asking questions about what

we're talking about, but I can't seem to form a single word now. All of them dead? How?

I want to ask so much more about what my uncle knows, but now that my mother has become curious, there's no way I can. It feels like the world is spinning out of control around me, and all I can do is fight to keep the tears from coming at the thought that King is gone.

Gone forever.

My hands shake uncontrollably, and I can barely lift the glass to my lips to take another drink. I don't want to be here. I want to go home.

I want to see King, but I can't. Not anymore.

Not ever again.

CHAPTER TWENTY-ONE

ophie

My mother hovers around me as my uncle studies me like he can't understand why I'd be in the least bit bothered by hearing that entire group of people I spent time around are now gone. And my father stands horrified at the mere suggestion that any part of my uncle's world still touches me.

"Victor, if you didn't order that done to the people who held Sophie, then who did?" he asks pointedly, signaling he's about a second away from blowing up.

My uncle merely shrugs, clearly not interested in discussing the topic further. "I don't know, but it wasn't me. I had plans to strike at Duke for a while now, but I guess that's been taken care of. However, that's not why I invited you all here. Tonight is to celebrate lovely Sophie's safe return and an offer from our brother to have her stay with him and Kaia to help out when the baby arrives."

I look around in shock at this news, my emotions suffering from near whiplash. I haven't seen my father's younger brother for years, and now he wants me to come live with him and his new wife? The man who wears the skull mask and terrified me when I was a little girl?

"What? Uncle Ryker got married?" I ask, unsure which part of all of this stuns me more.

My father shakes his head and smiles. "Not married, but he and Kaia are due to have a baby any day now. He asked me if you'd be interested in coming to live with them last week, but I didn't know if you felt up to it."

"I'm not a nanny, Daddy. I don't know the first thing about helping with a newborn."

"Not as a nanny," Victor explains to correct me. "Ryker tells me Kaia has been sick or something the whole nine months, so I think it's more for company. I can't imagine he doesn't already have someone all lined up to handle the actual baby."

The way he says that—the actual baby—makes me smile, and I see my mother nodding like she thinks this is all a good idea. Is this some plan to keep me safe because they all think I'm in danger?

"I don't know. I like my place. I know I took the summer off, but I had planned to do things at school over break," I say, just wanting to leave this house as my emotions begin to bubble up inside me over the news that King is gone forever.

But I can't show any of them how I truly feel, so I push it all down and pretend to be fine.

My mother sits down next to me and pats my hand in that way she likes to when she's worried. "From what I've heard, she's had a terrible time of it with this pregnancy. You'd be perfectly safe there, honey, and she is close to your age."

"Really?"

I silently do the math in my head as I remember how much younger Ryker is than my father and his other brothers. It makes sense that he'd be with someone closer to my age than my parents or Uncle Victor's.

Then my mother's words about being perfectly safe ring in my ears. But safe from what?

"Is there something you're all not telling me? Why would I have to worry about being safe now?"

Victor answers abruptly before my parents can come up with something to soothe my mind. "They never found out who killed Duke and his men. Your uncle and I are concerned that you may have seen something that could put you in danger. It's more a cautionary measure than anything else."

"So the whole bad pregnancy thing was a lie?" I ask the three of them.

My mother quickly shakes her head. "Oh, no. Kaia has been sick for months, the poor thing. Her blood pressure skyrocketed, and she's been forced to stay in bed since April. They were afraid she might lose the baby."

She pauses and then adds, "I think it might be nice for everyone involved. You'd get a change of scenery, and she'd get a new friend."

The last thing I want to do now is go live somewhere strange to me and make friends, and the idea that a pregnant woman consigned to her bed might not want to entertain a new friend or anyone else doesn't seem to have figured into my family's planning. A memory of all of us visiting Ryker's home right after my grandfather died when I was a little girl flashes through my mind. The estate was big. Maybe it would be nice to go somewhere new for a few weeks.

Somewhere I can get lost.

Somewhere to forget.

"I need to be back for when school starts next month, though. The semester begins the last week of August, so I want to be home by mid-August at the latest."

"Then it's settled. Tonight, we'll celebrate, and then tomorrow you can go to Ryker's," my uncle announces before his maid appears with a tray full of glasses of champagne.

None of this feels like the way I wanted to spend my summer, but I can't deny that sitting in my house watching out the front window for any sign of King isn't how I wanted to spend the next couple months either.

I catch myself as I think this and wince at the pain that settles into my chest. Is he really gone?

My Uncle Ryker's living room hides the fact that like most of the rest of our family, he's a man involved in what my father likes to say is a life of crime. Beautiful furniture and artwork make it look like he's a man of culture, but I know better.

The last time I saw him I was ten years old at my grandfather's funeral. While my father and Victor seethed at one another, Ryker stood off to the side alone, wearing that terrifying skull mask and unwilling to join in with any of the family. He looked like some angry specter amidst all those people telling stories about my grandfather and what kind of man he was. Now, eleven years later, here I sit in his home waiting to see him for the first time since that day and unsure what to expect.

As I think about that horrible day so long ago, he strolls into the room and stops dead in front of me. I look up to see him unfasten his mask, letting it drop into his hand before stuffing it into his suit pocket.

"Sorry about that. Kaia made me promise that I'd take it off before walking in here, but old habits die hard. I'd know you anywhere, Sophie. You look like the spitting image of your mother. Thank you for coming to stay with us."

He extends his hand to shake mine, and I notice the tattoos that extend onto his wrist as his suitcoat and white dress shirt ride up on his arm. I'm struck by how different he is from my father.

But he looks like my father with the dark eyes and

strong jawline my mother always says makes him the most handsome man in the world. Now without the mask, I can see how my uncle could be that too for many women.

"I'm happy to, Uncle Ryker. I was sorry to hear Kaia had such a hard time, but my mother told me the baby finally came yesterday. Congratulations!"

The man beaming his happiness at the birth of his first child looks nothing like the surly man who wore that skull mask that day so many years ago. Smiling, he nods to thank me.

"Maxim Dmitri Varens came into this world yesterday afternoon with all the fight I expected him to have, and now his mother gets to rest for a few days to recuperate. She tells me sleep for us is a thing of the past, but that's all he seems to do right now. I have to admit I spend more time than I should staring into his crib, to be honest."

I can see why my parents like this brother better than Victor. Ryker is charming and sweet, in the way only a bad man can be, of course. The same can't be said for my other uncle.

"Well, I feel sort of like I'm intruding on a personal time, to be honest, Uncle Ryker," I say, suddenly unsure I should be hanging around their house at that moment.

Shaking his head, he continues to smile, probably more about the birth of his son than anything I'm saying. "First of all, you can just call me Ryker. We're family, and you're a grown woman, so no more uncle stuff. Save that for Victor, who I know still insists on that kind of thing."

I can't help but laugh at how true that is. "He really does get into that uncle stuff. I guess because he's so much older than us."

Ryker rolls his eyes. "Probably to get under your father's skin, too."

"I know! It's like a death match when those two are in a room. I was afraid of who was going to throw the first punch last night."

As much as I want to ask Ryker if he knows what the source of the bad blood is between my father and Victor, I don't. Somehow every time anyone brings that brother into the mix, things get ugly.

"And Sophie, please don't feel like you're intruding at all. Part of the reason why I invited you here is to get you away from everyone else in the family, who I suspect have been hovering over you like a bunch of mother hens since you came home. Feel free to think of this estate as your own escape from the world. If you want to go anywhere, someone will escort you since I promised your father I'd keep you safe, but other than that, go anywhere you want on the estate. Jaxon and Cason work for me, so you'll see them around, along with my other men, but you have free run of the place. I had one of the rooms in the east wing made up for you, but if you need anything, just come find me at my office down the hall."

He chuckles and then says, "Or in the nursery since I spend a lot of time there too."

"I will. Thank you so much, Ryker. I think I'm just

looking forward to some time alone after all that happened," I say quietly as I tug on my sleeves to make sure my forearms are completely covered, suddenly embarrassed by what I went through.

But unlike everyone else with their soft tone when they talk to me about that, Ryker says in a voice that seems downright defiant, "This world we Varens live in can be ugly, but like I told your father, not everyone is Victor. Protecting family comes first before anything else, including business."

I'm not sure I understand what he means, but his hard expression tells me he believes in something his brother doesn't when it comes to family. I like that. It makes me feel safe here, something I didn't realize I needed until I left my house today.

When he pulls me into his arms for a hug, I can't help but relax. I can't place how, but he reminds me of King.

"Okay, I have more baby gazing to do before I get to work," he says with a smile. "Remember, do whatever makes you happy here. Think of this as a vacation from the rest of the family and the world. I'll catch up with you later today, but in the meantime, enjoy yourself."

"I will. Thanks!"

He leaves me standing there in his gorgeous living room wondering if I'll be able to do the one thing in this place that I couldn't do at home.

Forget King.

I wander out into the hallway and realize I didn't ask Ryker where my room is. The east wing, he said.

Didn't he? Or was it west wing? Looking left and then right, I can't even figure out where west or east is.

Making my way toward what looks like a stairway at the end of the hall, I peek into each room to see if it's Ryker's office but one after another turns out not to be what I'm looking for. A dining room and then a library I instantly think I want to take a better look at are followed by what looks like another living room. Finally, I hear men's voices and poke my head into the last room to find Ryker sitting behind an enormous cherry wood desk. He's put on his mask again and looks like that stern man from years ago, so much so that I hesitate to intrude.

"Sophie, you look lost," he says with a smile in his voice.

"I forgot to ask where my room is exactly. I'm sorry to bother you," I say as I inch into his office.

Three huge men turn to look at me, and I suddenly feel about as big as an ant. My reaction is to shrink even more as they stare in my direction like they've never seen a woman before.

"Gentlemen, this is Sophie," Ryker says, making all three heads snap back in his direction. "She's going to be living here for a while, so you'll see her around the estate. She is to be given free run of my home and the grounds."

After each man nods, Ryker waves his hand and sends them away. I watch as the three men dutifully file through his office door on the other side of the room, impressed with how much power he exudes from behind that desk and behind that mask.

"I didn't mean to interrupt your meeting, Ryker. I'm so sorry."

He shakes his head. "No worries. Let me take you to your room. I should have done that before."

I follow him toward the door out of his office the three giant men in suits just left through, but behind me I hear a noise and turn my head just as another man enters from the other door. I only get a quick glance at him, but I'm surprised at how striking he is. The last I see of him is when he stops dead in front of Ryker's desk and I hurry into the hallway.

"Somebody walked into your office as we were leaving," I say when I catch up to Ryker, who's made it halfway up the stairs before I reach him.

Looking back at me, he nods. "You'd be surprised at how many people I have to meet with day in and day out. I'm going to have to hang a schedule on my door so people have to make appointments now that Maxim is here," he says with a deep chuckle.

We walk in silence until we reach a door at the far end of the hallway on the second floor. He stops and turns to look at me, a smile wrinkling the skin around his eyes. "I'm not sure how I thought you'd find this all on your own for the first time. Kaia's right. I clearly have to work on my manners. Again, if you need anything, just let me know."

"Thank you, Ryker. I'm sure I won't have to bother you anymore."

With a gentle pat on my shoulder, he chuckles again. "No bother. Now back to work for me, unless

Kane is back, which means I can go spend some time with my son and his mother."

For a second, my heart skips a beat until my brain corrects what I thought I heard. Kane, not King. God, will I ever forget him?

CHAPTER TWENTY-TWO

ane

My heart slams into my chest, and I press my palms to the top of Ryker's desk as the room feels like it's spinning around me. This isn't happening. It can't.

I must be wrong. I haven't been able to get her out of my head for the past month and a half, so that must be it.

Fuck, it has to be it.

"Kane, what are you doing?" Ryker asks as he slides behind his desk and sits down like he does a hundred times a day with me standing in front of him like I do every day.

"Who was that you were walking out with a second ago?" I ask, barely able to contain my emotions as the words rush out of me.

For once, I wish he wasn't wearing that fucking

mask. I need to see his expression, and right now, just seeing his eyes isn't enough.

"Sophie. She's staying here for a little while," he answers, making my heart slam into my ribs again.

"Why?" I croak out, barely able to say that one word.

Ryker leans back in his chair and folds his arms across his chest in that way he does whenever one of his men asks him something they shouldn't. But I'm not just one of his fucking men, so he needs to goddamned answer me now.

"I'd think of all the people in the world, you'd understand why she could use some time away from her family and everything else."

"Her family? You're her fucking family. Did you somehow forget she's a Varens?"

"You know what I mean. Between Victor and my brother and sister-in-law, I don't think she's had a moment's peace since she got home. Here she can relax and still be safe."

"Why did you do this, Ryker?" I ask before stumbling back into the leather chair against the wall.

"I think I just answered that question, didn't I?"

"Stop. I'm not one of your fucking lackeys you can brush off with that bullshit."

"I thought you'd be happy to see her, to be honest, Kane."

Fuck. He says that like any part of Sophie and me could ever end up anywhere close to happy. This is what happens when men fall in love. They think others should too, even if it's the worst idea they've ever had.

"You should have told me she was coming."

With a shrug, he asks, "Why? So you could come up with some reason why you need to suddenly be somewhere else? No, I need you here."

"That isn't the reason and you know it," I say through gritted teeth, barely controlling my anger at this whole fucking thing he's done.

Ryker lets out a heavy sigh and nods before dropping his arms from his chest. "You're closer to me than nearly anyone in the world. Only Kaia is closer, and in many ways, she doesn't know me like you do. You're like my right hand. I'd be lost without you, Kane. In the same vein, though, that means I know what you've been going through like no one else. You can't stay like you've been for the past few weeks."

I don't bother saying anything to that. Either he's got his head filled with joy from the birth of his son, or he's trying to get back at me for that time I said I wanted Kaia when he was falling in love with her and thought nobody was noticing. It doesn't matter what he's thinking. It won't work.

Happiness and I don't go well together. We never have. We won't this time.

The problem is he's set Sophie up for nothing but disappointment.

Standing, I try to keep my emotions in check as they begin to spiral out of control. "You must not like this girl much, Ryker. I never thought of you as a dick like this, but whatever. I told you what she went through, and still you brought her here. You know who I am and you did this, so when it all fucking falls apart, I hope you have the right words to say to her."

Ryker sighs again. "Kane, say the word and I'll send her away. The family has other houses where she can go to be safe and still not have to deal with Victor and her parents hovering over her like some broken fucking bird. Say the word and she's gone."

God, I want to say that word. I want to use that card that someone who's more like a brother than merely a friend after all we've been through gets and tell him to send her away. To make him see that my past and all he knows about me should have stopped him from ever thinking she should be anywhere near me.

But I can't. Everything I want to say gets trapped in my throat, caught in emotion I hate and know will do nothing but hurt everyone involved.

"Not everyone gets the kind of happiness you have, Ryker. It's a mistake to think someone like me will."

"Do you remember the first time you saved my life?" he asks in a low voice. "Do you remember what I said that night?"

I don't have to think back to that night to remember. That moment in time remains frozen in my mind like some still picture that never leaves me.

"That you'd owe me for the rest of your life."

"And I do for that time and all the other times after that. You are the closest thing I have to someone who knows everything about me, and that includes Kaia.

You're nothing less than my blood brother, Kane. I'd give my life for you, and now that I have a son, I know you understand what those words mean. But I would because you've been the one constant in my life since that night when I was sixteen. I love my brothers and my family, but no one has been there for me like you have. We weren't born brothers, but you are that to me. And because of that, I can't help but want to see you happy. Can you honestly say that you didn't feel some real happiness with her?"

I shake my head at that description of what happened between Sophie and me at that fucking place. If that's happiness, I don't know why anyone would ever wish for it.

"Nothing that happened to her was anything close to happy, Ryker."

"You protected her."

"I protected her because she's a Varens and I committed myself to protecting you and all your family that first night."

Ryker shakes his head and abruptly stands from his chair. Glaring at me, he barks, "You protected her before you even fucking told me they'd grabbed her. By the time I heard about it, she was already in your apartment, safe and sound."

"I don't need a fucking order to do what I'm supposed to, Ryker. I've been working for you long enough that I know what to do. Stop trying to make this something it wasn't."

"And stop acting like you were just doing your job, Kane. I know why you keep this whole suffering lonely guy thing going, but isn't it time to stop? Don't you think you've done enough penance for one moment in an entire lifetime?"

With one question, he cuts to the heart of what's wrong about having Sophie here.

Pacing across his office, I stare him down as my emotions unspool inside me. "Some mistakes don't ever get to be forgiven! You know that as well as I do. Just because you're walking on air and living the fucking dream with Kaia and your new baby doesn't mean you don't know reality, does it?"

"I know no one deserves a life sentence simply for something that went horribly wrong. I knew that before Kaia and Maxim too, so don't blame my wanting some fucking happiness for you on them. Not that you should be ungrateful for them making me think I should do something to bring it about, for fuck's sake!"

Hanging my head, I try to find some sense of calm in the middle of this. Fuck, I miss life before we all decided happiness was a thing bad men got to have.

"This won't turn out well for her, and you know it," I quietly say as I stare at the floor.

"She thinks everyone died that day, you know that? Her father told me Victor just fucking announced what you did when he had them over and she nearly passed out at hearing the news."

I look up at him and say the most honest words I've ever had to. "It would be better off if she believed I was dead."

He and I stare at one another for a long moment

before he asks, "Is there something you didn't tell me about what happened there?"

Ryker has no idea what he's asking. Yes, I told him everything I found out at Duke's the months I was there. That was what I was sent there to do. And I told him the truth about why I killed Tap and the rest of them, something I wasn't ordered to do but did anyway.

Well, almost the truth. He knows about what that fuck did to her and how much I hated the rest of them, enough to kill every single one of them that day.

But he doesn't know what happened between Sophie and me. Ryker is that blood brother he called me. I've put my life on the line for him countless times and will again because it's my duty to him. Sophie and how she made me feel is something else, though. Something sweet I want to keep to myself.

"Don't make this something it isn't. You know me better than anyone in the world. If you care at all for her, you should hope she and I never see one another while she's here."

He sits down behind his desk and lets out a heavy sigh. "You decide how you want to handle things. She's in the east wing and has free run of the estate, so I suspect you'll run into her at some point."

I take a deep breath in and blow the air out of my lungs. "Tell me you have some job for me that will mean I can be gone from here, Ryker."

With a shake of his head, he says what I already know. "You're needed here. What I don't understand is why you want to avoid someone you risked your life to protect. I'm wondering what you left out when you told me about your time at Duke's."

If she was anyone else, I'd tell him every last detail. But she's a Varens, a member of his family, and even more, she's the only woman I ever let in.

The only one I've ever wished I was someone else for.

STARING UP AT THE CEILING ABOVE ME, I TRY TO think of anything but her. The same as every night since I returned here. Is she okay? Fuck, how the hell could she be?

My mind fills with the image of those cuts on her arms from when that fuck Tap carved into her skin. I clench my hands into fists and struggle not to jump out of bed and beat the hell out of something.

Anything.

Anyone.

This is who I am. A violent fucking monster. Instead of thinking of the good moments between us back there, all I can think of doing is hurting someone whenever I remember how broken she looked sitting in that bathroom while I bandaged up her arms.

I try to go back to how she felt next to me or how she made me feel like maybe life wasn't all pain and hurt. I want to relive all of that goodness, but the man I am crowds out all of it, leaving nothing but anger.

Anger at Tap.

Anger at how she was hurt by him.

Anger at how she'll be hurt by me if I don't stay away from her.

Fucking Ryker. Why couldn't he just leave her safe where she was? He knows there's no reason for her to have to be here. Keep her out of danger? Who's going to hurt her? The guy who killed everyone at Duke's is me.

I'm the fucking danger.

Pulling my arm over my eyes, I try to push all of it out of my mind. If I can just get to sleep, maybe I won't have to think about her and how much I fucking miss her.

That won't happen. She got under my skin, and now nothing is the same without her.

I sit up and swing my legs off the bed. East wing, Ryker said. No, I can't do that. I can't get to sleep either, so I may as well go down to the office and do some work since I know he didn't get it done with all the baby watching he's been doing.

On my way out of my room, I grab a black T-shirt and slip it over my head. I glance down the hallway at where Sophie probably sleeps and shake my head.

Bad men don't get to be happy. Not like that.

I head for Ryker's office and correct myself. Bad men like me don't get to be happy like that.

The door is closed, and when I open it, I see the room's dark. Once upon a time, he spent nearly every minute of the day and night in here. How the fuck he plans to move on Victor keeping bankers' fucking hours is beyond me.

Then again, who can blame him? A beautiful

woman to share his bed and a new son make wanting to spend endless time dealing with business the last thing on a man's mind.

All the better that he left so much undone today since I won't be sleeping any tonight. I search through the stack of papers next to the laptop as an idea about how to avoid Sophie hits me like a bolt of lightning. I can just work all night and sleep during the day. It's not like Ryker will need me to do much while the sun's up anyway. Jaxon and Cason handle much of the part of the business that requires day work, and if I need to be available before nightfall, it can be arranged.

Problem solved.

A noise outside in the hallway catches my attention, pulling me from the surveillance photos of Victor and his newest girlfriend, and when I look up, I know nothing's been solved. If anything, life just got a hundred times more difficult.

"King?"

CHAPTER TWENTY-THREE

ophie

MY FEET WON'T MOVE, LIKE THEY'RE ENCASED IN concrete, forcing me to stand there in the doorway to Ryker's office as I stare in at the man seated behind his desk and question whether I'm seeing a ghost or just losing my mind.

"Is it you?" I ask, my voice shaky as my emotions begin to overwhelm me.

His hair is shorter, and the beard is gone, but with every second that passes, I know it's him even before he answers. I want to touch him, to feel his arms around me so I know he's real and not just some wishful figment of my imagination, but I can't move until he speaks.

And then I hear his voice and he's there with me again.

"Sophie…"

I stumble into the office shaking my head in disbelief that he's right here in front of me. "You didn't die. My uncle told me everyone was massacred at Duke's. How did you get away?"

He doesn't answer. He doesn't get up when I stop in front of the desk either. Why is he acting like this? He knows my name. He said it. This is King. Why doesn't he stand up and take me into his arms?

Staring down into his eyes, I see no hint of the green that enchanted me so much. Was I mistaken? Does this man just look like the person I haven't been able to forget since my time at that terrible place?

"Are you him?" I ask as a sob threatens to make speaking impossible. "You look like him. Are you? If you are, why are you acting like this?"

The room falls silent as our gazes lock. I wait so long for him to answer that I question if this is real, if it's happening or if I'm dreaming, but finally he nods and says the words that make my heart soar.

"It's me, Sophie."

"How? Why are you sitting in my uncle's office like you belong here? How did you get out while everyone else died?"

He stands and walks around the side of the desk away from me, like he needs to put some kind of barrier between us. What's happened to make him act like this toward me?

When he turns to face me, I see the unhappiness in his expression and can't understand. Why wouldn't he be as happy to see me as I am to see him?

"Sophie, my name is Kane. I've worked for Ryker for years. I was sent to work for Duke by him."

I hear the words coming out of his mouth, but I can't process them. "So your name isn't King? You work for Ryker?"

"Yes. I've worked for your family since I was fifteen," he says in a low voice. "I couldn't tell you my real name when we were at Duke's."

A million questions swirl around in my head, but one surges to the forefront. "Why don't you seem happy to see me?"

His face twists into a look of pure anguish before he shakes his head. "It's not like that."

"Then what's it like?" I ask as I begin walking toward where he stands on the other side of the desk.

He backs away from me, but a leather chair stops him. I reach out to touch his arm, needing to feel him against my skin again, and he reacts by wincing, like I'm causing him pain.

"Why are you acting like this, King?"

His dark gaze meets mine, and he answers, "Kane."

"Fine! Why are you acting this way, Kane? Why are you acting like you don't even know me? Like you haven't thought of me not even once since that day you took me home from that horrible place? Because I've thought of you. When I heard everyone there had been killed, I felt like someone tightened their fist around my heart and squeezed so hard that my chest hurt. Now I see you alive and well and you don't even want to be near me. Why?"

I wait to hear his answer, but he stays silent. Hurt and anger twist inside me, but I can't keep them inside anymore and lash out at him.

"Say something! What happened to the man who held me in his arms and cared for me? Or is that your job you do here for Ryker? Is that it, Kane? Do you have the job of rescuing women on my uncle's order and then you don't give a fuck once they're safe? Tell me, do you include as part of your knight in shining armor service fucking them, or was I special? No, I guess I wasn't special since you can't even stand the idea of being next to me, much less showing me you gave one fucking damn about me!"

My words fly out of my mouth like bullets, each attack hitting him just like I want. I watch him wince once and then twice just before I finish, but still he says nothing.

I want to hit him. To hurt him like he's hurting me. I thought he cared during those days he kept me. Kept me safe. Kept me his.

Tears burn my eyes, but I won't let him see me cry. Fuck him. He can't have my tears now. I'm not that captive girl in this house. Here, I'm free to do as I want, so I run out of Ryker's office away from the man I've missed for weeks.

By the time I reach my room, I can't keep up the pretense of being strong anymore. My emotions take over, and I collapse into a heap onto the bed. I've wished to see him, thought about what it would be like if I ever could and then silently mourned his death, and now that I see he's alive but doesn't want me like I want him, all I have left is humiliation and sadness.

The door flies open, startling me, and the next thing I know, there he is standing in front of me. Gone is the tortured expression he wore just a minute ago. Now it's replaced by that look I remember all too well from those hours we spent together.

But still he has no words for me.

"Go away, whatever your name is."

"Sophie…"

I leap up from the bed and rush at him, pressing my flattened palms against his muscular chest to force him to go. I want the man who cared for me standing here, not this person who seems like a hollowed out version of him.

"Go away! Stop saying my name and then nothing else! I get it. You lied. For whatever reason, you lied when you made me believe I meant something to you. Joke's on me. I get it. Just go."

His gaze drifts down over my arms to where my hands sit on his chest. "I didn't lie."

He says those three words so quietly I almost don't hear them. I stop pushing against him and take a deep breath in, trying to control my emotions as they continue to unravel.

"Then why do you act like I'm some stranger you don't know?"

I hate how weak I sound when I ask that, but I need to know. Was I the only one who felt something in those days we spent together?

"You don't know me, Sophie. I'm not that man

here," he says flatly, like he has no emotion to spend on his answer.

Or is he trying to contain how he feels like I am?

I move my right hand so it's covering his heart and feel it beating beneath my touch. "Why would you be anyone other than the man you were at that place? Why aren't you that man here?"

"Because I can't be."

I don't understand anything he's saying. God, all I want is to feel his arms around me again.

"Don't you miss me?"

He winces again, like I'm hurting him. "We can't be, Sophie. We just can't. I'm not the man I was before. Here I'm someone else."

Covering my face, I don't hold back the tears anymore. "You were the only part of that whole terrible thing I didn't hate. Why are you saying these things? Is it because of my family? Is that it?"

I drop my hands to see him shaking his head. "Then why?"

"I can't explain it, Sophie. Just know that you're better off without me."

Each word stings so much that I want to lash out and hurt him, so I push hard against his chest and yell, "I wish you had died at that place! I wish whoever killed the rest of those fucking monsters had killed you too!"

His dark eyes fill with hurt for just a second, and then it's like he hardens over. "Have a good life, Sophie."

He turns to leave, hesitating for the briefest

moment, but I don't stop him. This person isn't my King. I don't know who this man is.

TILTING MY HEAD BACK, I FEEL THE SUN ON MY FACE warming my skin while I sit on a bench in the very fancy garden on the estate. I'm more of a wildflower kind of girl, so the regimented lines of this place feel too formal to me, but I can't deny how relaxing it is to sit in the midday sun as I try to forget everything that happened last night.

My chest aches at the thought of King now. Not King. Kane. A simple change of name and he's a completely different man. Must be nice. I don't have that option, so I'm left with my memories of him back at Duke's and wishing I'd never let myself care for him.

The sound of a flip-flop tears me from my daydreaming, and I open my eyes to see a beautiful brunette slowly walking toward where I sit. Her hair sits in a loose bun on the top of her head, making her look disheveled, and her jeans shorts and pink T-shirt make her look casual and relaxed.

I quickly stand up and smile, sure this must be Kaia. "Hi! I was just taking advantage of the beautiful setting and the sun."

She stops in front of me and smiles as she extends her hand. "I'm Kaia. Ryker told me you'd arrived a couple days ago. I'm so sorry I haven't had a chance to see you before this, but after giving birth to Maxim, I felt like I could sleep for a month. When I saw you from my window, I wanted to come down and say hi. I get the feeling you're a girl after my own heart. I love this garden too. It's one of my favorite spots on the estate."

I shake her hand and return the smile. "I was just thinking it's a little more ordered than I usually like in my flowers, but it is beautiful. I remember my grandmother loved this garden."

"Ryker's told me that. He doesn't like it much at all and rarely comes out here, so I'm usually the only person to spend time here. Well, me and the landscapers."

She chuckles, putting me at ease, and motions toward the bench behind me. "How about we sit down and get to know one another?"

We take our spots on the seat and begin talking. Within minutes, I understand why my uncle is so crazy about her. Kind and funny, she's sweet and just what I need to soothe my sore feelings today.

Taking a deep breath in, she lets the air out slowly and tilts her head back to look up at the sun. "I love how natural it smells here. Every time I come out to this garden, I feel rejuvenated."

"I could use that today," I say before mirroring her to inhale a deep breath of the garden's air. It's a hot and humid day, but the sweetness of what may be honeysuckle registers in my brain.

"I hope you won't feel like I'm intruding, but Ryker told me all you've been through. Thank God Kane was there to keep you safe."

The air in my lungs leaves my body in a frustrated rush. "I guess."

Kaia doesn't respond to my lackluster opinion of Ryker's second in command. Instead, she lowers her gaze and turns to look directly at me.

"Do you know the story of how I came to be here?"

Shaking my head, I smile, hoping she doesn't think I'm impolite when I say, "No. In fact, I don't know how my uncle could meet anyone wearing that mask."

A sweet giggle from her tells me my comment didn't offend. "I guess it's a bit intimidating. I've gotten so used to seeing him in it that I don't think twice about it. He doesn't wear it when we're alone, so I don't see it much anymore. But he did wear it when I first met him."

"That only makes me more curious. Like, was he out at a club and wearing that? I guess that could be intriguing. It certainly would set him apart from the hoard of guys who go to bars."

She shakes her head and smiles broadly. "No, we didn't meet at a club. We met when my husband gave me to Ryker to pay off his debt to him."

My mouth drops open in shock. "Oh my God. What kind of man does that to a woman he married?"

"Not a good one. Definitely not a good one. And I wasn't exactly given the royal treatment when I arrived here. I was a captive to a terrifying man in a mask."

I don't know what to say to her. This story sounds horrifying. I know I shouldn't ask, but I can't stop myself from wondering aloud how they moved from that to being in love with a new baby boy.

"What happened that things changed to how you two are now?"

Her smile lights up her face as she answers, "We fell in love. We didn't start out like anything that could be considered love, but it happened. I got to know the man behind the mask and realized I didn't want to be with anyone but him."

"You were lucky it was Ryker. If it was my other uncle, I can only imagine what might have happened. You got the good Varens. Well, other than my father."

Nodding, she says, "Oh, I know. I shudder to think of what might have happened if the people my husband got into debt with weren't as good as Ryker. I know what he does, but there's good in him."

"Oh, I know. Ryker is more like my father than Victor. He's awful. You're with the better brother, for sure. And you don't have to make excuses for what he does. I know what the Varens family is, even if my father isn't involved in the family business."

For nearly a minute, she doesn't say anything else and I worry I've said something wrong. I truly don't hold what Ryker or even my Uncle Victor do for a living against them. Maybe I should, but it's been a part of life in my family for so long that I don't give it a second thought.

As I struggle to find the right words to apologize and break the silence, Kaia says, "I guess I thought you weren't happy about what Kane did for you because of what he and Ryker are. If that's not it, then why don't you seem to like him?"

I let my gaze drop to the brick pathway and shrug. "I thought he was a different person. The man I met at that place cared for me, but now that I'm here, he barely has a word to say to me. I let myself feel something for him, but obviously, he didn't feel the same for me once everything was over. No happy ending for me like you and Ryker, I guess."

"Oh. Well, Kane is different than Ryker. His past is very different. I don't know everything about it, but from what Ryker has told me, he's been through a lot."

That doesn't explain why he seems so disinterested in me now that I'm not being held captive, but I nod and force a smile. "I guess."

"Have you tried to speak to him?"

"Yeah, but it didn't go well. I'm thinking it would be better if I go home, to be honest," I admit sadly. "You and Ryker are very nice to let me come here, but I think I should leave."

Kaia covers my hand with hers, a gentle expression of her sympathy for me. "I'm sorry to hear that, but please know you can come here any time. I know we just met, but I like you. You're a breath of fresh air compared to all the men who are always here."

I look over at her and laugh. "A real sausage fest, huh? I like you too. You're sweet, and you clearly are crazy about Ryker. I like that. The last time I saw him before this I would have bet he'd be alone forever. He seemed so cold and surly behind that mask. I'm glad you two found your way to one another."

As soon as the words come out of my mouth, I know I should apologize. "I'm sorry. I didn't mean I'm glad your ex-husband gave you away to someone. I definitely didn't mean that."

Kaia shakes her head and gives me one of her gentle smiles. "No, I know what you meant, and he's not my ex-husband. He died before I could divorce his rotten ass."

"Oh."

I don't know what else to say about that. I have a feeling I know without asking that he didn't die of natural causes. Ryker may be a good man to those he loves, but to those he doesn't, he's very much like my other uncle.

"Well, I better go back inside. It's just a few minutes difference between sun-kissed and red as a lobster for me," she says as she stands to leave. "Remember, the offer to come here and stay whenever you want is open-ended."

"Thanks so much. Now might not be the right time for me to be here, but maybe in the future."

"Whenever you want. Be sure to stop in and see the baby before you leave."

"I will. Thanks!"

After she takes only two steps back toward the house, Kaia turns around wearing a far more serious expression than just a second ago. "I don't know if you know this, but it was Kane who took out all those men at Duke's because of what they did to you. Ryker told me he didn't order him to do that. That was all Kane.

From what I heard they did to you, they had it coming, though."

Left alone in the garden, I can't help but wonder why the man who can't even be bothered to speak to me now was willing to kill anyone to avenge what they did to me.

 ophie

I WANDER AROUND THE ESTATE FOR AN HOUR OR SO enjoying how good it feels to be outside. The late July heatwave finally broken, the temperature hits the mid-eighties, but compared to the near hundreds we had for days, this weather is downright delightful. Ryker's home and expansive grounds give me a chance to have the freedom I hadn't been able to have even after returning home weeks ago. My parents watched over me day and night, so even a walk around the block meant I couldn't be alone.

As I linger near a large tree enjoying the shade from the afternoon sun, I hear someone calling my name. Turning toward the sound, I see my cousin Jaxon walking across the grass coming from the house.

I can't help but notice how similar he looks to Ryker now. The dark hair and way he wears a suit like it's the only thing natural for him, he strides across the lawn like he owns the place.

It's been a long time since the two of us were children and his father would bring him over to our house to visit. Nearly as much older as my uncle to me, Jaxon always seemed younger because he was willing to play with a little girl, even when he was a teenager.

"Little Sophie, I heard you were here. Did you come to see the new Varens?" he asks with a chuckle and opens his arms to hug me.

I rest my cheek on his chest, the expensive Italian suit gently brushing against my skin and reminding me of his father. Maybe I'd been wrong in my initial opinion a minute before. Perhaps he looks more like him than Ryker.

When he releases me from our embrace, he steps back and shakes his head. "I can't believe little Sophie is all grown up. How are you?"

I force a bigger smile than I feel like giving at the moment and tug on my sleeves to make sure they cover all the way to my wrists. "I'm okay. You know, after everything."

His smile fades as he nods somberly. "Fucking Duke Cantorini. He and all those son of a bitches got what they had coming to them, thanks to Kane. We're all just glad he was there to watch over you."

A fleeting thought about what Kane actually told everyone about exactly what he did to watch over me at that place makes me consider asking Jaxon, but I dismiss that as quickly as it comes. My cousin isn't that boy who played tag with me anymore. He's a grown man in the Varens family business and likely wouldn't be willing to tell me much of anything about what goes on.

"So you work for Ryker?" I ask, eager to change the subject, even a little.

Jaxon shrugs. "Him. Victor. I bounce back and forth, especially since Cason only works for this side of the family now."

I shake my head, unsure what he means by that. "This side of the family? I thought it was all Varens family business. I didn't realize there were sides."

"Oh, trust me. There are definitely sides in this family, and if Uncle Victor doesn't start understanding things can't be like they've always been, the situation is going to get ugly and soon."

The darkness in Jaxon's expression frightens me. "Ugly? What do you mean?"

Leaning in toward me, he whispers, "This family can't have two heads like it does now. One has to go. Willingly or unwillingly. I expect that things are going to get hot very soon."

None of this makes sense to me, but my instincts tell me this can't be good for anyone, especially Kane. Things getting hot may mean he'll have to do something like he did at Duke's for Ryker.

Something that may get him hurt or killed.

"When is this going to happen?" I ask, my heart racing at the thought of Kane in danger.

But Jaxon is through sharing his opinion and simply smiles. "Don't worry, Sophie. We'll get through whatever happens. We Varens always do, right? Be sure to look for Cason. He and his girlfriend live in the carriage house with their kid Lukas, and I know he'd love to see you. I have to get back to work, but I'll see you again."

He walks away before I can ask him more about what might happen, leaving me anxious and wanting to talk to Kane more than ever. Whatever happens, I can't let him go to battle for my family without him knowing that I didn't mean what I said last night.

I don't wish he died with Duke and his men. I said that to be cruel, but now after what Jaxon told me, I know I have to try at least one more time with Kane.

AFTER TWELVE PASSES UP AND DOWN THE HALLWAY outside of Ryker's office, he appears in the doorway on my thirteenth time and lowers his mask into his hand before smiling at me. "Do you need something, Sophie?"

Feeling foolish, I lie. "I was just getting the lay of the place. You know, it's big. It takes some getting used to."

"Oh, okay. I thought you might have been looking for me." He stops for a moment and then adds, "Or someone else."

I feel my cheeks heat from a blush and shake my head. "No. Not looking for anyone in particular. Just checking everything out. I'm sorry if I disturbed you."

His knowing smile tells me he doesn't buy a word of my poorly constructed excuse for lingering in this hallway for the last twenty minutes. "Not at all."

Looking around for some escape, I point toward the staircase. "Maybe I could go up to see Kaia and Maxim."

"I'm sure they'd love to see you. I think he's up from his afternoon nap by now."

As subtly as I can, I ask, "Do all the people who live here have rooms up on the second floor? I mean, I know I do and you and Kaia and the baby do, although Jaxon told me Cason and Lily and their baby live in the carriage house, so I guess not."

So much for being sly with that question. Rambling is not subtle in the least.

"Thinking of pacing the full length of the hallway up there?" he asks, cocking a dark eyebrow in what looks like an expression of how much he doesn't believe my question is merely idle curiosity.

Before I can think of an answer, he smiles in that way that makes him look kind and points toward the end of the hallway opposite from where we stand. "I think the room you're looking for is in that direction. It's the last door before the stairs."

Ryker turns away and walks back into his office, thankfully saving me from having to claim I wasn't looking for anyone in particular. I hurry away as I wonder how much he knows about what happened between Kane and me, and as I race up the stairs, I hope he didn't get every last detail.

Men say they don't gossip, but I know better. I can only pray Kane didn't tell Ryker everything.

I reach the top of the stairs and see the door to Kane's room. Closed, it feels like a symbol of him now. Somehow I'd imagined maybe it might be open so I could just knock quickly and then walk in.

So much for things being easy. But I can't let what I said yesterday remain without telling him I didn't mean that.

Lifting my hand to knock on the door, I see my fingers shaking. As much as I feared him at times at Duke's estate, now he terrifies me more because of how distant he's been. I don't know if I can handle him being so cold again.

I lightly tap on the wooden door in front of me and whisper, "Please be here and be the man you were."

The words barely leave my lips before he's standing in front of me wearing only a pair of jeans. My gaze moves up his muscular body to his stern expression, but in his eyes are hints of what I hoped for a moment ago.

He doesn't say a word, so I smile and ask, "May I come in?"

My heart races as my question hangs heavy in the air between us for a moment before he steps back to allow me into his room. Decorated almost exactly like mine with cream colored walls and dark curtains on the windows that match a navy blue bedspread, it should feel familiar but it doesn't.

Because of him. Because he's not the King I fell in love with back at that place.

Kane closes the door behind me as I survey the room and wonder what to say next to get him to speak to me. I turn around to see him walk past me toward the bathroom and remember that last night we spent together after he bandaged me up from what Tap did.

Instinctively, I pull the bottoms of my sleeves down past my wrists to hide the scars. When I look up, he's watching me, his gaze practically searing a hole through me.

"Can we could talk?" I say quietly.

"It's got to be nearly eighty degrees out. Why are you wearing a long sleeve shirt?" he asks with such coldness that I wince.

Why is he asking a question he already knows the answer to?

Hanging my head, I tell him what he wants to hear. "I always wear long sleeves now."

Before I know it, he's marching over to where I stand and grabbing my wrists. I look up in horror as he pulls up the white fabric covering my forearms and stares down at them. The scars from the words Tap carved into my skin have begun to fade, but the S in SLUT and N in CUNT are still clearly visible.

Kane's gaze moves back and forth from one arm to the other, and then he looks up at me. "This is why we can't talk. It's why you shouldn't be here in this house. Why you should be safe in your own house away from all of this, Sophie."

His deep voice breaks when he says my name, and in his eyes, I see the same look of hurt and anger I saw that night he crouched down in front of me and cleaned me up after rescuing me from Tap's basement. If what happened bothers him so much, why won't he show me an ounce of kindness like he did that night?

I open my mouth to ask him that very question, but the words get stuck in my throat when he tenderly runs his thumb over my ruined skin. My emotions are on the verge of unraveling all over the place at the very touch of his hand on me, a touch so filled with love and care.

"Please talk to me, Kane."

But he doesn't. Instead, he dips his head and presses his lips to those scars on my right arm, kissing them softly. I watch with tears in my eyes for how gentle he can be.

"There's nothing to talk about, Sophie," he whispers before lightly kissing the scar on my left arm.

"Yes, there is," I insist, unable to control my emotions anymore as I tear my arms from his hold. "Please, just talk to me. Is it that you're angry that I said I wished you died last night? I didn't mean that. I'm sorry."

"I don't blame you for saying that. You should hate me and everyone else at that fucking place for what happened to you."

I reach out to grab his arm, afraid if I don't he'll walk away again. His skin is warm and instantly I'm transported back to the time we spent together in his apartment so far from this house.

"But I don't hate you! Why won't you listen to

me? I keep trying to tell you I miss you. I love you. My heart was broken when I thought you were dead, and then it was like it fused back together and began beating again when I saw you in Ryker's office."

In his eyes, I see how he truly feels, even if he won't admit it. He misses me like I miss him.

"Why aren't your eyes green at all now?"

My question catches him off guard. "Contacts. I had to look different enough, so my hair was longer and I had green contacts," he explains with a sigh, like he's exhausted from being someone he truly isn't.

"Did you feel anything for me, or was that fake too?" I ask, even as the real fear that he'll finally admit it was all an act settles inside me.

Kane doesn't answer at first, and with every second that ticks by, the hurt grows more and more. Finally, he shakes his head and frowns. "Don't do this, Sophie."

"Don't do what?"

"Don't ruin what we were by thinking it wasn't real. It was."

"Then why can't it be that way now? You say you're different here, but how could that be a bad thing? You're accepted here for who you are. Is it that you think Ryker wouldn't approve of us being together? Because he was the one who told me where your room was."

Shaking his head, Kane steps back away from me. "Ryker needs to stop thinking everyone gets what he has."

"What do you mean? Like someone who loves him

even though when she first got here he was just a man in a mask holding her against her will? If they can be happy, why can't we?"

Kane rolls his eyes. "Christ, it must be something in the Varens blood. You and I aren't like Ryker and Kaia. That was completely different."

I can't go on fighting him like this. All I want is to have his arms around me holding me tightly to him.

Pressing my hand to his chest, I let myself revel in how incredible he feels. Closing my eyes, I say the one thing I need him to know. "Kane, I love you."

He takes me into his arms, and for the first time since that last night we spent together, happiness fills me. I open my eyes and look at him and see he feels the same way.

"Sophie, I love you, but we can't be together here or anywhere. I can't put you in danger like that. You mean too much to me."

And with those words, my sadness rushes back.

"Why? Doesn't it matter that we love each other?"

He kisses me softly on the forehead and sighs. "That's why we can't. I love you too much to do that to you."

As much as I want to stay there in his arms, I push him away and shake my head. "We have a chance to be happy, and you won't take it. All your talk about loving me and then you say you don't want to be with me? No. You don't get to have it both ways."

He hangs his head and sighs. "That's the only way it can be."

Before my tears overwhelm me, I run out of his

room and down the hall toward mine. I can't do this anymore. I have to leave this place or I'll never be able to get over him.

Even if I'll never stop loving him.

CHAPTER TWENTY-FIVE

ane

FOR THREE DAYS, I'VE BEEN SUCCESSFUL IN avoiding Sophie. It's all for the best. My sleep schedule is fucked up, but once she leaves, everything will go back to normal.

I roll over in bed and look at my phone. 8:50. A little late, but nothing too bad. If Ryker needed me, he would have called, so it'll be fine. Even better, getting to the office at nine will probably mean I won't have to deal with anyone tonight since there's nothing planned.

A quick shower and I'm ready for work, so I throw on jeans and a T-shirt, another benefit of working at night since unlike everyone else, I have no interest in wearing a fucking suit all the damn time. Everyone else can act like we're in some remake of Reservoir Dogs, but I'll stick to clothes I like.

By nine o'clock, I head down the stairs and make my way to Ryker's office, expecting to find it dark. Before I even reach the doorway, I know that isn't the case, though. Who the fuck is working this late?

I spy Ryker sitting behind his desk and breathe a sigh of relief. Maybe we're back to doing our jobs like we're supposed to?

"What's going on? Did Kaia throw you out of the nursery?" I ask with a chuckle.

He laughs, which is good since we've been on edge with one another way too much lately. "No, and fuck you. Just wait until you have a child. Then you'll understand why I want to be around him all the time."

Sitting down hard on the leather chair in front of him, I lean back and relax. "Okay, well then why are you still here at this time of night? If you haven't been expelled from Maxim gazing, why aren't you upstairs with him and Kaia?"

"I had some things to finish up, and I waited to talk to you. I have something I need you to do tonight."

Curious, I lean forward and rest my elbows on my knees. "I'm all ears. I don't remember seeing we had anything planned for tonight. What's up?"

"Well, I haven't seen much of you since you decided to be exclusively a nocturnal creature, so I didn't have a chance to tell you Sophie's leaving."

Just hearing her name makes my heart skip a beat, but I don't want him or anyone else to know the effect even talking about her has on me, so I work to keep my reaction as subdued as possible. With a shrug, I say, "Okay. What does that have to do with what we're doing tonight?"

"Not we. You. I want you to take her home. She's all packed and ready to go."

I hang my head and sigh. "Have Jaxon do it. Have Ivan do it. I'm not her personal driver."

"You drive me around all the time, Kane. What's the difference?" Ryker asks with a hint of amusement in his voice.

Why he's enjoying this I have no idea.

My gaze meets his and I see the skin around his eyes creasing from a smile that's hidden by his skull mask. "That's different, and you know it. I'm sure Jaxon would like to spend some time with her. They're cousins, so I bet they have a lot to catch up on."

"No," Ryker says flatly as he shakes his head. "You're the one I want to drive her. Victor's going to have someone watching her house from now on, but I want to make sure she arrives home safely. After you get back, feel free to take the night off."

"Safe from who? I fucking killed them all, Ryker."

"You didn't get that one guy, so you didn't get them all."

My mouth drops open in shock. "Stills? That old fuck isn't giving anyone payback. He's probably holed up in his house shitting his pants and wondering if I'm coming back to get him. You and Victor don't have to worry about Stills, although I owe him for messing up my leg when he stitched me up, that asshole."

"This is how Victor wants to play it, so humor me. Drive her home, make sure she gets into her house safely, and then you can have the night off."

"Since when do we give a fuck about how Victor wants to play things anyway? Aren't you hard at work consolidating your power against him, or has that plan been tossed out the window now?"

I stop myself from saying now that you have everything you've ever wanted in life with Kaia and Maxim. It would only sound jealous, and that isn't how I want it to come off.

Ryker folds his arms behind him and tilts his head back to stare up at the ceiling, almost as if he's looking up toward the two most important people in his world now, before leveling his gaze on me. "Nothing's changed. Victor's days as the head of this family are numbered. I just haven't decided what that number is yet."

"So this placating thing with him isn't something you believe in? Because you can trust me, Ryker. She's not in any danger from Stills."

"I do trust you, Kane. Never more than I do right now. But this is how he wants to run this thing with Sophie, so take her home and make sure she's tucked into bed and all her doors are locked, okay? I figured you'd be happy that she's leaving. At least then you don't have to live like a fucking vampire anymore."

As much as I'm pissed he's forcing me to drive Sophie back to her house, I have to laugh. I should have known he wouldn't have missed the real reason why I changed my schedule.

"Fuck you, and maybe I like nights better."

"Well, I like you around during the day, so enough of this Kane after dark shit, okay? Take the night off when you return and be back here in the morning."

"Fine. Have her down at the car in ten," I say as I head toward the door.

"Cheer up, Kane. It's not like I'm ordering you to kill anyone, for Christ's sake. It's just a car ride."

I don't bother responding to any of that. I'm not interested in cheering up, and I'd rather kill someone than have to do this.

Fuck. The last thing I want to do is spend an hour alone with Sophie. Why the hell is Ryker continuing to play fucking Cupid like this?

CHECKING THE CLOCK IN THE SUV, I SEE IT'S BEEN nearly fifteen minutes since I left Ryker's office. I feel like some kind of fucking chauffeur. Forget about all I do for this goddamned organization. Tonight, I've been relegated to driver for anyone who wants to go for a fucking joyride.

The passenger side back door opens, and without even a hello, Sophie climbs in with her suitcase. I guess it might have been nice if I waited outside to help her with that. She struggles with the bag, grunting and groaning until she finally sets it down hard on the seat next to her.

I watch all of this in the rearview mirror and don't

look away fast enough when she gets settled. With a simple glance, she flashes me her hatred and then follows it up by mumbling, "You're a real great guy, Kane. Maybe you'd like it if I was forced to run beside the car all the way home. You're probably the kind of guy who ties dogs to the back bumper and then drives away."

As that horrifying thought crosses my mind, I shake my head. "I love animals, so no, I would never do that to a dog."

Sophie quickly picks up on how I never said anything about her running beside the car, something I also would never do. Huffing in disgust, she mumbles, "Real humanitarian."

When I start the car, she screams, "Stop! I forgot something!" and throws the car door open to jump out. I watch her run back toward the house and disappear as my irritation grows by the second.

She didn't forget anything. This is just her way to grate on my nerves. Reason number 8577 why women don't belong in my world.

Three minutes later, she climbs back into the SUV and says sweetly, "Okay. You can drive now."

I glance back at her in the rearview mirror and see a smug look on her face, like I'm merely some hired hand who works for her family and she's deigned to be kind to me, the help. I put the car in gear and press on the gas, just wanting to get this over with.

"I'm not your personal chauffeur, Sophie. I'm just doing this as a favor to Ryker. Don't get this confused in your head."

Why I say any of that I have no idea. Maybe if she hadn't treated me like some mere driver I wouldn't have.

Her response only serves to make things worse, though.

"A, you do seem to be my personal chauffeur, Kane, since you're the man driving me as I sit in the back seat, and B, don't you worry about my head one bit. I know exactly what you are, so there's not an ounce of confusion with me. Now if you don't mind, I'm going to be relaxing back here with my headphones, so you don't have to bother saying another word because I won't hear you."

I open my mouth to snap back at her, but nothing comes out. When was the last time anyone—male or female—put me in my place like that? I can't remember. At least I can't remember the last time I let something like that happen without pulling my gun on the person. Leave it to Sophie to make me speechless even as I want to stop this car and show her exactly who the hell she's dealing with.

Just drive. What the fuck do I care about her not wanting to talk to me or treating me like some help her family employs to cart her sweet ass around? After tonight, we'll both be back where we belong in the world and things will go back to normal.

As much as I wish they didn't have to.

Shaking my head, I try to push that thought out of my mind. It doesn't matter that Ryker has Kaia and Maxim and Cason has Lily and Lukas. I still don't think this life we all lead has room for women and love and kids, no matter what those two seem to think. Our world is full of danger and death. Adding to those protecting a woman or kids means we lose focus. I can't afford that.

Not that it doesn't seem nice to have someone who cares for you at the end of the day. And to have someone who helps you forget all the ugly and terrible shit we see in this job wouldn't be bad. I get that.

I watch as a car passes by and glance back at Sophie sitting there with her eyes closed listening to music. She looks just like she did when I'd wake up in the middle of the night and see her sleeping next to me in my bed at Duke's. There in the moonlight streaming through the window, she was like an angel beside me. As much as I protected her, she made me feel like my existence wasn't merely that death that surrounds me so often.

She made me wish I could have more.

But I can't. Some people don't get that kind of life. Karma or whatever the fuck it is that shows you the truth of what you've done makes that known, even to those of us who wonder if someone like Sophie might be something we could have.

Anyone who gets close to me has to be strong. Those who aren't suffer or die. That's what my history shows. My family found that out too late. Ryker knows that, despite the fact that he seems to want to play matchmaker.

Sophie shouldn't have to be that strong to be loved. She deserves a man who will spoil her so she forgets that time she spent at Duke's. Not that I wouldn't try to do that. I'd give her anything she wanted. I'd fucking kill for her. Again. But it's not the same as what she could have with a man who doesn't live the life I do.

Some nice guy who has a normal job. Who wants to go to the movies with her. Some nice guy who doesn't face the threat of dying at the end of some enemy's gun more often than he'd like.

An audible groan escapes my throat as I think about this nice guy. I fucking hate that guy. He better treat her right when she lets him into her life or I swear to God I'm going to fucking rip him apart.

I look up toward the rearview mirror and see her looking at me, those dark eyes of hers full of the sadness I saw in one form or another for those ten days we spent together. My chest contracts at seeing it, but it's just proof that I'm right.

She and I can't be together because she'd have that sadness more than any kind of happiness I could try to give her. Better for her to go home tonight and forget me.

Even if I'll never be able to do that with her.

By the time I reach her house, I'm exhausted from thinking. Thinking of how much I wish things were different. How much I wish I wasn't the man I am. How much I can't change the way life is.

How much I'm going to miss her. Again.

I stop the car and turn the engine off, ready to be the good guy as she leaves that I should have been back at the estate. Turning in my seat to tell her I'll get her bag, I see her jump out and slam the door.

And there goes my chance to say goodbye. It's probably better off this way.

Yet as I watch her walk up the sidewalk to her front door, I can't help but wish there was any way we could be together.

I wait for her to turn around so I can wave and smile like a normal person seeing someone they love walking away, but she doesn't give me that either. The front door slams behind her, and with it, the last chance for Sophie and me.

Just like the last time I watched her walk out of my life, I feel lost as soon as she's gone. My chest feels like whoever was carving out my heart with that dull knife finally finished the job, leaving me hollow.

And just like that time, I say the same thing to myself this time. "It's better off this way."

With one last look at the house, I wait for the light in her living room to flicker on and blow the air out of my lungs. "Have a good life, Sophie."

CHAPTER TWENTY-SIX

ane

I PUT THE CAR INTO DRIVE, BUT OUT OF THE CORNER of my eye, I see something strange. Turning to look at Sophie's house, I see the light flash off and on again once and then twice. Something's wrong. I feel it in my gut.

Jamming the car into park, I jump out and rush up her sidewalk to the front porch. A sound like crying hits my ears and makes my blood run cold.

Sophie's crying.

A second later, I throw open the front door and tear into the house to see Stills standing next to the kitchen counter holding Sophie to him and a gun to her head. I pull my Glock and aim it squarely for his forehead.

"Let her go, man. This doesn't end well for you if she's hurt. Trust me."

Stills flashes me a look that says he knows how bad this is going to end. My fear is he's accepted his fate and thinks he can set Sophie's too.

Not today, old man. Today, I finish what I started back at that fucking shithole.

"I should have known you'd be close by. From the second this bitch showed up, you changed. The King we all knew and trusted turned into a fucking pussy because of her."

For a moment, I take my eyes off Stills and his ugly face to look at Sophie. She's terrified and looks like she's about to burst into tears at any moment.

"It's okay, Sophie. He's not going to hurt you or he knows what I'll do to him."

"The same thing you did to everyone else, you fucking traitor!" Stills barks, frightening Sophie.

"Then you know what I'll do to you, so let her go. She's no part of your gripe with me. Let her go now, Stills, and you may not have to deal with the Varens family hounding you day and night for the rest of your life."

Tightening his hold on her, he squeezes her hard so she screams. The sound cuts through me like a knife.

"Shut up, bitch!"

"Let her go, man. I'm the traitor. Kill me, not her," I say calmly as I quickly scan the room for anything to change this situation to my benefit.

Right now, he's got a gun pressed to her temple and I've got mine aimed directly at the center of his forehead. I'm a good shot, but Sophie's too close for me to risk taking that shot and him moving her even an inch or two so she gets it and he doesn't.

"I get Tap, but why Marsh and Duke?" he asks, his voice cracking on both his friends' names.

"Let her go and I'll tell you everything you want to know. She's not part of this, Stills. You know that. Just let her go and take your shot at me. I'm the one you want to kill, right? You want me to feel what Marsh felt. She didn't kill them all. I did."

On the counter, I see a pair of scissors on top of a pile of mail. It's within her reach, but I need to make her know they're there and to keep Stills right where he is. If he moves even half a foot, she won't be able to grab them.

Sophie's teary gaze meets mine, and I glance over toward the counter for a brief second before returning my focus to Stills. I hope she understood.

"I'm going to kill her and then you, fucker," he snaps at me. "She gets it just for causing trouble, and you get it for what you did. We trusted you, King. Every day for nearly a year we worked with you. I sewed you up more times than I can count. So did fucking Marsh! And how did you pay us back? A fucking bullet. Well, now that's what you and this bitch get."

I see Sophie side-eye the counter and then look at me with recognition in her eyes. She knows what I want her to do. Now we just need Stills to loosen his hold on her just a little.

"Then kill me first," I say, hoping he'll take me up

on my offer and move to change his aim. That should give her the space to grab the scissors and stab him with them, even if he does get off a shot at me.

Stills seems to consider the idea, and for the briefest moment, he drops his arm holding Sophie. I open my mouth to yell for her to get the scissors, but the words never get the chance to come out before she spins in his hold, grabs them, and then a second later spins back around. With more force than I can believe she possesses, she buries them in his neck.

He screams out in pain, but only for a second as blood gushes from his wound and he drops to the floor. Sophie staggers back from him, slamming into my chest, as stunned as I am at the scene in front of us.

Turning to look at me, she screams and pushes against my chest. "He was going to kill me! I felt the gun against my head. I saw you look at the scissors and knew what you wanted me to do. Oh my God, Kane! I thought he was going to kill me!"

Shaking her head wildly, she's terrified and stuck in fight mode. I know how she feels. I remember the first person I killed and know just what she's going through.

But I can't have her yelling and attracting attention from her neighbors, so I clamp my palm over her mouth to stifle the noise and hold her tightly to my body. "Sophie, it's me. Kane," I whisper in her ear. "It's okay, baby. You're okay. He's not going to hurt you anymore. I'm here, Sophie. I'm right here holding you."

She tries to talk, but nothing makes sense through her sobs. Her body shakes uncontrollably against mine, but I don't let go because I know she'll likely collapse if I do.

"It's okay, Sophie. I got you."

Her arms flail in front of her, and she begins to hyperventilate, so I spin her around and cradle her face in my hands. Stills' blood covers her, but in her brown eyes, I see the same Sophie I fell in love with.

"I'm here, Sophie. You were so strong. So brave. I know men who wouldn't have been able to do what you did, baby. You're okay. I'm here."

Her tears roll down her cheeks, creating pale streams through the stain of blood on her face. Nodding, she frowns as she tries to speak.

"He had the gun...I saw you look over on the counter...I saw the scissors."

As I suspected, she doesn't have the strength to stand and collapses against my body, but I've got her. Holding her to me, I set my gun down on the counter and grab my phone out of my pocket.

Ryker answers a few seconds later, but I don't give him a chance to make small talk. "I need Jaxon and Cason out at Sophie's house. Ivan, too. Hell, send everyone out. We've got a mess here that needs to be handled."

"What do you mean? What kind of mess?"

"Stills was waiting for Sophie when she got home. I came in, but he had her. She grabbed a pair of scissors off the counter and stabbed him in the neck.

Unless we want the police here, we need to get this place cleaned up and the body out of here now."

For a few moments, Ryker says nothing and then when he does, I hear the panic in his voice as he asks, "Is she okay? What about you?"

"We're fine. I'm going to bring her back to the estate, but we need to go now. Send everyone we have because if the police…"

I don't get a chance to finish before Ryker says, "I know. Okay. They're on their way. Get out of there and bring her back here, Kane."

I stuff my phone back into my pocket and press a kiss to the top of Sophie's head. "Come on, baby. We have to go. We can't stay here any longer."

She doesn't answer but merely nods. As we walk out, I grab her suitcase like I should have an hour ago back at the house.

Tossing her bag into the back seat, I get her settled in the passenger seat and then hurry around to get behind the wheel. The sooner we get out of this suburban neighborhood, the better.

Sophie begins to cry again, so before I drive away, I turn toward her and take her face in my hands again. "Look at me, Sophie."

She obeys, for once, and stares at me, her eyes still filled with terror from all she's been through. I lean in and kiss her for the first time in too long and press my forehead against hers.

"I'm right here, baby. I'm so proud of you. You stayed strong and brave. I mean it, Sophie. I'm so proud of you."

In a tiny voice, she says, "I was so scared, Kane. I thought I was going to die right there in my kitchen and you wouldn't know I needed you."

"I know. But you didn't need me. You took care of him all by yourself."

"When I saw you come in, I knew you wouldn't let him kill me. Just like before, you protected me."

Leaning back, I smile at how much she believes in me. "I wouldn't let anyone hurt you, Sophie. No one. I swear. Now I'm going to take you back to the estate and get you cleaned up. I promise, I'm going to be right there with you, okay?"

Sophie nods and covers her face as she begins to cry again. I get it. No matter what anyone says, killing another human being takes a toll on you. Even if it's in self-defense.

I CARRY HER INTO THE HOUSE AND UP TO THE ROOM she left a couple hours ago. She needs a shower and someone there to take care of her, but I need to find out from Ryker that everything's been handled. Sophie doesn't need cops searching for her looking to pin Stills' murder on her.

Setting her on her feet in the bathroom, I turn the water on and turn to face her. "I just need to run down to the office for a few minutes. I'll be right back. I promise. In the meantime, get in the shower and clean yourself up, okay?"

"Okay."

I kiss her again and push her damp hair off her

face. "It's going to be okay. I'm taking care of everything. Just get into the shower and let the water rinse everything away."

"Okay."

This time her voice sounds stronger, so I feel safe leaving her for a few minutes. I race down to Ryker's office, taking the stairs by twos and threes, and find him pacing back and forth. He stops dead when he sees me and shakes his head.

"We could have lost both of you tonight. I let myself get distracted, Kane. I'm sorry."

"Stills wasn't fucking taking me out. Not tonight or any night. But this turned out as good as it did because of Sophie, not me, Ryker. She must have ice water running through her veins because she watched me glance over at those scissors no more than twice and understood what I wanted her to do. Then when Stills loosened his hold, she didn't hesitate. Fuck, she was braver than I've seen most guys be on their first kill."

"How is she now?"

"She's cleaning herself up. I just came down because I wanted to know how things went back at her house. Did they handle everything?"

Ryker nods and then lets out a heavy sigh. "They're taking care of it. I'm dreading the call to Joseph. He stayed away from the life because he thought it would make his family safe."

"Give her until tomorrow before she has to deal with her parents. I know you have to tell them, but give her a little time. She's been through a lot tonight."

"Yeah. I don't want to lie to my brother, but maybe I'll just tell him she decided to stay a little longer."

Patting him on the shoulder, I smile as relief washes over me. "She's going to be okay. She's tough. She's a Varens, no matter how much her father tried to shield her from all of this."

"Go take care of her, Kane. I'll check in on her tomorrow, but for tonight, make sure she's okay."

He doesn't have to order me to take care of Sophie. I know my job. I also know I want to protect her as much as I did back at Duke's.

When I get back to her room, I hear the water running and walk in to find her still dressed and huddled in the corner of the shower, her head hidden in her knees. Rushing in, I crouch down in front of her, the hot water pelting my back, and put my arms around her.

"Sophie, I'm here. Just hang on to me and let me stand you up."

She looks up at me with wildness in her eyes. Shaking her head, she sobs, "I can't get the blood off. It's in my skin, Kane. It won't come off."

Tugging her shirt up her body, I whisper, "It's going to be okay. Let's get these clothes off and then you'll be able to clean up better."

I toss the soaked shirt and the rest of her clothes out of the shower and grab the bottle of shampoo. "First, we need to wash your hair, baby."

After maneuvering her out of the water, I take a handful of shampoo and rub it all over her head. It's a simple motion, but as I do it, she stares up at me wide-eyed and so scared.

"I know how you feel. I do. The first time I killed someone I couldn't stop shaking. This won't last, Sophie. I promise."

"I don't know what to do, Kane."

"You don't have to do anything. Ryker and I are handling everything."

"What happens now? How can I ever go home and live in my house knowing what happened there?"

"Now you stay with me here. That's what happens now. You stay here and I'll take care of you."

I see the confusion settle into her expression. After how I've acted since she came here, I understand why.

"What does that mean?"

Gently, I turn her around so I can rinse the shampoo out of her hair. "Close your eyes."

This gives me a few moments to find the right words for what I want to say to her. I don't want to fuck this up, but wanting someone like I want her is new to me. I hope she understands that.

Opening her eyes, she searches my face for the answer to her question. "What did you mean you'll take care of me?"

With her face finally clear of all the blood, she looks like the woman I fell in love with, and I can't help but smile at how sincere she sounds. "It means I don't want you to go. Stay with me. Let me do what I never thought I could. Let me show you how much I love you every day and every night."

"You love me and want me to stay?"

"I love you. I loved you when it was just the two of us in that apartment fighting to stay alive. I loved you when you came here, even though I tried everything not to. I loved you tonight when all I wanted to do was protect you from Stills. I don't pretend that I'm the kind of man you should want. All I know is you make me think there's some good left in the world, and I want that in my life."

As I watch, she begins to cry, her tears mixing with the water as it flows down over her cheeks. She's the most beautiful creature I've ever seen in my life, a beautiful soul I love.

"You love me," she says on a sob. "I've wanted to hear the man I knew back at that terrible place speak to me again, Kane. I thought you had disappeared forever, though. Now you say you love me and want me to stay here with you. I don't know what to say."

"Say you will. Say whatever you want. Just say it here with me."

Her smile lights up her face when she answers, "I loved you when you were King at that place and protected me. I loved you when I found out you weren't dead. And I loved you for coming to my rescue tonight. I love you."

She loves me. Kane, a man who hasn't believed he deserved love since that night all those years ago, the night that brought me to this place.

Sophie loves me.

ophie

I CLUTCH MY KNEES AND TAKE A DEEP BREATH IN AS Kane handles some issue on his phone. I'm safe here at Ryker's home. My family will protect me. I'm strong.

For all those years, my father's grumbling about the Varens' family business never made me think any of us would ever be touched. I doubt he thought his eldest child would ever experience what I have in the past few months.

"Okay, that's done," Kane says with a smile before crawling up the bed toward me. "Are you hungry?"

He sounds like the man I spent those terrifying days with back at Duke's. Still gruff and hard, his gentleness comes out when he tries to take care of me. I see it in his dark eyes that once enchanted me but now soothe me more than he can ever know.

I love the contrast in him, the hardness that makes the kindness even more pronounced.

Shaking my head, I stretch my legs out in front of me so his T-shirt comes to the middle of my thighs. "I'm not hungry right now. Maybe later."

"Okay. Just let me know. If no one's around in the kitchen, then I can make you something."

He sits far enough away from me that he's out of my reach. Or is it that I'm out of his reach? Does he have a problem being close to me now?

I look down at my bare forearms and cringe before folding my arms across my chest. "Is something wrong, Kane?"

Leaning back just the tiniest bit, he puts more room between us. "I just want to make sure you're okay."

"Why do you keep moving away from me then?"

I see the worry in his eyes. It makes them look sad. I don't understand why he'd be sad, though. He said he was proud of me for being strong and brave, but now it's like I have the plague and he needs to avoid even touching me.

"The first time I killed someone, I wanted to run away and hide. I didn't want anyone near me. I just thought that maybe I should give you some space right now. It's nothing else, Sophie. Honest."

Reaching out, I touch my fingertips to his forearm, loving how warm his skin feels. I hold my breath as I wait for him to flinch or recoil from me, but he doesn't move, almost as if he understands how much that would devastate me.

"It just feels like you don't want to be near me right now," I say quietly, hoping I'm wrong.

A second later, he crawls up the bed to sit next to me and presses his leg against mine. "What did I tell you about whenever you're around?"

I look away, afraid to answer his question. I remember what he said, but maybe everything that's happened since then has changed things. Maybe seeing what happened tonight made him realize he loves me but that's more about protecting me than anything else.

His fingers gently touch my chin and turn my head to face him. "Hey, what's going on? Tell me. Whatever it is, we got this, right?"

Closing my eyes, I answer his question the best I can. "I just thought maybe you feel different than you did back at Duke's."

"Nope. If I was being truthful, I would have told you back then that I loved you. The only thing different is now you know. But I guess there are other things that have changed."

I knew it!

My eyes fly open to see him smiling at me. Confused, I shake my head as tears burn the back of my eyes. "Like what? I had a feeling there was something wrong, but you just said I could tell you. Well, you need to tell me."

Kane leans in and kisses me softly, making my heart flutter at the feel of his lips on mine. "Back there at Duke's, I felt like I could fall in love with you because I didn't have to be me there. I got to be someone else, and King could fall in love with the beautiful girl he held captive. I never believed I could feel that way about someone and be happy as Kane living here and being the person I am. That's all changed now."

"Why?"

"Because the moment I saw Stills holding that gun to your head, I felt like my entire world was being threatened. I couldn't bear the thought of losing you."

"But why does that mean you can be with me now?"

He hangs his head and says nothing for a long time, and when he finally answers my question, my heart tightens. "The first time I killed a man it wasn't a man at all. It was my brother."

"Your brother?"

Nodding, he continues, "He came at Ryker with a knife to kill him."

"Why?"

"After my mother left when I was ten, my father, my brother, and I ended up homeless. I was fifteen and living on the streets. My brother was nearly eighteen and lost to drugs, along with my father, but I was still trying to go to school. I was barely hanging on, but I had one friend. Ryker. My brother and father knew he was from money, so they planned to kill him and take whatever he had on him. I couldn't let them do that. He was my only lifeline to anything but living on the streets."

"Is that why you're so loyal to him?" I ask as I weave my fingers through his to hold his hand.

"Yeah. We were just kids, but he was more like my brother than my own brother. Ryker and this house showed me that I didn't have to stay where I was. I pledged my loyalty to him that night, but I also swore to myself that I wouldn't let anyone else get close to me ever again after what I did to my brother."

"You were protecting your friend. How was that bad?"

Kane winces like he's in pain. "In my head, I equated love with that. I loved my brother and he knew how much it meant to me that I had a friend in Ryker. Love couldn't be trusted. I didn't see what he and my father planned to do until the last second because I couldn't believe my family would ever do that to me."

"So you decided to be alone instead of risking loving anyone ever again," I say sadly, completing his story for him.

"The life I lead doesn't allow for love. At least, I never thought it did."

"But you love Ryker. You were willing to risk your life and go undercover at Duke's for him."

"That's different," he says with a shrug. "He's a blood brother. When no one else was there for me when I was on the streets, he was. It was Ryker who gave me a place to live and a focus for my life. I'd be dead if it wasn't for him. I'm not exactly someone who did well with homelessness."

"That's what love is, though. It's exactly the idea that someone who loves you is there when no one else is."

"Well, I didn't think that could ever happen to me."

"Love can happen for anyone," I say softly before bringing his hand to my lips in a kiss.

He pulls me onto his lap, my legs straddling his hips. Looking up at me, he smiles in that way that is nothing less than sexy and takes my face in his strong hands. "That you believe that about me is one of the reasons I love you, Sophie. You saw something in me when you shouldn't have. You didn't know I was trying to protect you and would have given my life for you then. Still, you saw what I didn't know existed in me."

"I believe in you just like I believe in love, Kane."

His expression grows dark as I finish saying what I truly feel. Before I can ask him what's wrong, he sighs and winces.

"You're young, Sophie. You have your future in front of you. You know what I am and what my life entails. I won't blame you if you decide in a couple days after you've had a chance to think about it that this isn't what you want."

As serious as he sounds, I can't help but laugh. "What is it about this house? I swear it makes the men here old before their time. You act like nine years difference between us is ninety. You're thirty, for God's sake. I'm not that little girl you liked to call me back at that place."

"Fine, but that doesn't change what I am."

"You're no different than most of my family, Kane."

He averts his gaze to the side of the room. "Your

father never wanted you around this. He won't be happy."

Truer words have never been spoken. My father has railed against the life Victor and Ryker lead all my life. That doesn't change how I feel, though.

"All my father has ever wanted for me is to be happy. Everything else, he'll get used to. Of course, if you break my heart, he'll make Victor his best friend and find a way to kill you in the most painful way possible. Torture should be expected."

For a second, Kane looks stunned by my teasing, but when I smile and giggle, he lets out a heavy sigh. "You are certainly a Varens through and through."

I don't know if that's a good thing. I grew up thinking it wasn't, but if it means that I'm strong and brave like Kane said I was, then I wear that name with pride.

Against his lips, I whisper, "What I am is crazy about you, through and through."

He lets out a sexy moan before lifting his hips from the bed, and I feel his hard cock press against me. "And I'm crazy about you, obviously."

"Well, at least one part of you is," I say with a giggle.

Sliding his hand around to the back of my neck, he pulls me to him and kisses me slowly, like he wants to taste me in a way he's never done before. When his tongue teases mine and he softly moans into my mouth, it's as if a jolt of need shoots straight through me. I roll my hips over his cock, loving how it feels as

I drag my pussy over it. His jeans and my panties only add to the feeling and my need for him.

He tightens his hand in my hair, twisting until delicious pain dances across my scalp. He's that same man I met at that terrible place in many ways. Beautifully savage and hard. Capable of cruelty in a way I've never experienced before. But those same hands that can inflict pain are the same that gently cradle my face as he professes his love for me.

"Fuck, Sophie. I'm not sure we should do this tonight," he groans as he loosens his hold on my hair.

I stare down at him in utter confusion. "Why? I thought you always wanted me whenever I was nearby. Isn't that true anymore?"

"Baby, it's as true now as it ever was," he says before lifting his hips off the bed to press his cock against my pussy. "I just don't know if I can be gentle tonight, and I think you need that after all you've been through. Killing makes me a little crazy, and not in a good way."

For a moment, I stare into his dark eyes and see this isn't some excuse. There's a wildness in them now.

"But you didn't kill anyone, Kane. I did."

He nods, but the harshness in him doesn't subside. "True, but I wanted to kill him, and that need to hurt isn't easily turned off with me."

"Don't turn anything off. You would never hurt me, would you?"

"Never," he says with a wince, as if the very idea causes him pain. "Not intentionally."

"Then don't back away from me now. I want all of

you, even the parts you don't think anyone should want to love."

"It's just that tonight I can't seem to…"

His voice goes hoarse before he can finish his thought. I don't care what he can't turn off. If it's anger, then it can join mine. If it's fear, then I want to feel it with him.

I kiss him hard, hoping to show him how much I want him. The good him. The bad him. All of him.

Weaving my fingers through his hair, I scratch across the back of his head until I reach his neck and press my nails into his skin. "Please don't hold back anything from me. I trust you now like I trusted you to protect me at Duke's. Don't be afraid to show me that man I met then."

Kane nips my bottom lip with his teeth and moans into my mouth. "I missed you so fucking much, Sophie."

I know just what he means. Knowing he was in this house, so close yet so far away, made me crave his touch, the feel of his mouth on me. Like a need I couldn't satisfy.

"Don't hold back. Never hold back with me."

The words barely leave my mouth before he flips me onto my back. His eyes fill with a need I know all too well as he stares down at me. He tugs my underwear down my legs and tosses them away as I wriggle out of his T-shirt that's too big for me. Naked beneath him, I reach out to pull his shirt over his head, but it's off before I can do the job myself.

My fingers fumble with the button on his jeans,

and Kane adds his to lower the zipper. I feel my heartbeat begin to race as he pushes his pants down his legs, inch by inch revealing all of him.

I'm barely able to take a breath before he's on top of me, his body covering mine and his cock pushing between my legs. He's thick and hard, and I feel the coolness of his piercings against my tender skin, sending a shiver of anticipation through me.

When he kisses me, his mouth takes my need to feel him inside me, feeding off it as he forces me to take every inch of him. With a single slow thrust, he buries his cock into my body, filling me so completely it takes my breath away.

In his eyes, I see he needs this rougher, harder than that gentle beginning he's given me. Arching my back, I press my heels into the small of his back and moan in his ear, "Fuck me. Don't stop until all I can think about is you."

I want to forget the feeling of a gun pressed to my head. How much I wanted to kill tonight. How terrified I felt that I might not get to see another day. God, I want to forget how much it hurt to see Kane but not touch him or have him touch me.

I want to forget everything but him.

He slides out of me and lowers his head to take a nipple into his mouth. His teeth bite down just hard enough to deliver the exact amount of pain and pleasure. Leaning back, he takes a deep breath in and shudders.

"I want to feel every part of you. To taste you on my tongue. Mark you as mine so whenever anyone looks at you, they know deep inside you want only me. Then I want to fuck you hard to show you just what I am and hope you don't turn away."

My hands claw at his body to bring him back to me. "Yes. All of it. Please."

He doesn't wait for me to finish speaking before sliding down my body to press his mouth against my pussy. The first touch of his tongue to my clit sends waves of need coursing through me, and I spread my legs as wide as I can, desperate to have him touch every tender inch of me with his lips and tongue.

Two fingers slide into me, curling up to reach a spot that sends my body into overdrive. He spreads me apart and sucks my clit hard into his mouth. When he bites down, every nerve explodes and I come hard. He rides my release like everything he's ever needed exists in that single spot on me.

"Don't stop…God, don't stop…oh…this feels so good," I moan as wave after wave of ecstasy rolls through me.

When the aftershocks finally subside, Kane moves up my body and kisses me. "Never, Sophie. You taste so fucking good I could spend the rest of my life licking your pussy."

I reach down between us and palm his hard cock, ready to give him what he's given me, but he narrows his eyes. "Tonight, I need something else. Roll over and get on your hands and knees."

Behind me, he leans over my back and kisses my ear. Sliding his hand around the front of my neck, he whispers, "You are so fucking beautiful. And mine."

With a single hard push, he fills me again, but this time there's no gentleness to him. His fingers press against my throat, and he pumps into me, powerful and commanding as my body welcomes each thrust. He fucks hard and ruthlessly now, but in my ear, I hear him whisper words that make my need spike with each syllable.

"That's it, little one. Take every inch of me. You feel perfect around me, baby. Feel that every time I fill you up?"

I whimper, silently praying for him to say more.

"No words? You like silent fucking?" he asks before plunging into me.

"No. Don't stop."

I feel him stuff his hand into my hair, and then he tugs hard, pulling my head back. "That's a good girl. You like when I talk dirty, Sophie? Does your pretty cunt get wet with every word? Good."

A tiny moan escapes from my throat at how fucking good this feels. I want him to make me his all over again.

"Remember when I told you I'd be thinking of you with pigtails dressed in a schoolgirl uniform?" he asks as his hand releases its hold on my neck, leaving me wishing for his touch once more.

"Yes."

"This is exactly what I thought of then, little one. You bent over in front of me and me fucking you like this. You look so beautiful, Sophie."

He stills inside me after that, and I turn my head to

see him staring at me. "Tell me what you want, little one."

Barely able to speak, I say with a sob, "Please don't stop. Make me forget everything but you, Kane."

Leaning forward, he presses a soft kiss to the spot below my ear and exhales a warm breath against my cheek. "There's nothing but you and me now, Sophie. You're mine, and I'm yours."

His hand returns to my neck, grounding me when he starts fucking me again. I feel the rage in him, but I can handle it. He needs me to take this part of him.

My muscles ache, but there's no pain. Only pleasure. Closing my eyes, I feel my orgasm begin deep inside me, a delicious sensation that increases with every time Kane's cock fills me and those piercings graze the most sensitive parts of me.

"That's it, baby. I want to feel you come hard on my cock. I love when your cunt milks me. Let go, little one."

With a gentle squeeze, Kane tightens his hold on my throat, and my body reacts instantly. Pushing back against him, I surrender with a tiny cry.

Moments later, he stills and his cock fills me one last time. With a sigh, he kisses me on the side of my cheek.

"I didn't hurt you, did I?"

The worry in his voice is real. I collapse to the bed beneath me and roll over to look up at him. "No. I'm strong, remember?" I say with a smile.

Lowering himself beside me, he takes me into his

arms and holds me before kissing the top of my head. "I didn't forget. I just wanted to make sure."

I curl up against his body damp with sweat and giggle. "You don't have to worry about me. I can handle a lot. I'm a Varens."

He pushes my hair back off my face and tilts my head so he can look down into my eyes. He's gorgeous and raw and everything I want.

"My beautiful, strong Sophie."

There, in his arms safe and sound, is the only place I ever want to be. I know what he is and what he's done, and I love him. I can handle the darkness that lurks inside him.

All my life, I've heard how wrong men like Kane are. I don't know if that's right, but nestled in his embrace as he whispers how much he loves me doesn't seem wrong.

ane

I SLIDE THE TIE FROM AROUND MY NECK AND TOSS IT onto the bed, happy to be rid of that noose after three hours. Sophie wraps her arms around me and presses her cheek against my back.

"No chance you want to keep it on for a little while longer? I like the way you look in a suit and tie."

Covering her hands with mine, I look back at her and smile. "Oh yeah? I hate dressing like this, but I might be able to be convinced."

Her chuckle resonates through my chest before she slips out of my hold and walks over toward the window. "I'm so glad it was a nice day for Maxim's christening. Late September can sometimes be iffy, but today was beautiful."

I shrug out of my suit coat and lay it over the tie on

the bed. "I thought Ryker was going to explode he was so fucking happy. Then again, I'm not used to seeing him not wearing that mask outside. I guess he didn't want to scare the hell out of the priest."

Sophie turns around to look at me and shakes her head. "I never thought I'd see him like this, to be honest. He and Kaia are over the moon about that little boy. I love that for them."

A sense of sadness creeps into her voice, even though she seems happy for the new parents. I hesitate to ask, sure her mood change has to do with me. I've seen how she adores Maxim. She spent the whole summer with him and Kaia. It's only natural that she probably wants to have one of her own.

Except that I haven't exactly shown myself to be the man to join her in that.

Not that I wouldn't be happy to have a son of my own. I never believed that my life had room for a woman, and I was wrong about that. Maybe a little guy to carry on my name would be nice.

"You okay? You seem off," I say in a low voice as I watch her grab my coat and tie off the bed and walk over to the closet with them.

"I'm good. Just tired, I guess."

She doesn't sound tired. She sounds sad.

"Do you want to forget about dinner? We can just stay here, if you want."

Now I sound sad. Christ.

With her back to me, she shakes her head. "No, I'm good."

Nothing between us seems good right now. I hate

seeing her like this. Maybe I was wrong thinking we could have a happily ever after like Ryker and Kaia.

Maybe I was wrong to think she could find that with me.

I pad up behind her and wrap my arms around her shoulders. Taking a deep breath in, I inhale the soft flowery scent of her perfume as I nuzzle her neck.

"What's going on, Sophie? I thought you had a good time today."

She lets out a heavy sigh and leans her head against my chest. "I had a great time, Kane. I loved seeing Ryker and Kaia so happy, and I had a great time with my mother and Selene. I just wish my father could have come too."

"I know, but for now the problem with Victor means your father needs to lay low."

Sophie turns to face me and nods. "I know. I get it. My uncle is a dick and he has no problem with killing off family members. I just hate that the thing my father feared the most is now happening to him."

"His oldest daughter in love with a bad man?" I joke, hoping to cheer her up.

Cradling my face, she smiles before kissing me softly. "No. What I hate is that my father has been dragged into this power struggle between Victor and Ryker when he spent nearly his entire life staying away from all of this. Instead of being with his wife and family, he's forced to hide away and my mother is forced to pretend he's dead. They don't deserve this, Kane."

"I know. It's just the way it has to be for now."

"What if I never get to see him again?" she asks, tears welling in her eyes. "I'll never forgive myself if Victor gets to him and I didn't have a chance to tell him how much I love him one more time."

For two weeks, I've been forced to give her the same answer about this. It's just the way it has to be. I understand why Ryker has him hidden away. I'd do the same thing for someone I love knowing how vicious Victor is lately.

But it doesn't change how much this breaks Sophie's heart.

I take her into my arms and hold her, but I want to do more. I'm supposed to protect the woman I love. That's what I swore I'd do if I ever got the chance to have Sophie in my life.

"What if he doesn't survive this, Kane?" she sobs into my chest. "What if my uncle finds him and kills him to hurt Ryker?"

"We won't let that happen," I say, wishing I had something more to reassure her. Smoothing my hand over her back, I feel her whole body tremble. "I promise we won't let that happen."

"I'm sorry. I should be stronger than this."

"You don't have to be sorry. I'm here and I'm more than strong."

Sophie sniffles and wipes under her eyes to dry the tears. "I'm glad I have you. You're what keeps me going when I don't think I can anymore, Kane."

I drag my thumbs across the tops of her cheeks and smile. "You'll always have me. Remember that."

For a moment, we stare into each other's eyes in

silence, and then she asks the question I've been wondering about since this whole thing with Victor began.

"How long can we all stay here, Kane? Guards follow my mother and sister around whenever they leave the estate, and Kaia and I haven't felt safe enough to leave in nearly a month. Lily told me Lukas needed to go to the doctor last week and she didn't know if she should take him or use Seymour, who is very much not a pediatrician, by the way. We're all hunkered down here because we need to be protected from Victor, but this can't go on. I know we get to talk to my father, but burner phones and all the fear?"

The image of Seymour treating a toddler flashes through my mind. For a doctor, he does a hell of a job with bullet wounds and all the other scrapes guys like me get, but he lacks the touch a child needs. He'd probably scare the hell out of the poor kid.

"It won't be much longer. Ryker's got to stop Victor, though. The time's come for him to be taken out. But these things take planning. Believe me, it's happening as fast as it can."

Hanging her head, she says in a tiny voice, "I know. I'm sorry for complaining. I just hate that my father has to be hidden away without all the people who love him."

Then she giggles and looks up at me. "Actually, he's probably happy as a clam not having to deal with my sister and me and my mother. All that estrogen nearly drove him nuts while we were growing up."

"I need to run down to Ryker's office for a minute. I'll be right back, okay?"

With a nod, she sighs. "I'm good. Don't worry about me. I'm just being a crybaby. Go, do what you have to do. I'm going to see if Kaia needs anything. Maybe we can get Lily and Lukas and take the kids outside for a little while before the sun goes down. Lukas loves to see the fireflies."

I kiss her, lingering on her lips before I leave. "I'll be back soon."

Despite the fact that today was probably the happiest day of his life, Ryker sits behind his desk with his head down focused on that laptop he stares at all the time. Without his mask, all he's going through is clear in his worried expression.

"No rest for the wicked," I say with a chuckle as I walk into his office.

He lifts his head and shrugs. "Well, that's what we are, so I guess it fits," he says somberly.

"Something up?"

Taking a deep breath in, he lets it out slowly as he sits back in his office chair. "Nothing new. Just crossing the T's and dotting the I's for when things do happen."

"Got it."

His expression turns quizzical. "Why are you down here? I figured you'd be spending the rest of the night with Sophie."

"I am, but I want to run something by you. Something I'd like to do for her."

A slow smile brightens his face. "Something you'd like to do for her? Are you thinking of popping the question, Kane?"

I can't stop my eyes from rolling back into my head. "I swear you say these things just to bust my ass. We've been together for like three months. Give us a little time, okay?"

Ryker smiles, knowing more than anybody else but Sophie how crazy in love with her I am. "Okay. Then if it's not that, what are you talking about?"

For a moment, I hesitate, but this is too important. "I want to take her to see her father."

"No. I'm sorry, Kane, but it's too risky."

"I'll take every precaution necessary. Nobody will know we're going to see him."

Still, Ryker refuses to agree. Shaking his head, he frowns. "Victor has his men all over the place. He'll find out and then Joseph won't be alive an hour later."

"You know I can do this. Ryker, she just wants to see her father. Let me do this."

"I can't risk it."

There's got to be some way to convince him. Leaning down, I set my hands on top of the edge of his desk and level my gaze on him. "I'll take full responsibility. If something happens, it's my life for his."

Now Ryker rolls his eyes. "As if I would ever risk losing you either. No. It's too risky. We can't afford to hand him over to Victor."

"You've got Jaxon protecting him now, don't you? What about if we met somewhere between here and the safe house. She just wants to talk to him in person. A few fucking minutes."

"A few minutes that can get him killed. You know this. Since when have you gone soft and worried about people missing one another? You think his wife doesn't miss him? Fuck, she and Selene are stuck here in a place they've never spent more than a couple hours years ago. I'm not even sure Selene has ever been here before now. Everybody needs to just stay put until this business with Victor is finished."

As much as I hate to admit it, Ryker's right. It's too risky. I would have seen that if I wasn't so blinded by wanting to make Sophie happy.

I pace back and forth across his office for a few passes trying to think of a way to give her what she wants and still keep everyone safe. Nothing comes to me until I remember a story Jaxon told me about how he and his girlfriend get to see one another when he can't drive down to see her in person.

Stopping dead at the edge of Ryker's desk, I spin around to face him and say, "What about if we did something remote? Is there any reason that can't happen?"

"Like what?"

"Remember Jaxon telling us how he talks to that girl at school? He and Tia get to see one another while they talk when he can't get down there. Is there any reason Sophie can't do that with Joseph?"

With a shrug, Ryker says, "I don't know. We'd

have to make sure there was no way to trace where Joseph was."

My hope soars at his answer. "So if we could be sure of that, it could happen?"

"As long as we're absolutely sure not to put my brother in danger."

I clap my hands together, thrilled I'm going to be able to do this for her. "Great! I'll have Jaxon look into it. If it's safe, I'll have him tell me what he needs and we'll do it that way. Don't tell Kaia, though. I want this to be a surprise for Sophie."

"You really are crazy about her, aren't you?"

The two of us have never really talked about Sophie and me. Ryker still doesn't know everything that happened back at Duke's, and he's never asked about it. I've never told him because it doesn't affect what I do for him and the organization. She just moved in after that night Stills tried to kill her, and since then, we've been together.

I can't stop myself from smiling when I answer, "Yeah, I am. And don't give me any shit about everything I ever said to you about Kaia and there being no room in our world for women or love because I'm not hearing it, okay?"

He gives me a smug look and shrugs. "Okay. If you're happy, I'm happy for you. No shit to give."

"I've got plans to set up, so I'll see you tomorrow, Ryker."

"I'll be here."

As I turn to leave, I tease him, "Unless Kaia or Maxim give you a reason not to?"

Sighing, he looks up toward the ceiling. "Someday I hope that can happen."

Two days later as the sun begins, I walk into the room I share with Sophie and find her curled up on the bed reading a book. Leaning over, I kiss her and take the book out of her hands.

"Hey! I was reading that."

"I have something for you, so reading can wait."

As she glares up at me, I hand her the laptop where I've set up everything for her to talk to her father. "I have something for you. Enjoy!"

Sophie looks down at the silver laptop and then up at me. "You're giving me a computer? Not exactly the sexiest gift, but thank you."

"Just open it, okay?"

With a look of pure disbelief, she lifts the cover and there waiting for her on the screen is her father, courtesy of Jaxon's help. Her eyes fill with tears, and she looks up me, unsure what's going on.

"I couldn't find a way for you to see him in person, so this is the second best thing. Jaxon helped me set it up. Talk to your father. I'll leave you two alone."

"Hi, Daddy. I miss you. Are you okay?" she asks and then reaches out to grab my hand.

"Hi, Soph. I'm okay. I'm so happy Jaxon set this up so we can talk. How are you, honey?"

"I'm okay. I want you to meet someone."

She tugs me over to where she sits on the bed and pulls me down next to her. "Daddy, this is Kane. He worked with Jaxon to set this all up so I could see you because he knew I missed you."

I give Joseph a smile and see him staring back at me with suspicion in his eyes. I don't blame him. He spent his whole life keeping his family away from men like me. To see his daughter seated next to me must unnerve him.

"Ryker's right hand man?" he asks as his focus shifts from me back to Sophie.

"Yes, Daddy. He's the man who saved me when Uncle Victor's enemies kidnapped me. He and I are in love, and I know what you're going to say, but I'm a grown woman who can make her own choices, and I choose him. I hope you understand that."

Time seems to grind to a standstill, and my heart beats wildly in my chest as she and I wait for Joseph to respond. As much as she says she's chosen me, I know how much her family means to her, and if her father disapproves of her being with me, I'm not sure what will happen next.

With a grimace, he finally answers, "You always were so headstrong, but you're right. You are a grown woman now, and I can't honestly object to you being with Kane since I was in the family business when your mother and I got together."

As Sophie beams a smile, Joseph turns his attention back to me. "And I'm sure he understands that even though my brother might not like it, if he hurts you, I'm going to get back into the family business, right Kane?"

Spoken like a true Varens.

"I understand you perfectly, Joseph," I say with a nod.

His expression instantly brightens. "Then I don't think we'll have a problem."

Leaning over, I kiss Sophie on the cheek. "Talk to your father. I'll be downstairs, so come find me when you're done. Take your time, though. You have a lot to catch up on."

"Thank you so much!"

I walk away and stop at the door to look back at her. It took so little to make this happen, but seeing her sweet smile makes me happier than I ever thought I could be. It's a very different life than I expected when I chose to work for Ryker. I've laid down my life over and over to protect him, but now I have another Varens to give my life purpose.

Whatever happens when Ryker strikes at Victor, I know where my loyalties lie now. With the friend I pledged loyalty for life and the woman I adore.

NEVER MISS A THING!

Be sure to subscribe to Abbi's newsletter to always be in the know about new releases! Visit her site at abbicook.com and subscribe today!

ABOUT THE AUTHOR

Abbi Cook grew up wondering if she was different because she always wanted to know more about the villain than the hero in the stories she read. When she got older, she found there were others in the world like her and devoured their writing, loving every dark word. She's written her own tales for years, but in 2019 she decided it was time to take the next step and publish them. She's never looked back since that day.

Readers can find her at her website at abbicook.com, on FB and IG, and through email at abbicookauthor@gmail.com

www.ingramcontent.com/pod-product-compliance
Lightning Source LLC
Chambersburg PA
CBHW020356260626
47156CB00007B/2131